Second Chances

Second Chances

A North and South Story

Diana K Cooper

First paperback edition 2023

Book design by Publishing Push

ISBNs:
Paperback: 978-1-80541-384-4
eBook: 978-1-80541-385-1

Acknowledgements

This novel is inspired by *North and South* by Elizabeth Gaskell, which was published in 1855 following its serialisation in the weekly journal *Household Words*. I hope that readers familiar with Mrs Gaskell's superb book, and those who are not, will enjoy my story which centres around some of the original characters and themes. *Second Chances* is a stand alone novel and requires no previous knowledge of *North and South*.

My appreciation for *North and South* has been expanded and enhanced by my fellow members of the Mill at Milton, a wonderful global community who love the original text and reading and writing about it. I am sincerely grateful for the unstinting encouragement and enthusiasm from my friends at The Mill, and special thanks goes to Roxana for her time, knowledge and commitment in helping me to achieve my dream of writing my own novel.

Finally, I would like to dedicate this book to my Mum and son Johnny, whose unconditional love and support are appreciated beyond words.

Chapter 1

January 1855

John Thornton loved Margaret Hale. It really was that simple. If you could see into his soul, it would be the defining essence of him. But John's great misfortune was that Miss Hale was as far from his grasp as she ever had been, or ever would be. He wanted to keep away, truly he did, if only to preserve a shred of self-respect, but he could not. He was incapable of resisting the seemingly magnetic draw that forced him out on nights like this, and propelled him to the small house in Crampton Terrace where the Hales lived. His head and heart demanded that he continue to torture himself on a weekly basis by attending his classics lesson with Margaret's father, Richard Hale.

Since he had left school prematurely to become the breadwinner of the family, John's aim hadn't been merely success. He aspired to be a better man, an educated man, and stretch his comprehension of mankind through studying the teachings of the Greek and Roman philosophers. He was well aware that his business contemporaries, all ten years or more his senior, thought him mad. John was the butt of his fellow cotton mill masters' jokes for taking to

Diana K Cooper

schooling after his workday ended, but John didn't care about their opinion; he was his own man.

John believed that persevering with his studies was a good thing. During these hard economic times, his continued lessons showed the world that John Thornton and Marlborough Mills were undisturbed, though the reality was as different as night is to day. From dawn till dusk he put every ounce of effort into keeping his factory alive. But in the evenings when he sat in the drawing room with his mother or, as now, on his brisk walk towards Crampton, Margaret pervaded his thoughts.

John was under no illusion. He knew very well that the primary reason for continuing his regular trips to Crampton was not his love of the classics, nor was it the need for tutoring from Mr Hale on the topic. In fact, he suspected Mr Hale was disappointed in the effort he made these days during the lessons, but was too polite to say so. No, the principal aim of this weekly pilgrimage was to catch a glimpse of *her*. If he was really lucky, and it hardly ever happened these days, she might welcome him into the house and take his hat and coat, her body in such close proximity that he might catch the delicate scent of roses that she favoured. Or, she might serve tea for Mr Hale and himself in her exquisitely genteel way; this simple task providing the evidence that she knew something about him, that he inhabited a small corner of her mind, even if it was only the way he liked his tea. Most treasured of all, she might remain in the parlour with them and participate in the debate which Mr Hale's lessons precipitated. Margaret, as Mr Thornton allowed himself to

2

think of her on occasion, although he had no right to be so familiar, was quite brazenly opinionated, and sparks fairly flew when they were able to voice their differing points of view under the benevolent guidance of Mr Hale. As John neared the house he lifted his chin and pasted on the armour of his neutral expression, ready to accept whatever disappointments he would endure this evening. It was possible that he might not see her at all.

Unless he was mistaken, Miss Hale had been avoiding him. She had been conspicuous in her absence on the evenings of his lessons ever since that terrible day, some five months ago, when he had presumed to declare his feelings for her. Why she should avoid him when he was the one to be so cruelly rejected he wasn't sure, but that was the truth of it. Miss Hale had made it abundantly clear that she had no higher regard for him than she had for any man, possibly less so, and would not entertain his affections. Her words to him that afternoon had upheld his abiding belief that as a mere man, even a good man, he was simply not good enough for Miss Hale and never would be. He knew that being in trade meant he was an unsuitable match for her, as society, and Miss Hale herself, didn't consider men like him to be gentlemen.

He had been encouraged to make an offer of marriage to Miss Hale by his own mother when Miss Hale's honour teetered on the brink of ruin having come to his aid. She had saved him from an angry mob amassed outside his mill, but he had misread her actions on the day of the riot, perceiving that she had done it out of care for him. He had foolishly allowed himself to think that she might return his feelings. He had been wrong. Even the risk of irreparable damage to her reputation could not induce Miss Hale to accept him, let alone welcome the force of his affection. But the worst part of the whole affair was that she had no comprehension of his ability to love. She had freely admitted that she didn't understand him or his love for her, and nor did she care to.

John passed several people on his way to Crampton, although his consciousness didn't register them as his mind was preoccupied with thoughts of what might lie ahead that evening. He, on the other hand, was noticed by all he passed by, as was usual. He wore his customary black frock coat, waistcoat and cravat – the everyday uniform of the mill masters, that was in stark contrast to the clothes worn by the townsfolk. He was easy to spot, the master of Marlborough Mills, as he strode about the town in distinction to his peers, as no other mill masters would be seen walking around Milton when a carriage could be taken instead.

John was unmistakable being tall and broad shouldered, with dark hair, stern features and strong chin, which was usually covered in stubble. Despite taking pains to shave each morning, it was not long before a five o'clock shadow appeared ahead of time. Notwithstanding, or perhaps on account of, his almost perpetually brooding countenance, he turned the head of many a woman in the town. It was rumoured that the high and mighty, if not refined, echelons of Milton eyed John as a suitor for their daughters. They cared not whether their daughters were compatible with or even liked him, though most young women whispered and tittered together at the thought of capturing his heart.

He had evaded marriage so far despite being over thirty years of age, and it was mooted that despite his legendary temper and battle-axe of a mother, the real flaw with John Thornton was that he was wed to his mill.

John sprang up the front steps of the Hales' modest home, unable to keep the excitement from his tread, and rang the doorbell. He frowned slightly and cocked his head to listen. Quite unusually he could hear some sort of commotion coming from within. He could detect raised voices and in the distance … wailing? *Dear God*. He rang the bell again and knocked firmly on the door. He felt a compelling urge to batter it down to discover what calamity had befallen the Hales, and how he could come to their aid. Fortunately for all concerned, Richard Hale himself opened the door a moment later, which was a curious occurrence in itself, and highlighted that something out of the ordinary was undoubtedly in progress.

'Ah, John. Come in, come in,' Mr Hale said distractedly.

Richard Hale was a slight man, grown frailer by grief, but John always felt at home with him, and fancied that his own sharp edges softened slightly by just being in the older man's presence. John likened Mr Hale to a kindly uncle or perhaps even a father figure, although he was nothing like John's father as far as he could recollect. Mr Hale had been a country village vicar in the southern county of Hampshire until he had felt compelled to renounce his position, though not his faith, due to a matter of conscience. John found this strength of character at odds with the gentle, meek man he had come to both respect and call friend.

'You have caught us at sixes and sevens tonight. I must apologise,' Mr Hale said, grasping the younger man's arm, not in the customary handshake, but in what felt more to John like an entreaty.

The caterwauling continued and appeared to be coming from the kitchen at the back of the house. John could make out Margaret's voice, which calmed him slightly as it clearly wasn't her howling, and a deeper voice. A man's voice. Indelicate as it was, he couldn't help looking down the hall and in the direction of the noise. Polite society might have contrived to ignore the disturbance, but John was not a gentleman, as had been made plain to him in the past. He was simply a man who loved the woman embroiled in some sort of disturbance not forty feet away, albeit that his love was not reciprocated.

'May I ask if I can lend my assistance? It seems there is some misadventure afoot,' suggested John.

'Our friend Mr Higgins—' began Mr Hale tremulously.

'Higgins?' interrupted John sharply, eyebrows raised. He trained his attention onto the male voice he had heard a moment before coming from the kitchen. It was raised now, along with Margaret's and the wailing person, and yes, he recognised it. It was Higgins' voice.

'Yes, yes,' continued Mr Hale. 'Mr Higgins happened upon an accident in the street. A poor animal, a dog, was knocked over and injured very badly indeed. Mortally, I fear. He brought the pitiful creature here not knowing what to do with it,' said Mr Hale, his voice gradually fading. The impending death of the injured animal brought to the fore thoughts that were never far below the surface as he still grieved for his dear wife Maria, whose death four months ago had affected him deeply.

'If you are agreeable, Mr Hale, I will offer my help,' said John, as a statement rather than a question this time, taking charge of the situation as was his wont.

He took off his hat and overcoat, and hung them up on the coat stand in the hall. He then shepherded Mr Hale into the parlour, and once his friend and mentor was safely situated in front of the fire, John ventured down the hall towards the voices.

Nicholas Higgins had been hurrying towards Crampton Terrace late that afternoon. After the mill whistle had sounded, signifying the half-day finish as was routine on a Saturday, Higgins had spent his leisure time at the Goulden Dragon, sinking an ale or two and putting the world to rights with his pals. Time had run away with him, and he was overdue to collect his daughter Mary from the Hales' where she had been earning some extra money by helping Miss Margaret and Dixon with the washing.

As he turned the corner onto Briarcliffe Road, he saw a sheepdog start to limp across it. Higgins noticed the animal as it was quite out of place there, being a farm dog, and a lame one at that. He had heard the children, who now lived under his care, talking about a stray black and white shaggy dog in the town, and that they had befriended it. He surmised this must be the animal they had referred to. Its belly was large, and Nicholas was just contemplating whether it was old and fat or if it was perhaps pregnant, when a carriage rounded the corner and overtook him. As the carriage sped up the street, the front wheel clipped the dog, knocking it over, and as the dog lay stunned on the ground, the rear wheel of the carriage had run over it. It all happened so quickly, and yet Nicholas had seen every horrific second as if it were slower than in real life, and he instinctively ran to where the dog lay motionless but panting in the dirt of the street, blood beginning to ooze from its ear and belly.

Nicholas took off his cap and scratched his head, glancing around for some assistance, but the scant few people there turned their gaze away from him and hurried on their way. He couldn't just leave the animal there to die alone on the street, and as the Hales were only a few minutes' walk away, he jammed his cap back on and gathered the stricken animal up into his arms, and made his way to the Hales' back door where he lay the afflicted dog in the backyard and knocked urgently for attention.

Mary answered the door ready to berate her father. She knew where he'd been. While she was earning a few extra pennies, he drank them back down again at the pub. At the sound of their heated exchange Margaret came to the door, wiping her brow with her apron. It had been exhausting work that afternoon, and in her slightly dishevelled state she was glad that it was only her friend Nicholas at the door. On hearing about the tragic events that had befallen the farm dog, Margaret insisted Nicholas bring the creature into the safety of the kitchen where they could attempt to tend to it. Dying as it may be, it was still one of God's creatures, and she would care for it as best she could.

Dixon's alarm at finding the filthy animal that had been allowed into the kitchen was eclipsed by the dread that the beast was in fact bleeding to death. Despite her usual bluster and resilient exterior, the Hales' maid found the shock of it all too much to comprehend. Her distress manifested itself as loud sobbing as she patrolled the kitchen doorway, caught between the urge to leave, and the voyeuristic demand to watch as the horror unfolded. Margaret and Nicholas attempted to persuade Dixon and Mary to leave them in peace, supposing that a crowd of strangers, not to mention the intrusion that Dixon's cries were causing, would add to the poor dog's distress. Mary was glad to take the opportunity to leave and scurried home to attend to her adopted brothers and sisters, leaving her father and Miss Margaret to tend to the animal.

The first pup was born almost ten minutes later, shortly followed by a second. Higgins and Margaret wiped the bloody mucous from the pups' little faces, but it was to no avail. The dog continued to pant, labouring along with the pain from the mortal internal injuries sustained in the carriage accident, and Margaret and Higgins did their best to comfort her. An hour filled with anguish passed, every minute feeling like an age, with the dog becoming weaker by the moment. And when eventually another bout of contractions came, two further dead pups were delivered.

Margaret's knees and back ached terribly from spending so long in one attitude. She and Nicholas had been thus occupied for nigh on two hours, but she would not complain, not when the poor creature in front of her was enduring so much worse. She bent over the animal's body, offering futile words of encouragement as another slippery corpse was birthed by the dying animal. Five tiny puppies lay dead, no doubt delivered too early, their births brought on by the catastrophic injuries sustained by their mother earlier that day.

John Thornton entered the kitchen to the unwelcome sound of the elderly maid causing such a commotion that Margaret and Higgins were having to practically shout to each other to be heard over the din. The sickly iron tang of blood permeated the air, foretelling the approach of death. Dixon was pacing near to the doorway, alternately dabbing a tea towel to her eyes and then pressing it to her matronly bosom. John's eyes immediately sought out Margaret at the far end of the kitchen. He saw that she was kneeling on the flagged floor opposite Higgins, one of his tacklers who, along with his daughter and adopted family, had been befriended by Margaret shortly after her arrival in Milton. Margaret had her back to him, and both she and Higgins were clearly focused on the injured animal before them. John's initial appraisal was that Dixon was not helping one jot. He had been in the room for only seconds and already her agitation and distress had his nerves jangling. John determined that it would be beneficial to remove her from the room, and thereby reduce her anguish and the intensity of her distress that they were all presently subjected to.

John took Dixon by the arm and gently but firmly began to lead her from the room. 'Come, Miss Dixon,' he cajoled. 'Come and sit with Mr Hale and keep him company. You will be support for one another during this most upsetting time,' he said, although he did rather doubt his own words. Dixon allowed herself to be led from the room by Mr Thornton, despite her deep disregard for him, and was stationed in the sitting room with Mr Hale.

'Oh Lord, God help us and save us! Miss Margaret! I have left her alone with that Higgins!' exclaimed Dixon, clutching the towel to her chest again.

'It's all right, Miss Dixon, I will accompany them. There is no harm done. I will fetch you some tea to calm you presently,' said John kindly, and he softly closed the parlour door and hurried back to the kitchen.

The atmosphere in the kitchen was much improved, and Margaret and Higgins were now speaking in hushed tones as they attempted to staunch the blood flow from the injured dog at their knees. John came to Margaret's side and crouched down to her level. He was more familiar with seeing her wearing gowns of muslin or silk, but today he noticed she was wearing a plain linen day dress with a pinafore apron which was hideously stained from her ministrations to the dog. Even in this harrowing ordeal she looked perfectly composed, but as she turned her face to him he was momentarily shocked by the sight of her. Her face was deathly pale, and her usually flawless complexion was marred by streaks of the animal's blood where she had wiped her brow with her hand. Her hair, which she wore in a plain bun, had become a little untidy from her vigorous housework that afternoon, and some of it was now loose at the nape of her neck. Margaret's luminous grey eyes, magnified with the sheen of her tears, met with his of clear blue. She had such a look of utter despair that John's arms ached to hold her and to comfort her. He looked across to Higgins who didn't seem to be faring much better either. He still wore his flat cap, pushed back on his head, and his clothes also bore witness to the animal's struggle for survival from its lethal wounds.

Higgins had the animal's head on his lap, and he patted it and soothed the wounded dog with quiet words of encouragement while it panted, chest heaving and tongue lolling from its gaping mouth. The dog had a mostly black long-haired coat with white patches to its face and front paws, although it was difficult to fully determine due to the blood that matted its fur.

'What can I do?' said John softly, his deep, smooth voice a balm to Margaret's anguish.

'Oh, Mr Thornton,' she said, looking at him with hopelessness for the loss of life in front of her. 'The poor thing. She is being so brave. Surely, she won't live. But, can you see, there are babies,' she said, her arm outstretched towards the mass of blood-covered remains lying next to the dog, and large tears finally breached her lower eyelashes.

Higgins glanced up at John, and the men gave a curt nod to one another.

''Tis right, Master,' said Higgins. 'Poor creature is dyin'. Looks like all her young'uns too.'

John observed the litter of five bloody pups lying lifeless next to their mother, who finally stilled, her suffering over.

'Oh!' said Margaret, putting the back of her hand to her mouth and closing her eyes tight, forcing a spill of tears to course down her cheeks. She tipped her head back and said a silent prayer for the tragic mother in front of her.

John could bear it no longer. He knew well that there was no occasion in polite circles that allowed an unmarried man to embrace a similarly unattached woman, but his heart gave him no choice. She didn't like him at any rate, so if she were offended then it would only be another nail in that coffin. So John threw caution and propriety to the wind and put his arm around her shoulders, and perceiving no initial objection, he hugged her to his side. Amazingly, she laid her head upon his shoulder, and he guiltily reflected on how delicate she felt against him. While it was not proper to have Margaret in his embrace, neither was it usual to be sitting on the floor with her and one of his hands tending a dead animal, and John rationalised that these were extenuating circumstances after all.

John was glad that Higgins was there. They had not always seen eye to eye, far from it, as Higgins had been a leader in the union that had brought about the strike of the mill hands across the whole town of Milton. It had caused both the near ruin of John's business and the riot that had dealt the fatal blow to his hopes of a romantic attachment to the woman currently within the protection of his arm. But due to Margaret, for Margaret, John had employed Higgins when no one else would. He had been rewarded with a reliable worker, and had developed something akin to friendship with him, as they toiled to keep the mill afloat. He knew that Margaret saw Higgins as her friend, and no doubt she was more comfortable to be in the older man's presence than his own.

After all the preceding commotion and activity, a quiet stillness now hung over the small group still situated on the kitchen floor. The three of them sat there for a few moments in silence, contemplating the unequivocal sadness of the tableau that they were a part of.

'What happened?' John asked Higgins quietly. 'Looks like a farm dog. A Collie,' he said, his arm still around Margaret as though it were the most natural thing in the world.

'Aye. Word 'as it, it were from Bonney's Farm, yonder past the fields behind t'church,' said Higgins.

'I know it,' replied John.

'It turned up on't streets 'ere a few month ago, our Mary said. Got chucked out 'cos it were lame. Kids 'ave been feedin' it. Then this afternoon I saw it get 'it by a carriage. I couldn't jus' leave 'er there.' He raised his eyes to Margaret in silent apology.

'No, Nicholas. You did the right thing,' replied Margaret, offering words of support to Higgins, while she in turn gratefully absorbed the strength provided by Mr Thornton's firm and steadfast arm about her shoulder. 'Birthing is a gruesome business. There is no dignity in it. Nor in death,' said Margaret, surprising her companions with her observations.

The two men locked eyes above Margaret's head. Only a brief time had elapsed since her mother had died, and both men were acutely aware that in her grieving state this further knock would be keenly felt.

'You have witnessed birthing before?' asked John, attempting to steer her thoughts away from death, but worried that the alternative choice of topic was not an appropriate one to have with her either.

'Yes,' said Margaret, her head still against his shoulder and her gaze fixed upon the dog. 'When Father was a minister, and I was home from London, I would help if local villagers needed it. Only a handful of times you understand. But, to counterbalance the distress was the joy ...'

Quietude fell upon the group again as they regarded Margaret's words. John contemplated her strength of character and this new facet that he had been previously unaware of. He tried to imagine his sister Fanny or his mother offering to assist with childbirth. He was sure that Fanny wouldn't, but he considered that his mother would attend if she was needed. She was a strong woman too. But as John looked at the dog laid out on the flags in front of them, he wondered if she would have tried to save this animal like Margaret had. Certainly she could, but would she? He doubted it. John realised that while Margaret had the strength that he admired in his mother, she also had the will to help, to love and to care. Just not for him.

Higgins was the first to move, breaking the spell, the stiffness in his joints testament to the length of time he and Margaret had tended to the injured dog.

'Beggin' your pardon, Miss Margaret, but I'll see to this,' he said, nodding at the bloody debris on the kitchen floor. 'Then I mus' get back to Mary and t'children.'

Margaret roused herself from the warm cocoon of Mr Thornton's welcome, if improper, embrace, and faced the reality of practicalities that must be attended to.

'Of course, you must get back, Nicholas. I can deal with this. You go.'

Higgins looked at the master. He would not leave her to this job alone, but he sorely needed to get home.

'It's all right, Higgins, I'll help Miss Hale. I'm in no rush,' assured John.

'I'll thank you, Master. Miss Margaret, I'm sorry for bringin' this on you.'

'No, no Nicholas. I'm glad we tried to save her. And at least she was not alone,' said Margaret, causing another tear to trace a shimmering trail down her cheek.

Higgins washed the blood from his hands at the kitchen sink, then bade Miss Margaret and Thornton goodnight. John took off his jacket and placed it on the back of a kitchen chair. A tea tray was partially assembled on the table, so he fetched the kettle of water from the stove and filled the teapot for Mr Hale and Dixon. He had to smile to himself; if his mother knew he was about to serve tea to Dixon she would likely be overcome with apoplexy.

'No, Mr Thornton, allow me,' said Margaret, frowning as she reached forwards to take the tray from him.

'I'll do it,' he said tenderly. 'It's no bother. Besides, you might set her off again,' he said, blinking, with a tiny smile reaching one side of his mouth. He nodded at the large patches of blood on Margaret's apron and dress where she had been kneeling in the pooled blood.

'You wash yourself up a bit, and then perhaps you could find something, maybe a vegetable sack, and we'll wrap up the poor old girl and her pups,' he said, glancing back at the dog on the floor.

'Of course,' said Margaret, comprehending the merit of his words and the mess she was in.

John delivered the tea tray to Mr Hale and Dixon in the parlour, where they had assumed their natural evening occupations of reading and mending. However, the fact that neither of them appeared to be surprised at Mr Thornton furnishing them with a tea tray, highlighted to John that the two of them remained somewhat dazed and disturbed from the evening's upsetting turn of events. On returning to the kitchen, he rolled up his sleeves as Margaret appeared out of the pantry with an empty potato sack in her hands. He knelt down and was just about to pick up the dog when he froze, startled. His odd behaviour made Margaret also still, and look at him in surprise.

'What is it?' she enquired.

'Wait,' he said, with his hand lifted aloft as he stared at the puppies. 'Yes!' he exclaimed. 'Look! One moved.'

Margaret fell to her knees again in a flash, and instinctively grasped John's forearm as she held her breath, her eyes keenly searching the bodies on the floor for a sign of life. One tiny, bloody body quivered.

'Oh, Mr Thornton,' she whispered, and their wide eyes met, full of wonder. John reached behind him for a towel from the stove door, picked up the tiny pup, and attempted to wipe off the blood and slimy membrane that were remnants from its traumatic birth.

'It'll need some milk,' he said, looking at Margaret.

Galvanised into action, Margaret scanned the kitchen for some way to fashion a feeding receptacle for the tiny pup. She made a cone from waxed paper and covered it in a muslin square, then poured a little milk into the cone and milk dripped through the muslin tip. While John held the pup in the palm of his hand, Margaret dripped the milk into its mouth and, quite incredibly, the little creature drank greedily. John and Margaret warmly smiled at each other, revelling in their combined triumph.

When the pup had had its fill, John handed it, still bundled in the towel, into Margaret's arms. She sat cradling it gently, while John went back to his grim job of wrapping up the bodies of the dog and her remaining pups. He left the parcel outside the back door and promised to arrange for it to be removed the following day. He filled a pail of water, and on his hands and knees, he wiped away the bloody, sickly smelling evidence of the horror they had witnessed from the floor.

After he had washed his hands and arms, John came up to Margaret, and with one long finger, stroked the little pup's head which peeped out from the towel. Its eyes were tightly shut but it wriggled in Margaret's hands.

'It's not out of the woods,' he said, as he looked into her eyes, anxious to not destroy this tender moment, but feeling the need to make it clear to her that the little mite was still in a precarious position.

'I know,' she said, and smiled hopefully at him. 'But as it says in Romans, "Where there is life, there is hope".'

John walked home a little while later once he had taken his leave from Mr Hale. The blood stains were barely visible on his trousers or shoes, though his shirt was another matter, and his mother would no doubt have something to say about that. His mother. Here he was, a grown man of almost thirty-two years, responsible for the livelihood of hundreds of hands, and yet he was still subjected to his mother's sharp tongue. He loved his mother and respected her opinion. He thanked her for helping to make him the man he had become, and welcomed her support. Yet sometimes he wished she were not so harsh, including with him. He hoped that another would be his confidant. A woman of his choosing. Margaret.

Margaret's words came back to him – *where there is life, there is hope.* She had meant it for the puppy of course, but surely he could apply it to his own existence in more ways than one. His business was edging towards failure but, while the mill continued, there was hope for a reversal in fortune. And with Margaret too, although he knew very well that she would never love him, perhaps there was a way for her to grow to like him. To be his friend. For him to be hers. Yes, while there was breath in his body, he had hope.

It was a clear night in Milton, with an icy wind that had chased away the smoky remnants from the sky. John looked heavenward at the multitude of stars and predicted the early morning frost to come. Tomorrow, he and his workers would be subjected to that further layer of discomfort, but tonight he was not troubled by the cold. His mind was preoccupied with the evening's extraordinary events. Margaret's acceptance of his embrace and resting her head against him. Touching his arm. Touching his skin. Good Lord, there were enough new experiences in that short period of time to last him, well, perhaps a lifetime. He may never have that level of intimacy with her again.

It felt to John as if he, Margaret and Higgins had been in a bubble, where for a short while they were just people able to relate to one another without the constraints of society. Different rank, education and upbringing had been of no consequence. He thought of the poor mother dog and her dead offspring. How he wished for the remaining creature to live. His mind raced ahead to visiting again tomorrow, as he had promised, and he prayed that the little pup would be thriving still.

Chapter 2

Margaret opened her eyes a fraction as Dixon bustled noisily around her bedroom, first clanking the water jug, and then the brass handle of the sweeping brush against the fire grate as she cleaned out the previous day's ash. Margaret's mind registered that, after a good night's sleep, Dixon had regained her vigour following yesterday evening's excitement.

'So, you are awake at last,' the maid commented impertinently, in an accusatory tone.

'I have been awake most of the night,' replied Margaret quietly, although she felt aggrieved to be on the receiving end of the maid's harsh tongue. Dixon's attitude towards her had never changed since she and her brother Frederick had been children. Although it had not jarred when she had seen her infrequently, now that they lived under the same roof, along with her father, the maid's surly comments felt less appropriate with each passing day. Margaret was at a loss as to how she should handle Dixon when neither of her parents had ever taken her to task about her manner towards their daughter.

'And sleeping in your day clothes? Your hairpins still in? I've never known the like. And your apron is ruined,' grumbled the maid. 'The missus would never—'

'I know, Dixon,' cut in Margaret, flinging a hand over her eyes as Dixon drew back the curtains. Weak sunlight filtered into the room, its strength already half blotted out by the smoke billowing from Milton's multitude of industrial chimneys. Remembering the reason for her disturbed sleep, Margaret looked down to the tiny soul next to her on the bed, still swathed in the kitchen towel that Mr Thornton had wrapped it in the previous night. The bundle started to wiggle.

'She is ready to eat again I think,' said Margaret, with a gentle smile. The pup had survived the night and Margaret's heart was gladdened.

'Good heavens above,' said Dixon, clutching her neck. 'Dogs sleep outdoors! If anyone were to hear—'

'Who will hear, Dixon?' she laughed, not rising to the bait. 'There are only you and I and Father in the house. I believe this secret is quite safe.'

'Humph,' grumbled Dixon, trudging testily out of the room.

Alone again, Margaret thought back to the puppy's dramatic arrival last night, and the tragic experience that she had shared with Nicholas and Mr Thornton. Had she really let Mr Thornton put his arm around her? She covered her face with her hands in mortification. Of course, he had only meant it in sympathy as she had been distressed. Surely, it was an act that she could compare with when she had shielded him from the rioters. Just as

22

she would have protected any man in danger if she could prevent them from coming to harm, then presumably Mr Thornton comforting her was a human reaction to a person in distress. Certainly, that must be it. She fervently hoped that he did not think she welcomed his attentions. She had been perfectly clear about that in the past, when he had so condescendingly offered for her hand in order to preserve her maidenly reputation.

There was no doubt that she had acted recklessly that day when the strikers were so passionately afflicted as they gathered at Marlborough Mills. Firstly, she had sent Mr Thornton out to face the angry mob alone to attempt to reason with them, and he had done as she asked. Then having realised the terrible danger that she had exposed him to, she had thrown herself against him, between him and the amassed throng to protect him. She had felt certain that they wouldn't harm a woman. She had clutched him with her arms around his neck in front of all who were there, and those of his household spying from behind the curtains of the house.

Margaret supposed that some might have looked on his subsequent proposal the following day as a gentlemanly act, and she fancied that perhaps it was. But to marry such a man, such a stern unyielding man, merely for society's approval, was abhorrent to her. She had heard many disparaging reports about the cruelty of the mill masters from the poor. Margaret had paid attention to their tales when she delivered baskets of provisions to relieve their suffering, and understood Mr Thornton to be one and the same as his contemporaries. She didn't wish to tie herself to this or any man just to save her reputation, although she had to respect him for making the offer.

In the end there had been no furore about her actions at the mill. The vast majority of those who witnessed her clinging to the master were factory hands who cared nothing about reputations, and she had heard a rumour that it wasn't she, but his sister that had protected him that day. She guessed that the covert watchers from the house kept the facts to themselves to protect Mr Thornton. Margaret's life with her father, a new and rare time, could carry on unhindered. After the tumult of the riot there had been no storm to weather, and her life in Milton had continued unchanged, except perhaps that Mr Thornton's mother, and sister Fanny, now held her in lower regard.

Although Margaret now wished she had repelled Mr Thornton's arm last evening, she recognised with some discomfiture that at the time it had been welcome; it had felt right. The circumstances had been so distressing that any offer of support would have been so. She wondered if Nicholas would have consoled her in that way if Mr Thornton had not been there. As he was a father she was sure he would have, although she couldn't envisage her own father doing so. Last night he hadn't. Nicholas' empathy for those less fortunate than himself was evident on a daily basis. That could not be said for Mr Thornton, who appeared to have little natural sensitivity, so she realised that she must have been quite a fright to have inspired such a reaction from him.

Mr Thornton had said that he would call again today, and Margaret was determined to show him that the previous night's need for his solace was an isolated incident, and that she was composed and capable once more. She would have no further need for his arm about her shoulders, no matter how surprisingly protective the gesture had been at the time. No doubt within the secrecy of Marlborough House, Mr Thornton embraced his mother and sister on a regular basis as some peoples' fathers, brothers or sons often did. She tried to picture Mr Thornton comforting his mother or Fanny, but she couldn't, though she wondered if that was because those women didn't appear to be the kind who would welcome such softness. Margaret had never been exposed to physical expressions of affection, and she felt it peculiar that an infamously hard man like Mr Thornton would be wont to such displays, especially for her, when no one else had been compelled to offer her similar support in the past.

Margaret readied herself for the day, and although she was fatigued from the night spent awake with the pup, once she was washed, in fresh clothes and with her hair neatly pinned in place, she felt ready to tackle whatever lay ahead.

Mr Thornton had promised to have the pitiful remains of the pup's mother and siblings removed and, sure enough, just after eleven o'clock there was a knock on the back door. Margaret was pleased to see that Nicholas had been dispatched to see to the task, and he was accompanied by the three elder Boucher children whom Nicholas had cared for as his own since their parents died.

'Nicholas, children, come in,' welcomed Margaret, opening the door wide to her visitors, letting a gust of icy air in with them.

'Think t'master thought you might prefer a friendly face,' said Higgins, with what Margaret perceived as a curiously teasing smile. 'Said to tell you 'e'll be along after t'whistle blows.'

Margaret was busy showing the sleeping pup to the children. She had it situated close to the stove for warmth. She held hands with the smaller two, while Tom, the eldest at seven years of age, stood on the opposite side of a pail on the floor with Higgins at his back. All five peered into the bucket, which was lined with rags from an old sheet and a towel, where the puppy lay.

By and by the pup started to wriggle and Margaret picked her up and let Tom hold her. She was so tiny that she fit into Tom's cupped hands, and he proudly and reverently allowed his younger sisters to gently stroke her. In truth, the children were somewhat disappointed in the puppy. She was not fluffy or playful. She was a very small black, white and pink blob, with sealed eyes, and ears flattened to her head. But they took Miss Margaret's lead, and if she was happy with it, then they would be too.

'Children, we need to think of a name for her,' said Margaret, smiling lovingly at the scene before her. 'Can you help me to choose?'

Three little foreheads creased as they gave Miss Margaret's question serious thought. Tom was the first with a suggestion.

'What about Victoria, after t'Queen?' he said boldly.

How the boy has come along, thought Margaret. The Boucher children had been lucky to be taken in by Nicholas, although she knew his decision to have them was partly driven by duty; he felt some responsibility for the death of Mr Boucher due to his association with the union and harsh words the men had exchanged after the riot. The ill-fated strike and subsequent confrontation had affected so many of them, quite profoundly, in different ways. The hopelessness of his situation had been too much for Boucher to bear, and in taking his own life he had left the children as orphans. But as well as feeling an obligation towards the children, Margaret also knew that Higgins' decision to look after them was because he was a good man. To take in these children, abandoned to the world by fate, was in Margaret's opinion an heroic act and she was glad of his selflessness. She was sad to think it, but Nicholas and Mary were perhaps doing a finer job of raising the children than Boucher himself would have done. She hoped that one day, these children would understand how fortunate they were to have someone who cared for them. Wanted them. What an uncommon and precious gift that was.

'Perfect!' said Margaret, clasping her hands together in delight. 'How clever, Tom,' and she smoothed his dark blonde hair affectionately.

The children gathered around and watched Margaret feed Victoria by means of the waxed paper and muslin cone that she had fashioned the previous night. They giggled behind their small hands when Victoria wet the towel on Margaret's knee. She then allowed the children to help her to settle the puppy back in the bucket bed before they took their leave.

By six o'clock in the evening, Margaret was exhausted. The lack of sleep from the night before had caught up with her, and the magnitude of the task ahead dawned on her for the first time. Victoria woke frequently, and when offered warmed milk she guzzled it willingly. To ensure the pup flourished, Margaret knew that she would need to maintain this level of commitment.

She was just dozing in the parlour, catching a few minutes rest before she must start heating milk again, when the jingling of the doorbell jolted her awake. *Mr Thornton*, she thought. Dixon huffed down the hallway to the front door and Margaret could hear his soft deep voice, although she couldn't make out his words. A moment or two later, Dixon knocked on the parlour door and introduced Mr Thornton with an air of irritation that both he and Margaret decided to ignore. Margaret rose to greet him, bobbing a small curtsy, and he bowed in response.

Throughout the afternoon, Margaret had anticipated Mr Thornton's visit, and now, just at the very moment when he had arrived, she felt nervous and on edge. She had known he was coming after work, as Higgins had told her so, but when she usually knew he was expected it had become her habit to keep in her room. She was ashamed to acknowledge that she had been hiding from him, ever since his proposal of marriage. While she had not regretted her refusal, she was sorry for her unnecessarily cruel words of rejection, and she had found it hard to face him afterwards. She had reflected on her words to him many times and knew that she must have hurt him even if, as was her belief, his protestations of love were false. He had taken her quite by surprise by his sudden and unwanted declaration. Although she had spent time in his company during his lessons with her father, she didn't know the man, let alone have developed a fondness for him, so she couldn't believe that he had genuine feelings for her. To say that he loved her, and so fiercely, was too much to bear. She would not be lied to. She would rather be alone than in a loveless marriage, and with that thought, for the first time in many months, Henry Lennox briefly flitted through her mind causing a small frown.

As John straightened from his bow, he immediately noticed Margaret's scowl and his heart plummeted. She didn't want to see him. It seemed that things between them had not improved, despite the intimacy of the previous night. It appeared that the truce between them had been called off.

'Begging your pardon, Miss Hale. I shan't trouble you,' he said, swallowing hard and retreating a few steps back towards the door. He would not impose himself where he was not welcome.

Margaret's countenance cleared as Henry Lennox was banished from her thoughts, and she bestowed a courteous smile upon Mr Thornton. He was always so inflexible, and yet yesterday she had seen another side to him. She watched him visibly stiffen and, blinking furiously, he stepped forwards again and put a large parcel down on the parlour table, and fiddled with the brown paper wrapping. Collecting himself, he stood straight and raised his chin. She'd seen that mannerism before, but she was at a loss as to why he should need to be defensive. Surely it was she who needed to show him her armour after letting her guard down so completely last night. She had offended him already it seemed, though she had no idea how, especially as he had only just entered the room.

'I am pleased to see you, Mr Thornton,' she assured him levelly, and he looked momentarily into her eyes to discern if she was simply being polite. 'Please do sit down. You must be excited to see Victoria,' she said, and the complete joy upon her face at the mention of the puppy encouraged him to comply and sit as requested.

'Victoria?'

'Yes, Tom Boucher named her. Isn't it a splendid name? Thank you so much for allowing Nicholas to come during the working day,' she said, and he merely gave a little shake of his head, deflecting her kind words.

Margaret reached into a bucket which he had failed to notice when entering the room, as all his senses were previously focused on Margaret. She extracted Victoria, unwrapped her and placed her in his hands.

'Would you please hold her for a moment? It's her feeding time, and I will fetch some warmed milk for her and tea for you, if you would like it?'

'Indeed,' was all he could manage to get out, so enamoured was he by Miss Hale's easy manner with him, following her initial apparently frosty welcome.

John peered at the pup nestled in his palm. It was a tiny little scrap, and with such a majestic name he mused, a small smile lifting one side of his mouth. He thought of Tom Boucher naming the puppy, no doubt with the grandest name he could think of to emulate Miss Hale.

While Margaret was out of the room, John inspected the little creature. Like its mother, the tiny pup was mostly black but had a white muzzle, chest and front legs, with further patches of white to its back feet and tail. It was so delicate with tiny pink paws and a pink nose where its fur had not yet started to grow. It wriggled over in his hand, and John's stern eyebrows drew down into a deep frown and he stilled. He caught his bottom lip between his teeth and stared hard at the pup, his mind and now his stomach in turmoil.

When Margaret entered the room carrying the tea tray, including Victoria's milk and feeding apparatus, she was completely oblivious to Mr Thornton's anguish.

'Would you like to feed her, Mr Thornton?' Margaret asked, pleasantly.

John's expressive eyebrows lifted, and he blinked twice.

'Miss Hale,' he said uncertainly. 'I think you may have to rethink the pup's name.'

'Oh? Do you not like it?' said Margaret, a little put out that Mr Thornton would question Tom's choice.

'You see,' he said, then paused. He swallowed and shut his eyes for a moment. 'The pup is more an Albert than a Victoria, if you get my meaning,' he said, and ventured a quick look at Miss Hale.

'Oh! I didn't see … umm …'

A hot blush was creeping up John's neck and his collar was suddenly too tight, making both breathing and swallowing quite difficult. 'Well, I'll grant you it's small. But he's only young.' *God almighty*, he thought, closing his eyes and covering them with his free hand. What on earth had possessed him? Why did he not just ignore it and let her find out in due course? Well, that was it then. There was no way he would be permitted into the Hales' parlour again. Referring to male organs of all things. *Good God.* John heard Miss Hale give a small, strangled wheeze. He dared to glance at her, and found her cheeks to be tinted a radiant pink as she held a dainty hand over her mouth to subdue what he assumed to be a further cough.

'I apologise, Miss Hale, for my … ungentlemanly conversation,' he managed, before shame caught his tongue again.

'Nonsense, Mr Thornton,' Margaret began, endeavouring to get her flush of embarrassment under control. 'You were quite right to point out my error. Well, it appears you have named him then. Hello Albert,' she said, and leant forwards to stroke the pup as he lay in Mr Thornton's hand. And there it was, the slight scent of roses that he ached for.

'Will you feed him, Mr Thornton and I will pour the tea and, I must say, I am intrigued by the parcel you brought with you.' Margaret handed the warm milk to John, and he fed the little fellow as he had seen her do yesterday, a little clumsily at first, but he soon got the hang of it.

Margaret unwrapped the brown paper parcel. It contained a small wooden crate with low sides, and a packet of cotton scraps to provide a warm and comfortable bed for the puppy.

'I can see you have already made arrangements,' John said, nodding to the bucket that Albert had been sleeping in when he had arrived. 'So don't feel obliged to use my offering. Although I have a steady supply of cotton bits when those need changing,' he said stiffly.

Margaret looked at Mr Thornton. How different he was both last evening and today. She couldn't reconcile this man with her previous experience of him. After her abominable treatment of him when he had proposed, he was behaving most graciously, kindly even, towards the puppy that they had saved, and it pleased her that he had been so thoughtful with his gift.

'I thank you, Mr Thornton. Truly. Dixon will be glad to get her bucket back, and Father will be pleased to put an end to Dixon's complaining about the loss of it. So, you see, your contribution will have far reaching consequences and it is most appreciated.'

John watched as Margaret made up a bed for Albert in the crate and placed a towel over the cotton padding. Then, when the pup had had his fill of milk, Margaret carefully took him from John's hands, her scent reaching him again as she leant towards him. Once Albert was laid snugly in his new bed, he immediately went to sleep.

'John!' said Mr Hale, as he entered the room. 'How wonderful to see you this evening,' and he reached out his hand to shake John's as he moved to stand.

'No, John, you stay there,' Mr Hale encouraged. 'Poor Margaret has been up all day and all night with the little mite. I don't know how we'll go on in the longer term,' he said, grey bushy brows coming together in consternation. 'We know nothing about rearing animals.'

Margaret wondered at the use of the word 'we' as her father had yet to involve himself in the care of the puppy.

'If I may,' said John. 'I would be happy to do some research on hand rearing dogs if that would be of help?'

'Yes, thank you. We would be most obliged,' agreed Margaret.

Shortly after John had shared a cup of tea with the Hales, he took his leave. Whilst he didn't want to go so soon, he was aware of the very little rest Miss Hale had had in the past twenty-four hours, and would not impose upon her any longer. He was encouraged by the request for further cotton scraps and information on rearing puppies that he would endeavour to investigate, giving him the opportunity to see Miss Hale again soon.

Chapter 3

Hannah Thornton despised Margaret Hale. How any woman could reject her son was beyond comprehension. The southern miss, with her superior ways, still dangled John's heart from her little finger, and it galled Hannah that she was powerless to turn him from her. Each week when he gathered his books and marched over to the Hales', half of her hated him for doing it, for grovelling for an ounce of affection from the girl who had broken his heart. Little did she know that these days John almost never saw Miss Hale on his visits to Crampton for his studies. Yet the other half of Hannah was proud. She was gratified that her son would stand tall and not be cowed or turned from the path he chose to better himself. Nevertheless, it was with some anxiety that Hannah watched her son ready himself to go to the Hales' for the third night in a row.

John's clothes had been all but ruined two days ago when he had become embroiled in the calamity at the Hales'. She would have to burn his shirt, and Hannah was further peeved with Miss Hale for the additional expense she had caused. Hannah had spied a parcel that John had taken to the Hales' the previous night, and her pride had prevented her from quizzing him about it. Tonight, John was once more getting ready to leave, although he had not changed from his work clothes, so she was somewhat relieved that he was not making a special effort for Miss Hale. Again she noticed a parcel in his hand, and this time she couldn't resist asking about its contents, so she intercepted him in the hall before he could escape.

'Cotton waste, Mother. That's all,' he said, as he pecked her cheek and strode towards the door.

'Are they so hard up that they can't provide a bed for one dog? Do they plan to have you walk over there every night to see to it?' she asked, her tone brittle and biting.

'I am happy to supply them with the scraps. The waste is of no value to us and it is a help to them. I go there because I want to, Mother. Goodnight,' and he left the house, banging the door closed harder than he had intended.

As well as the cotton parcel, John also had some information to impart to Miss Hale. Firstly, John had spotted Tom Boucher waiting for Higgins to finish work, and had broken the news to him that the puppy wasn't female and so an alternative name had had to be chosen. Rather than being disappointed, Tom was quite pleased that the puppy was a boy dog, and he was equally glad that they had kept a regal name. Secondly, John had gained intelligence on dog rearing as he had promised. During the break for the noon meal, John had asked Higgins for help in identifying any hands who knew about caring for puppies, and he was directed to two men, a father and son who worked in the weaving shed but had previously worked in farming. Both men had been most anxious at seeing the master bearing down on them in the canteen, but to their relief he had only questioned them about dogs.

John had listened intently as the senior of the two men, named Ernest Bailey, explained the pitfalls, and his son Edwin joined in with little facts that his father had missed. The crux of the tale, for the time being at least, was that Albert would need feeding every two to three hours, day and night. Margaret's current feeding technique appeared to be sufficient for now but soon he would need bottle feeding with a teat. It also appeared necessary to help the pup to relieve himself. John blanched. That was going to be an uncomfortable topic to broach, but he armed himself with cotton, and set out with purpose to see the Hales.

Dixon let him into the house, a disapproving look on her face. The survival of that puppy, though pleasing to Miss Margaret, was causing the maid concern as it brought about more frequent visits from Mr Thornton. Although she had not confided in her, Dixon had been under the impression that the mill master had a soft spot for Miss Margaret, and Dixon had been pleased that she appeared not to have entertained his affections. Miss Hale was a lady, the granddaughter of Sir John Beresford, and she had been brought up for finer things, not the likes of a rough tradesman like Mr Thornton.

Mr and Miss Hale were seated in the parlour, and both stood to welcome their guest. After a few pleasantries had been exchanged, Mr Hale excused himself from John and Margaret's conversation regarding the puppy as he had a lecture to prepare, so moved away from them to a chair near to the window to concentrate.

'He is well, Miss Hale?' asked John softly, not wanting to disturb Mr Hale's engrossment. 'Are you managing all right with his feeds?'

'He is doing well, thank you, Mr Thornton. I must admit it is very tiring as he needs frequent attention.'

John imparted the information regarding the feeding schedule that Albert would require for some weeks yet, and Margaret nodded in understanding as she listened to him. He then moved onto the more daunting information.

'The hands, a father and son called Bailey,' he began, 'have also mentioned, umm, something else.' Margaret watched Mr Thornton as he blinked and ran a finger underneath and along his collar to loosen it a little before he continued. 'Bitches, umm, mother dogs, lick their young, and the Baileys have suggested this can be simulated by stroking the pup underneath with damp cotton wadding.'

'And what is the purpose of it, Mr Thornton? Is it to establish a bond between the mother and her young?'

How he wanted to say yes.

'Well maybe it would do that. Umm, but no,' he said, and he glanced at Mr Hale hoping for some interruption from him, but none came as the elder man was absorbed in his book. 'It stimulates the offspring to … to …'

Margaret leaned closer. 'To?' she urged gently.

'Void,' he said, in a hoarse whisper.

Margaret sat back. 'Oh! Well, Mr Thornton, I can report that so far, Albert has had no difficulty in … voiding, as you put it,' and her cheeks bloomed into a delightful blush, as once again she and Mr Thornton had to overcome their joint mortification.

Miss Hale was the first to recover, adopting a business-like approach. 'But I will do as instructed. And I thank you for the provisions. Truthfully it is the two hourly feeding that is the bigger problem. I have always marvelled at the fortitude of mothers, and now my appreciation of them is further enhanced.'

'Perhaps it is more convenient and natural to feed one's own young. Physiologically speaking.' *Good god almighty*, he thought.

'Indeed,' agreed Margaret, and she couldn't look at him, for she knew she would see the evidence of his embarrassment, and that she would be unable to quell the giggle that bubbled beneath the surface.

Mr Thornton had become most perplexing, a conundrum. She had always understood him to be a principled man, through listening to his conversations with her father. Even Nicholas had ventured that he was a decent man and employer, but she had always imagined him before to be so cold. Her opinion of him was being forced to be changed as she had experienced at first hand his kindness, and he had caused amusement on these past two evenings, even though the subject matter was not something she could repeat. Her cousin Edith or Aunt Shaw would be scandalised by the unfortunate subjects he had been required to address. He had not shied away from them though, even when he was clearly uncomfortable, and she surmised that she respected his honesty.

Later that evening as he walked home, John Thornton smirked. It appeared Miss Hale had a sense of humour, he just wished his humiliation had not been the cause of her amusement. In the last few days he had alluded to male organs, toileting needs and breastfeeding. He wondered if he could be any more embarrassed, or if there were any further scenarios that he would blindly stumble into showing up his ungentlemanly and rough nature. And yet she had taken it in her stride. Thank the Lord she had not taken offence, or he would never be able to explain to his mother why he was no longer welcome at the Hale household whether for lessons or otherwise. It would be a few days before he could visit again, and he hoped by then he would have managed to control his mouth from venturing onto unseemly conversation.

Chapter 4

It was another cold morning with wintry gusts from the north, and grey storm clouds further darkening Milton's smoky sky. Despite the biting chill, John refused to have the fire lit in his office as his workers had no such luxury in the sheds and warehouses where they toiled. If they could endure the hardship day in and day out, then he could too. The risk of fire that any flame posed in the mill was great indeed, with the promise of catastrophic consequences should the cotton fluff catch alight. He didn't suppose that any of the workers paid any attention to his, the master's, comfort. However, it sat better with him that he was not privileged when they had no such benefit, whether they discerned it or not.

John was an expert in self-denial having spent most of his youth and all of his adult life to date exercising it. As a lad he had needed to do without so that his meagre wages both supported his family and could be saved up to pay back his deceased father's creditors. Self-control was a well-honed tool that John had used to raise himself, his mother and sister from near ruin to the pinnacle of his career to date, and now it was a way of life. Townsfolk would look on John Thornton, the severe and driven master of arguably the premier cotton mill in Darkshire, as a successful man. But triumph and wealth did not make you a gentleman and nor did manners. The title of gentleman was the birthright of those outside John's circle, a club that he could not infiltrate, and until he met Miss Hale he couldn't have cared less.

The incessant, rhythmic clatter filtered through to John's office as he sat at his desk with the ledgers open in front of him. It was no good, he couldn't balance the books, but the unrelenting clamour from the weaving shed comforted him. At least for now the mill was still living and breathing. He had tried, and still endeavoured both day and night, to turn the fortunes of his mill around. Its failure would not be through lack of effort, and a lesser man might have given up and cut his losses before now. But John was a formidable man, described by some as a bulldog. Although he was physically strong, John's real might was in his strength of character and dogged determination to develop. He perpetually looked to move forwards, progress and improve, not just himself but everything in his power, most especially the mill.

The strike had caused seemingly irreparable damage to his business. Of course, he understood that the workers wanted higher wages. It was perfectly understandable; he would have felt the same way in their shoes. But with the increased price of raw cotton from America, all the mills had no choice but to cut wages simply to survive. He knew well that a strike would deal a hammer blow to the mill, and he had tried to prevent it by negotiating with his fellow masters. When that failed, he had felt forced to import Irish workers to replace those who banded together in the industrial action.

But while his tactic had worked in that the strike had ended, he was on the very edge of bankruptcy, and the resulting humiliation that would taint his mother and perhaps even Fanny by association. The penalties for missed deadlines, late payment for orders, and vast quantities of cotton unusable due to the poor workmanship of the inexperienced Irish workers, had all compounded with the unmanageable market forces. His hundreds of workers would be thrown into destitution without the jobs he provided. And to add insult to injury, the strike, and Miss Hale's perception that he was cruel to his workers, had fuelled her disdain for him.

He thought back to his doomed proposal, tormenting himself, running over the words they had spoken to each other, as he was wont to do. How could he have ever thought to win her hand? The tiny flame of hope that had been within him, that a woman such as Miss Hale could love him, had been fanned by Fanny's firm opinion that she was sure that Miss Hale was attempting to catch him, and her actions of putting herself between him and the rioters proved it. John laughed sadly to himself. She need not catch him, he was already hers, body and soul. The wildfire of passion for Miss Hale had compelled him to offer for her hand, and he had been duly crushed by her rejection.

He had used every last speck of his courage to see her that day, and to expose his closely guarded inner feelings to her. Overcoming his almost debilitating shyness with the opposite sex that he usually tried so hard to conceal, had taken considerable nerve. He had learnt to hide his self-consciousness behind a carefully constructed wall of brusque civility, and yet on that day he had dropped his shield and had spoken to Miss Hale of his passionate love for her. Her disgust at his words of love, words he had never said before, a feeling he had never felt before, soundly annihilated any hope of winning her, and he had retreated, wounded, back behind his barrier. He wished he had never uttered those words that she found so repellent, but it was no good looking back. Time could not be reversed and neither, in his experience, did it heal.

She would never have him, he knew that with complete certainty. He was a nobody who pulled himself and his family out of the gutter that his father had left them in, and through determination and hard work he had succeeded. But success was not a quality that Miss Hale valued. She knew of the deficiency in his education due to his early removal from school, and most damning of all, the disgrace of his father's suicide after having lost everything by gambling on a speculation. He shook his head. Early in their acquaintance she had even refused to shake his hand, and since then he had been careful not to offend her with his evidently uncouth ways. He had been deluded to believe that she could ever hold in high regard a man such as him.

Nor was Miss Hale's head turned by his looks and he was glad of it. He was not what might have been described as a ladies man. Although his shyness prevented him from conversing comfortably with women, it was a fact that he had previously neither had the time nor inclination for a romantic attachment. John found his apparent appeal to the fairer sex to be something of a curiosity, and thought it likely that their interest was more to do with him being a prominent figure in the town, and that he was still single, than his attributes. In truth, the fact that he paid the young women of Milton no heed only increased their fascination with him. Nevertheless, John felt his features were all too extreme – too dark, too stern – and yet there was nothing he could do about it. There was nothing average about him. To tone down his appearance he chose to always dress very moderately and in complete contrast to his sister. Fanny Watson, formerly Thornton, adored attention of any kind and dressed to be noticed and admired.

That a woman should want to marry him for the way he looked was detestable to him. Fanny had married a man for his money, and John found that equally distasteful. Certainly, Margaret Hale was the most beautiful woman he had ever laid eyes on, but she was so much more than that. He adored her spirit, her intelligence, her conversation and her kindness. He couldn't imagine Miss Hale marrying a man for his looks or his money, and he felt certain that she would want a man who understood, respected, and cherished her. Good Lord, he could do all of that. He did all of that and more already. If only her heart answered the call of his.

John's mind ran over their meetings over the last few days for perhaps the millionth time. How right and in keeping with her temperament it was that she championed the puppy. That she would strive for it. Love it. It was another reason why she could not, and would never love him.

Despite the reality of the impending failure of Marlborough Mills he would come out of it fighting. Margaret Hale didn't need to fight his corner, so sided with those who needed her support, and they were supremely lucky to have her patronage. He couldn't change his character; both nature and nurture had fashioned him that way.

Despite being so out of Miss Hale's level of society, he would help her as much as he could. His heart would let him do no less. He wanted the puppy to survive, not just for her, but for the creature itself. The unconditional love between an animal and its master or mistress was something he had never experienced, though he had longed for a dog of his own when he was a lad, but his mother had never allowed it. Helping Miss Hale would be a privilege. He would take comfort from assisting her, and would save up all of their meetings in his heart, and pull out each memory from time to time to examine and enjoy. If that was all he could have of her, then it was enough. He would accept any time with her with silent gratitude, and perhaps she might soften to him a little and not dislike him so much. That would be a victory. He could not fall out of love with Miss Hale, she was indelibly imprinted on his heart, but he must accept that he was too far removed from being the gentleman she deserved.

He closed his eyes and brought to mind his favourite moment with Miss Hale that had occurred a few days ago, when she had allowed him to put his arm around her. It was such an outrageously forward gesture, but she had accepted it, so distraught had she been at the time. Had Nicholas Higgins been next to her, then John thought it probable he would have done the same thing. John realised that he would not have begrudged Higgins the action. Indeed, Miss Hale would likely have felt more comfortable accepting the older man's fatherly embrace than his own. But she had accepted it, and had rested her head on his shoulder in her distress. He remembered the feel of her body, soft and nestled perfectly against his. What he would give to repeat that intimacy, but he knew he never would. He hoped Miss Hale was never in a position where she needed comfort. He would not wish that on her, especially not simply for his gain.

As Miss Hale had made it crystal clear that he would never be suitable as a husband, John's mind wandered to others who might be singled out by her as a partner. Certainly, no man that he knew of in Milton would suffice. Men of a similar standing to himself, arguably the best that Milton could offer, were few and far between, and were liable to wish for a more obedient wife, preferably with a dowry to bolster their coffers. All the other mill masters were already married, and he knew that some of his contemporaries, the likes of Slickson and Hamper, had they been available, would not have entertained Miss Hale. They were not likely to appreciate her opinionated conversation, yet it was one of the things he liked most about her.

Many months ago, John had heard the Hales mention a man named Henry Lennox. This unseen man was notable in that Miss Hale referred to him as 'Henry', not Mr Lennox. He had paid close attention to the description of this gentleman's relationship to Miss Hale, and he understood him to be a relation by marriage to Miss Hale's cousin, Edith Lennox. The familiarity of calling this man by his first name had irritated John to an absurd degree. Miss Hale also called Higgins by his Christian name. It was a sign of her friendship with him, a sign of her affection. That said, he had not heard mention of Lennox for several months, but that was most probably because Miss Hale had been absent from his lessons for that duration too.

She had been much more welcoming of him the last few times he had seen her, and he realised that a friendship of sorts had formed between them. Perhaps with time, she would feel as comfortable with him as she did with Higgins and Lennox. He smiled wryly to himself as he mused that his financial ruin might actually make her more sympathetic towards him.

Unless an investor came forward soon, in a matter of weeks Marlborough Mills would close its gates for the last time, and any foolish fancy his lonely heart had for Miss Hale would be obliterated once and for all. He would have nothing material to offer her, and she did not want or accept his love. She deserved better than a coarse man like him. He hoped for her lasting happiness in finding a gentleman she could love and respect, and who felt the same for her. He just hoped with all his faithful heart that he would not have to bear witness to it.

John slammed the ledgers closed. He'd wasted enough time daydreaming again. He needed some relief from Miss Hale and his financial predicament, so he scraped his chair back from the desk and stood, rolling up his sleeves. What he needed was some hard physical work to warm him up and divert his mind, and he knew of a shipment of cotton in need of dispatching that would do the trick. Banging his office door closed behind him, John descended the stairs to the mill yard where the daily bustle was in full swing.

The hands nodded to the master as he passed them by. He was something of an enigma to his labourers. Thornton could nigh on blister the paintwork with his temper when it flared, but no other mill masters took their turn with the hard physical graft. No other mill masters had occasion to sit and eat their meal with the workers in their canteen, or even provided a canteen for that matter. No other mill master contributed as many safety measures, including the 'wheel' to remove excessive cotton fluff from the environment that was notorious for clogging healthy lungs. If it weren't for the pitifully low wages that all Milton mills paid, the hands at Marlborough Mills would be bordering on content with their lot.

Chapter 5

Margaret had spent the two days since Mr Thornton's last visit tending to Albert with unrelenting diligence. She fed him every two hours and swabbed him with the cotton wadding as Mr Thornton had explained, and the little chap continued to thrive. Help from either her father or Dixon was neither requested nor offered, so Margaret shouldered the burden alone. However, the lack of sleep over several days, with an hour snatched here or there, was taking its toll. She was utterly exhausted and almost fell asleep at the dinner table; the steady ticking of the clock and the uninterrupted stillness of the room lulled her into slumber. Mr Hale watched his daughter from across the table as she swayed, nodding off to sleep upright in her chair, then jolting awake again seconds later. Richard Hale didn't wish to see his daughter so debilitated, and so he resolved to fix the situation.

Margaret and her father retired to the parlour for a little while together before he went out to deliver the lecture that he had been preparing for a gathering at Milton's Lyceum.

'Margaret, my dear,' Mr Hale broached benignly. 'I think it would be better if the creature was tended to by someone more able.'

'Able?' Margaret was suddenly wide awake, startled by her father's words, and she sat up straight in her chair.

Mr Hale fidgeted with the book in his hands, staring at it, unable to meet her gaze as he turned it round and round, and searched for his next words. Margaret could be quite forthright, and he needed to tread carefully. He didn't feel particularly capable or adept at handling his daughter who had become almost a stranger to him, having spent so long living apart from her parents. His motivation for making the decision on the future of the puppy was because he wanted to make life easier for Margaret. She already worked so hard in the house assisting Dixon with household chores, and he was sorry about it. He was ashamed that he could not provide a better life for them, having given up his position as vicar in Helstone a little over a year ago. But before he could summon up the right words, Margaret spoke up.

'Father, I am able. I am tired, that is all. You would have me give him up? I can't, Father. Don't ask it of me, please,' said Margaret, impassioned.

She reached down into Albert's crate and picked up the sleeping puppy, clutching him to her breast as though her father was about to snatch him away at that moment.

'I think it is for the best, Margaret. Sincerely, I do. I would have suggested Mr Higgins might have it, but he will not appreciate another mouth to feed. I will ask at the assembly tonight if anyone can take it in. If no one there is able, then I know that Mr Thornton will be of assistance in finding a home for the animal. It will be for the best.'

Margaret was incensed. His constant referral to Albert as 'it' further inflamed her ire.

'Father, have you decided this already? Without asking me?' she said, getting to her feet. Margaret could barely comprehend his words. That he would do this to her, to Albert, felt underhand and uncalled for.

The strange fact that neither her father nor Dixon had offered to help her with rearing Albert, despite him being unquestionably adorable yet helpless, occurred to her for the first time. Even a man such as Mr Thornton had immediately warmed to him, and Margaret believed the sincerity of his feelings for the pup. She wondered if her father had asked Dixon to side with him on this matter. Could it be that he, or they, wanted her to fail? Margaret had the grace to perceive that her paranoia was more than likely due to her overwhelming fatigue than the truth of the matter. Her father was not a bad man by any means, but Margaret was horrified by his words, and a sick feeling washed over her, and yet ... how typical.

As much as she loved her father, and he too loved her, she knew that with complete certainty, he would not fight. He would not fight for her, he would not fight for his faith and now he would not even fight for this little pup. It was a trait, a flaw of his character which had resulted in Margaret spending the majority of her childhood wrenched from her family, as he had bent to the will of her mother's relatives. Both her parents had. Margaret had been sent to London to grow up apart from them and her dear brother, Frederick.

Margaret had been singled out to be her cousin Edith's companion, and it had stung sharply. Her parents had managed without her so that Edith could have her simply as a playmate. Instead of her fate, Frederick had been favoured with their parents' love and attention, and was brought up in the bosom of their family. Although Margaret had spent long periods of time separated from Frederick, she had always held him in the warmest regard, having enjoyed joyous times together in their childhood.

Margaret had been devastated when Frederick had left to join the navy, and her worry for him was realised when news of his death was received by the Hales. If that were not terrible enough, it was reported that he had been involved in a mutiny aboard the 'Russell', although the details were scant and failed to satisfy the questions this occurrence raised with the family, and which would never be answered. He had been tragically killed during the revolt, and reports from the survivors suggested that Frederick had been an instigator of the mutiny. His name would be forever linked with the disgrace, and it cast a spectral shadow upon his memory.

While in the household of her Aunt Shaw, Margaret had benefited from an education, fine clothes and upper-class society. She had learnt to be a lady, and yet it was of little use to her now. She was in a limbo between Aunt Shaw's influence on her upbringing, and the reality of her adult life which would be spent apart from that elite set. She was a parson's daughter, and although she had some high-class pedigree, she had no fortune to make her an attractive match for those in her aunt's circle. While her beauty had brought her to the attention of some gentlemen, her lack of money soon cooled their interest. In fact, she had been utterly blindsided when Henry Lennox had proposed. She had had no inkling that he had any romantic feelings for her. And of course, more recently she had received Mr Thornton's unexpected and wholly unwanted offer.

Margaret did not believe the sincerity of Mr Thornton's protestations of love. In her view he was doing what society expected of him, and in offering her the protection of his name, he would gain a wife above his station in society. Perhaps he would see that as a fair trade. But Margaret wished for a partnership, a mutual affection and trust, which was as far from Mr Thornton's ideal as it could possibly be. Even Henry Lennox would be a preferable alternative. And yet when she thought back to her relationship with him, the insipidity of his suit also repulsed her. Margaret fervently wished for the opportunity to be independent, but it was impossible. She must marry, for once her father had passed, she would be without means. How she wished that she and her father could live safely together, forever.

While Margaret viewed Henry Lennox as a friend and someone she had shared light-hearted jokes with during Edith and Sholto Lennox's wedding, she had no desire to marry him. He was amiable enough, but she did not love him. As nice as he was, Margaret found him bland and completely lacking in dynamism or drive. She found she was comparing him with Mr Thornton who had too many of those qualities! Surely it was normal to compare these men as they had both offered for her. The compelling feature of her parents' marriage was that it was bound with love, and Margaret felt that this was an essential requirement for both the success of the union and happiness of husband and wife; she would settle for no less. Mr Thornton's proposal had been altogether different from that of Henry's. The violence in both words and manner when he had declared his passionate love for her had been shocking and offensive. She would not willingly give herself over into the hands of such a man, most certainly not Mr Thornton, to be subject to his will, and to pledge before God to obey him. Margaret felt as though she had become a piece of merchandise, something to be moved from place to place to fulfil a function. Others made decisions about what she should do, and how she should spend her time. What she really wanted was to be able to choose for herself.

Her father had made it clear that he was certain that Mr Thornton would help him take Albert away from her. Margaret thought it was likely that he would help her father and side with him. Her father and Mr Thornton had formed a friendship, and he had already found men who had experience with puppies at his mill. She was sure that it would take little pressure from him to get the labourers in his employ to agree to his wishes and take Albert. Of course he would. They would ally themselves against her as everyone always did. For all the kindness he had shown her since Albert's birth, Mr Thornton's true colours would prevail; he would be no better than the rest.

Margaret felt helpless. Although she could challenge the unfairness that she saw about her, and experienced herself, she was under the control of her father and had no power against his authority. At least, on this occasion, her father had not presented this to her as a fait accompli as had happened in the past. It still wounded her so deeply to have been sent away to London as a child. Again recently, when she was no longer required by Aunt Shaw and Edith, and had been permanently reunited with her parents, she had been uprooted once more. She had had no say in the Hales' removal to Milton, and had not known about the arrangements until it was too late. All she could do was to go along with it, be brave and try her best. She had helped her father with the relocation, and supported him when her mother could not. She was ashamed to admit, if only to herself, that she had wanted to please him; she wanted him to be glad that she was there, and see her worth.

Richard Hale took the path of least resistance. The only exception being his marriage to Maria Beresford when love had truly conquered all, and she, a great beauty and daughter of Sir John Beresford, had married a lowly parson far beneath her own standing in society. But Margaret wondered, had the tables been turned and her father had been the aristocrat, whether he would have battled to make Maria his wife. Perhaps it had been her mother who had fought for him. She would never know.

Now that Margaret was opposing his plans to be rid of the puppy, Mr Hale's resolve faltered. He wondered if he had been a little high-handed. Perhaps this was not a contest that he needed to win. Harmony and understanding were important principles after all, and as he still grieved the loss of his dear wife, Mr Hale did not have the heart to bring about conflict. Margaret may need to reach the decision that she could not care for the dog herself. Margaret's exhaustion suggested to him that her dedication to the puppy would soon wane. However, Mr Hale was not well acquainted with his daughter, or her tenacity.

'Well, Dixon and I will not have the time to help. So if you are set on going down this path, then …' said Mr Hale, his words fading to silence.

'I will manage, Father,' she said, more determined than ever.

~

'I don't know what you see in the girl. She refused you, John. She doesn't know your worth,' spat Hannah Thornton to her son. She stood with her arms crossed, the customary black silk of her dress rustling as she moved, barring the door to the hallway and thereby preventing John's escape. She would have her say and he would listen, whether he liked it or not.

'I am well aware of that, thank you, Mother,' countered John. He had heard it many times before and now he merely deflected it. There was no merit in expounding Margaret Hale's virtues to his mother, as her indisputable dislike for Miss Hale was deeply entrenched. Today however, Hannah would not be easily fobbed off and she needled him further.

'And now she, the daughter of a disgraced parson who gave up his living for a "matter of conscience", so high and mighty that she would not have you, suddenly decides to click her fingers and you come running,' sneered Hannah, clicking her own fingers for emphasis.

John took a breath, determined to stay calm in the face of his mother's antipathy towards Miss Hale. 'She is too good for me, Mother. I respect her decision and I understand it. She is right. Look at Fanny, Mother. She has married a man over twice her age, a man old enough to be her father. She doesn't love him. I doubt she even cares for him. She cares for his money, and if that is all she wishes for then I am pleased for her. But Miss Hale did not accept me for my money, and God knows it's just as well seeing as I'm about to be ruined. But don't you see? She wants more. She needs a man she can respect and love, and she doesn't see that in me. I am reconciled with it, pleased even, as I wouldn't be able to give her the life she deserves. Not now.'

'Deserves?' huffed his mother angrily. She knew that she was pushing John close to his limit over Miss Hale. She almost wanted to make him snap, make his temper flare so that he would show his unrefined side to Miss Hale this evening when he visited her, and put himself even further from her grasp. But John's mention of the fading fortunes of the mill softened her tone.

'You speak as though the mill failing is a certainty. Are you sure nothing can be done?'

John ran his hand through his hair, disturbing its perfect neatness. It was a habit that his mother had attempted to quash in his youth, but which surfaced when he was troubled.

'It is likely, I won't lie. But I will do my damnedest to keep going as long as I can. Now, excuse me please, Mother,' he said, and she stood aside to let him pass.

It was a blow to Hannah that John felt the mill would fail, although it was not completely unexpected, as he had discussed his concerns with her before. His worries became her worries, and for the life of her she could see no merit in his continued visits to Miss Hale when it would do him no good, and if nothing else, would lead him to further upset. He may well protest his resignation to Miss Hale ever accepting him, but Hannah's sharp senses detected her son wearing cologne, and her heart ached for the further disappointment that the girl would inflict upon him.

Hannah watched John straighten his cravat in the hall mirror and flatten down the tufts he had created in his hair. He put on his overcoat and hat, picked up the now familiar packet of cotton wrapped up in brown paper, bade her goodbye and set off for the two-mile brisk walk to Crampton without a backward glance.

'You'd best come through to the parlour,' said Dixon, her nose in the air as she led him through the house to wait for Margaret and her father.

John sat on the faded and threadbare green velvet settee in the cosy sitting room, where he had spent many hours conversing with Mr Hale and Miss Hale prior to his proposal, after which she abruptly stopped participating in his lessons. It was a small room which his mother and Fanny would no doubt find wanting, but John found it comfortable in that it held a warmth, not simply from the fire, but from the feeling of being lived in and familiar. He was all nervous energy as he waited to see if Miss Hale was still of a friendlier disposition towards him as she had been on the last few occasions when he had visited. He held on to the cotton wadding parcel on his knee and waited.

Above his head he could hear footsteps, light ones, and he imagined Margaret preparing herself to come downstairs to see him, and his heart lifted his lips into a small smile. He wondered if she would make any special effort to check her appearance before meeting him. John chided himself; she was not interested in him, and he needed to remember it. He had no idea if Margaret would feel any gladness that he had come, as he had told her he would, or if she dreaded his visit as he presumed she used to do. The steps became louder as they approached down the stairs, the click of heels on the wooden steps, and then Margaret entered the room, her arms full with the crate that he had provided, and which now contained Albert.

'Miss Hale,' said John, standing. A little crease appeared on his forehead as he appraised Miss Hale's countenance. She was dressed in her usual demure and neat way, with no flounces or ruffles required to enhance her appearance, but her beautiful face was ghostly pale, with dark purple smudges beneath her eyes. In truth she looked utterly worn out.

'Are you well?' he enquired, his deep voice softened with concern.

Quite out of character, and to both Margaret and John's mortification, she promptly burst into tears. Loud trembling sobs crinkled her face and turned her nose and cheeks immediately pink. He stepped towards her, feeling the need to do something but having no idea how he might alleviate her sudden distress. He reached forward and gently prised the crate from her hands.

'Allow me,' he said, taking possession of the crate containing Albert, which was surprisingly heavy, and tucked it under his arm. John noticed a stoneware hot water bottle in the crate near the puppy to keep him warm. Margaret pulled a delicate handkerchief out of her sleeve, and covered her face and her embarrassment with it.

'I'm so sorry. Please forgive me,' she said, her words muffled by the handkerchief.

John cautiously reached out with his hand that was not engaged in holding Albert in his crate. He took a gentle but firm hold of Margaret's upper arm, and led her towards the easy chair by the fireplace to sit down.

'Can I help you, Miss Hale? Some tea or a sherry perhaps?' he said, glancing around the room, hoping that some kind of remedy would appear to him. 'Is it Albert? Is he well? I am sorry I couldn't come for a few days.'

Margaret calmed and attempted to pull herself together, quite surprised at her lack of poise. She was making a fool of herself, and yet subconsciously she did not anticipate his censure.

'He is perfect,' she said, her bottom lip beginning to quiver, signifying that she was perilously close to crying again.

John's urge to comfort her was almost impossible to fight, and he was relieved when Mr Hale entered the room.

Margaret's father would be able to provide the solace that respectability prevented him from offering, and he was glad of it.

'John, John how splendid to see you. Again, you find us wanting. Margaret is worn out I'm afraid, but she will insist on caring for that dog,' he tutted, shaking his head in exaggerated disapproval. 'I must be away to my lecture, so do call for Dixon, dear, if you need company,' he said, patting Margaret's shoulder gently. With that Mr Hale exited both the parlour and the house, seemingly not noticing, or perhaps not acknowledging, the evidence of Margaret's upset.

John was nonplussed and stood looking at the vacant doorway where Mr Hale had departed, his mouth slightly open in astonishment at both Mr Hale's egress, and at being left alone with Miss Hale. With Margaret now sitting stoically in her usual seat, John took his on the settee again and placed the crate on the floor between them. Albert was deeply asleep and thereby unmoved by the anguish in the room. Margaret would not meet John's eyes, no doubt mortified by her emotional outburst, and he marvelled at her bravery. Just to stay in the room with him showed remarkable fortitude. He couldn't imagine Fanny sitting with a visitor, thinking she had embarrassed herself with a tearful outburst, particularly if the said company was one she did not like at that. But Fanny was wholly different to Miss Hale. Fanny was all dramatic flounces and annoyed foot stamps, whereas Miss Hale was subdued and silent in her misery. However, John did not want Miss Hale to be ashamed of shedding tears in front of him. Whatever the troublesome issue was that caused her distress, he merely wanted to make it better if he were able.

In Margaret's stillness while she composed herself, emitting small hiccupping breaths smothered by her handkerchief, John turned Mr Hale's words over in his mind and realisation dawned on him.

'You have been tending to Albert every two hours for days now,' he stated quietly, leaning towards her with his elbows on his knees.

Margaret nodded, unable to speak in case she cried again. Needing to do something, she leant down, picked Albert up and held him to her. John noticed that Albert had grown already, even in the two days since he had last been here. The pup's eyes were still closed fast but he looked bigger.

'And it looks like you have done a fine job. The little mite is thriving,' he added in gentle encouragement.

That Mr Thornton would show her more tenderness than her own father was almost too much to bear. His kindness was feeding the sorrow she felt so deeply, and she had to change the dynamic of the conversation or else she would dissolve into uncontrollable weeping. So, Margaret employed attack as her defence.

'I have had a disagreement with Father,' she said, her eyes fixed on the crate as neutral ground between them. 'He wishes to be rid of Albert and would garner your complicity in doing so.' She raised her chin in defiance, and engaged his eyes accusingly, unknowingly using the same gesture as he when challenged. 'What do you say to that, Mr Thornton? Will you be stealing him away against my wishes in collusion with my father?'

John was momentarily knocked off guard. He had offered his help to her, and somehow he was being accused of some dastardly act that he had no knowledge of. Despite the injustice he remained calm so as not to distress her and bring on more tears.

'I am oblivious to this plan, Miss Hale,' he said with candour. 'I have not been approached with such a request, I assure you. I understand that your opinion of me is that I am ungentlemanly, and I dare say that has a ring of truth to it, but I am an honest man if nothing else.' John pushed his fingers through his hair making shiny tufts. Margaret was fleetingly distracted by the sight of his tousled hair, and she had a startling urge to mess it up further. Unaware of the diversion his mannerism was causing, John continued, 'I don't understand, Miss Hale. Why would Mr Hale want to get rid of him?'

'He believes it is too much for me. It is a lot of work to be sure. Father and Dixon can't help,' she said forlornly, the fight gone from her voice as quickly as it had appeared. His heart constricted with the need to console her, despite her prickly demeanour only moments ago.

'I can see that you are tired,' he began, and noticed her back stiffen in an unspoken rebuke to his comment. 'It is understandable. I would be weary after days without proper sleep myself. Anyone would. I am not criticising, Miss Hale. Just saying that I understand.'

A moment's silence passed before she voiced her heartfelt concern. 'Mr Thornton, what if he is right?' she said, and fat tears started their trail down her cheeks again.

John reached out his hand as if to offer his strength but then withdrew it, uncertain whether his touch would be welcome.

'Now then, you don't want to be drowning him in the meantime,' he said, with a tiny half-smile, and Margaret managed a watery smile in return.

John reached into his waistcoat pocket and withdrew his handkerchief, and Margaret accepted it from his proffered hand; her own handkerchief was now completely wet through and no longer of any use.

'I can think of no one more capable than you, Miss Hale. The little fellow is in good hands, but you don't need me to tell you that. If it sets your mind at rest, I will promise to help you if I can, seeing as Mr Hale and Miss Dixon are unable. I give you my word that I won't go behind your back to take him away from you. I can see what he means to you. I think Albert is a lucky chap. First to be saved and then looked after by you. I don't presume to know you, we both know that I don't, but I have faith that if anyone can do it, it will be you. If you would accept my help, I will willingly give it. No strings attached, as we cotton manufacturers say,' he said, and succeeded in winning another smile from Miss Hale, this time big enough to display the charming dimples in her cheeks, and with it came an accompanying little laugh.

'You saved him, Mr Thornton. You noticed he was still alive when I did not,' she pointed out, sniffing and dabbing at her eyes.

'Well then, I think that grants me a vested interest in his upbringing don't you? And I did name him, don't forget.'

John reached forward and took Albert from the warmth of her hands, their fingers grazing momentarily.

'Go and rest,' he said tenderly.

'I'm all right.'

'No. Go and rest. I will feed this little man for the next two times, then I'll ask Miss Dixon to deliver him to your room. So you should get perhaps six hours of sleep. I know it's not much …'

Margaret's soft grey eyes met his, and John thought he had never been looked at with such warmth in his entire life, and his heart swelled further with love. That a small gesture from him would engender such a look from her was wondrous, and he would stow this instance with the other special moments in time that he'd shared with Miss Hale, and held in his memory for safekeeping.

In the solitude of the Hales' parlour John took off his jacket, loosened his cravat a little and rested his head back on the settee. Albert snuggled into the crook of his arm and John dozed, aware of the sounds of Dixon moving around the house from time to time. His mind naturally wandered to matters of work awaiting him at the mill tomorrow. If he had not come to the Hales' tonight, he would have been working, poring over his paperwork to glean any financial advantage possible.

Prior to the strike, John had planned to increase productivity. He had modernised his machinery, as well as installing safety equipment including screens and the wheel. He had taken out a large bank loan to help cover the initial outlay, and now it was clear that he had overstretched. His expenditure was much greater than the other mill masters as he alone had paid out for the Irish workers. While this had broken the strike and benefitted all of the mills, John had been left with the unskilled labourers who ruined large quantities of his cloth. These factors, along with the commitment of the bank loan, weighed heavily on John. He mused that this break, just sitting quietly, was good for him, and he was grateful for the peaceful interlude.

When it was the puppy's feeding time, John managed comfortably in finding the necessary equipment in the kitchen. He was pleased not to encounter the formidable maid while he was there, and Albert seemed not to notice the difference in the provider of his food. He swabbed the puppy and smiled when the procedure had the required effect. John felt a blush creep up his neck as he recalled having to describe the method to Miss Hale a few days before. At least he had managed not to stray into indelicate conversation tonight. He had a mind to report back to the Baileys regarding the effectiveness of their advice to date. He would seek them out tomorrow and offer his thanks.

After the following feed, John refreshed the water in Albert's hot water bottle and took his leave from Dixon on the understanding that she would place the crate containing the puppy in Miss Hale's room and not disturb her. It was late by the time he started his walk home, but John was filled with a sense of well-being. He had hardly seen Margaret this evening, and yet he was pleased more than he could say, as he had been of assistance to her when no other had, and he felt blessed to have been able to do so.

Many months ago, Miss Hale had made it clear that she didn't like him, but John liked her. He loved her. He would walk to the ends of the earth for her if she commanded it. Mr Hale and Dixon's unwillingness to help Margaret with Albert left a gulf that John could fill, and he would do it willingly, gladly stepping into the breach. He would help when he could, as much as he could, within the confines of Miss Hale's wishes. John's business may be failing, and his life ruled by relentless hard work and struggle, but this opportunity to help Miss Hale and Albert offered him a glimpse of happiness that was sorely missing from his life, and he would grasp it and hold it fast to his heart.

Chapter 6

One hundred and ninety miles away in the capital, Henry Lennox sat at his desk. This was a most uncommon occurrence. Henry could rarely be found at his place of business, an attorney partnership situated in Middle Temple, beyond noon each day. For at that time, without fail, he removed to his gentlemen's club. His office was an impressive room, spacious and dominated by his large mahogany desk, which was adorned with a green tooled leather top. Bookcases lined the walls, containing legal tomes which were rarely used for reference. He closed his eyes and was faintly aware of the smell of beeswax that was used to polish the furniture each and every afternoon. He was here at this late hour because today had been an exceptional day, a pivotal day in the life of Henry Lennox. It was possible, no, highly probable, that all his dreams had been answered, and his mind buzzed as it turned over and over the most exquisite information that had come to him that morning.

Henry was a gentleman by birth. He was a second son, and had been astonished when his elder brother, Sholto, had entered the military. Sholto had the opportunity to live the high life, but wasted his time by obtaining a commission and entering the army where he acquired the rank and title of captain. If Henry had been first born, he would have found no trouble in filling his days between gentleman's clubs and the entertainments on offer there. Not only did Sholto pursue his ambitions as a soldier, but he would inherit their father's estate. Being the heir, his elder brother had also been able to attract and secure the hand of the wealthy, charming and beautiful, if a little flighty, Edith Shaw. Of course, Sholto's blue eyes and blonde hair were attractive to women, as well as his easy charm and future inheritance.

Henry considered himself to be a tolerably attractive man. He was of average height, slim and always smartly dressed. He was intelligent, and as he must take up an occupation he had decided to become a lawyer. Henry was a junior partner at the attorneys, and had begun to make a name for himself within legal circles. A favourable reputation was required for substantial financial benefits to follow.

Margaret Hale had come into his acquaintance around two years ago when Sholto and Edith Shaw, Margaret's cousin, began courting and subsequently married. Sholto joined the Shaw household in Harley Street, and Henry had become a regular there too, cultivating an association with the family. Mrs Shaw's hospitality created multiple opportunities for the young lawyer to mingle with wealthy socialites and the gentry, which in turn further increased his prospective elite clientele.

On meeting Margaret Hale, Henry was immediately captivated by her astounding beauty. She was not pretty in the conventional sense like Edith, but was strikingly handsome. With her fine figure, lustrous hair and demure countenance, Margaret was a sought after young woman, until her flaw was discovered; she was penniless. It had been a great disappointment to Henry, as her notable ancestry would further bolster his standing if she were his wife, and he agonised for several weeks as to whether he could risk marrying her or not. He would come into a small inheritance on his marriage, but not enough for the life he intended to lead, not when he could see the lavish lifestyle that the likes of the Shaws and his own brother now benefitted from.

In the end, the draw of her beauty was too great, and Henry considered there would likely be room in the Shaw residence for himself and Margaret once they were wed, so all was not lost. Her pedigree and beauty would be enough. It had therefore been a most grievous blow when she had actually turned him down flat.

He had visited Margaret at her lowly country parsonage home in Hampshire, grasped her hand and had spoken words of love that he assumed she would accept with gratitude, but she had refused him. Henry had been dumbfounded, as Margaret had even implied that a marriage proposal from him would be welcomed by talking to him about weddings and then suggesting he call upon her. He wondered if she were being coquettish but, no, she had meant it. Never for a moment did he think she would reject him. He was not heart-sick of course, but he thought she liked him well enough, and he was certain she wouldn't get a better offer. It was auspicious that he had approached her in the seclusion of her family's home and not in London where his humiliation would have been harder to conceal. Sholto had not teased him about it, so Margaret had clearly kept the debacle to herself. He supposed she yearned for a love match, but he wondered, if that were the case, why she would not look to her own mother's example and see the folly in it. Although he didn't love Margaret Hale, in spurning his attentions, she had become the itch that he had to scratch, the prize that he must win. He would have her. She would marry him. He would triumph, and woe betide any hapless fool that stood in his way.

Due to his links with the Shaw family, Henry had been introduced to Mr Adam Bell, and it was from this gentleman that the delicious news of this morning had sprung. Mr Bell, it transpired, was Miss Hale's godfather and long-time friend of Mr Hale. They had known each other from studying in Oxford, from where Richard Hale had diverted into the church. Mr Bell had remained as a tutor and had become both a learned fellow and a wealthy man with investments and properties, mostly in the North. After dinner at the Shaw residence one evening the previous week, Henry was fortuitously engaged by Mr Bell for his services as an attorney. Henry had willingly agreed to act on Mr Bell's behalf on the writing of his will. The meeting to draw up the legal document had happened that very day, and Henry's desire for Margaret Hale had become all-encompassing. She was to inherit all. Every last farthing of Adam Bell's fortune would be hers, and no one, apart from himself and Bell, knew about it.

While he was not so unkind as to wish an early demise upon anyone, Henry easily concluded that Mr Bell was of advancing years, and he might need to wait but a short time before Margaret would inherit. The one thing she must not do under any circumstances was to marry someone else. As things stood now, he felt Margaret was relatively safe. She had no money and therefore was not in demand, but when she came into her inheritance it would be a different situation altogether. With her beauty, breeding and money, she would have half of London trailing after her, and he would have no chance whatsoever in securing her hand. Henry deduced that he must form an attachment to her before Mr Bell died. Henry didn't consider himself to be a bad man, but he was a realist, and he would use his privileged information about the destination of Adam Bell's wealth to his benefit. In his opinion, there was no use in knowing confidential information if you didn't use it to your advantage.

Shortly after his ill-fated proposal, Henry had learned from his brother that Mr Hale had done the most extraordinary thing. He had denounced his position as a clergyman in Margaret's idyllic village, moved the family to Milton and had become a tutor. According to Edith, Margaret was residing in this common, dirty town, with no polite society to engage with. She apparently spent her days delivering food parcels to the poor, and running her father's meagre household since the death of her mother some months ago. While at first Henry found this to be quite outrageous, and joined the Lennoxes in their dismay on the degradation of this splinter of the family, he began to feel somewhat gratified by the turn of events. If Margaret Hale could not find a suitable match in London or Hampshire, there was little to no hope of her finding an attachment in Milton. He almost wanted to rub his hands together with glee.

Henry was sure that once Margaret had lived in the oppressive Darkshire town for a little while, she would soon see the error of her ways and practically beg him to repeat his declaration. Miss Hale would be safe in Milton, the lowly daughter of a disgraced vicar, with no dowry or friends. Henry would reintroduce himself to the Hales through his association with Mr Bell, and his attendance in Milton would highlight to Margaret the dreadful mistake she had made in rejecting him. Henry would be her salvation and marriage to him would offer her a way out, and a way back to London society which she must be sorely missing. Henry chuckled to himself. This was going to be delightful. He would get revenge upon Margaret for dismissing his proposal when all of her wealth became his, and he would acquire the most physically desirable wife of any of his contemporaries in the process.

Henry closed the leather document pouch on his desk that contained Mr Bell's will, and locked it in his desk drawer. The document was so precious to him that he considered taking it home with him for safekeeping. Tomorrow he would have it stored in the company's safe, so that neither flood nor fire could destroy it, and then he would begin his plan to capture Margaret Hale.

Chapter 7

A snuffling, squeaking sound gradually seeped into Margaret's consciousness as sleep finally receded. She sat bolt upright, immediately awake. *Albert.* Her eyes found the crate on the floor by her bed and the puppy was wiggling, presumably in search of food. Margaret lit the candle on the table beside her bed and looked at the clock; it was just before three. She had been asleep for almost seven hours, and whilst she could not say she felt refreshed, she didn't feel the tiredness that had infiltrated her bones the day before. She rose from the comforting swaddle of the bedcovers into the icy room, wrapped herself in her woollen shawl, and crouched down to check on the puppy. His hot water bottle still held a little heat. *Mr Thornton*, she thought.

Margaret slipped silently downstairs to the kitchen, illuminated by the moonlight that peeped through chinks in the curtains. She heated the puppy's milk and refilled his stoneware hot water bottle, then hurried back towards her room, anxious to get back into the warmth of her bed. As she passed the hall table at the bottom of the stairs she spotted a piece of paper. Stopping to see what it was, she held it up to the pale light of the moon's beam and read

'Miss Hale', written in large bold copperplate. *Mr Thornton.* She placed the note back on the table and raced back upstairs to her room. Margaret picked up Albert's tiny warm, firm body, and propped herself up in bed beneath the sheets and blankets that still held her body heat. She fed the ravenous pup until he'd had his fill, wrapped him up in his towel and cradled him, stroking from the tip of his tiny pink nose to the crown of his head until he drifted back to sleep. After placing Albert back in his bed, Margaret blew out the candle then lay waiting for sleep to envelop her again, but it didn't come, couldn't come. Huffing, she crept back down the stairs to retrieve the note from the hall table and then retreated back to bed. She re-lit the candle and read the short note addressed to her.

Miss Hale,

I hope you found the short respite from your caring duties for Albert to be of benefit.

If it meets with your approval I will return tomorrow (today?) in the evening to offer similar assistance.

Please do not hesitate to send word if you would prefer otherwise.

John Thornton

Margaret carefully folded the paper back up and blew out the candle. *Mr Thornton.* He had been such a help last night. By enabling her to rest, he had not only allowed her to cope with her commitment to Albert, but he was giving her the opportunity to succeed. She would be able to care for Albert against the odds stacked against her. Mr Thornton was empowering her to have some control and if, as his note suggested, he was willing to do it again, it gave her hope that she would win this battle and be able to provide a home for the puppy. She would love Albert, and that love would be reciprocated.

Mr Thornton had inconvenienced himself by no small measure for her. No, for Albert of course. She had cried in front of him, repeatedly, yet he had borne it with soft kindness. The Mr Thornton of last night and the past few days was at odds with her previous impression of him. Or perhaps it was not her experience of *him*, but her knowledge that Mr Thornton was well known for his brooding manner and stern ways with his workers. She had heard all about the mill masters of Milton and their reputation; they were shrewd industrialists with a fervent desire for making money at the expense of the poor. Mr Thornton was one of them, and just because he had been considerate to both herself and Albert, it didn't mean that these other facets to his character did not exist.

Margaret contemplated the kindness he had shown despite their tumultuous history. After all, in the not too distant past she had treated him atrociously. But she reasoned that she had been cruel to him because he had offended her. She thought back to his presumptuous declaration, that no doubt he had been compelled to make, merely because she had defended him like she would defend any man if it was in her power to do so. That he would deliver his proposal with feigned affection was insulting. She must remember his duplicity; he had falsely professed his love for her. Margaret frowned. The fact that he was her father's friend meant that his well-meaning assistance to her now might as soon be withdrawn, if pressed by her father. Margaret curled into a ball facing Albert who made faint snorting noises as he slept. She needed to keep matters in perspective. Her father loved her. He would not be underhand and spirit Albert away. She merely needed to show him that she was coping and all would be well. She would accept Mr Thornton's offer of further assistance again, as it wouldn't be long until Albert didn't need round the clock feeding anymore. She closed her eyes and willed herself back to sleep, knowing that she would be disturbed again in a few hours' time.

John woke with the early morning whistle, and heard the steam engine come to life under the authority of the mill's stoker. The rhythmic pumping of the engine as it gained heat and power receded from his consciousness with its familiarity, not unlike the ticking of a clock. He had an hour before the workers would arrive. Despite his later bedtime due to helping with Albert at the Hales', he felt both at peace and energised at the same time. To have been of service to Miss Hale and the puppy had been a privilege, and it had lightened his heart and his mood.

He wondered if she would send word today that he was not required again tonight. Surely he was good enough to assist her in tending to the puppy. Would she refuse help because it was he that had made the offer? Perhaps in the cold light of day she might regret accepting aid from a man such as him. She may think he had taken advantage of her by exploiting her weariness to insert himself into her life where he was not welcome. He had not of course, but he could see how his actions might be misconstrued. He had yet to run the gauntlet of his mother's biting opinion this morning, and he closed his eyes and wondered why he put up with it.

John took longer than usual to get ready for the day ahead. He needed to hide his excitement at the prospect of seeing Margaret tonight with his customary mask of stern control. However, he could not subdue the joy from his step as he bounced down the stairs to the dining room where his mother already sat in wait for him like a great black bird of prey.

'Good morning, Mother,' he said, taking his seat and reaching for the tea pot.

'Is it? I'm surprised you're so chipper, seeing as you got back after midnight.' She fixed him with her disparaging stare.

John stopped stirring his tea. 'Mother, I am over thirty years of age, not thirteen. However, since you have brought it up, I will be going to the Hales' again tonight and may not be back till late, so don't wait up. I'll eat in the canteen at lunchtime.' He gulped down the lukewarm tea in one go, extracting a tut of displeasure from Hannah.

John stood up and put a piece of toast in his mouth and held it there between his teeth while he put on his jacket. He knew very well that he was irritating her, and they both knew that he was doing it on purpose, demonstrating his uncouth ways that she had tried so hard to drum out of him as he grew into adulthood. But John was rough around the edges and always would be. His mother was aware of the fact and so was Miss Hale, and because of it he was doomed to a life of solitude.

John's thoughts of Miss Hale were soon banished from his mind as the thunder of clogs on the cobbled streets of Milton gradually increased in volume. The workers of Marlborough Mills spilled through the gates, and the jostling and banter quietened down as their day of toil commenced. There was a large order to get finished and dispatched that day. They were on time with it, and John had the hope that payment for this consignment, which would not incur a late shipment penalty, would assure the continuation of Marlborough Mills for at least another month.

The Hales' kitchen was humid despite the chill of the late January day. Margaret sprinkled water over the pillowcase before running the hot flat iron over it again, smoothing out the creases with a hiss of steam. Her back ached from the stooped position she had been in all afternoon, and her arm trembled with fatigue from repeatedly lifting the iron on and off the hot stove, but she would not stop. She would not cry off this chore and be challenged that Albert was the reason for her exhaustion. Indeed, it was not the case. The mountain of washing she had worked her way through was enough to tire the most efficient laundress, and she had commenced the task with vigour thanks to the rest she had been afforded by Mr Thornton's intervention the previous night. The next item on the pile of ironing was the handkerchief that he had kindly lent her last evening. She sprinkled it with rose water then applied the hot iron, pressing precise creases at the folds and smoothing out his embroidered initials with care.

Dixon pummelled the dough she was working on at the kitchen table and broke the silence between them. 'I don't know what the mistress would 'ave made of it. God save us, she might be turning in 'er grave this very minute at the thought,' she grumbled, apparently to herself, but hoping to catch the attention of Miss Margaret whose mind appeared to be away with the fairies.

Dixon's mention of her mother succeeded in diverting Margaret's attention. 'What did you say, Dixon?' she asked, meekly. 'I'm sorry, my mind was elsewhere.'

'And I bet 'that' Mr Thornton's mind will be elsewhere today an' all!' exclaimed the maid.

Margaret stiffened at the mention of his name, astonished that Dixon had hit upon the exact thing that she had been thinking about at that very second.

'What about Mr Thornton?' she asked, affecting a casual tone.

'Well,' said Dixon, warming to her subject and stopping her kneading so that she could give Miss Margaret her full attention. 'You 'ave to question his reasons, don't you?

High and mighty Mr Thornton who is supposed to be some kind of northern gent! I don't think so. You need to watch 'im, Miss Margaret. There is only one thing he's after, and it's the honour that your good name, your breeding what was passed down from my dear mistress—'

'What are you talking about, Dixon?' asked Margaret, unable to make head nor tail of Dixon's rambling.

'Do you think he wants to stop up 'alf the night just to look after that dog?' she said pointedly, throwing a disdainful look at Albert in his crate. ''Course he doesn't. He wants to wheedle 'imself further into your good books, so that all around can think what a gent he is 'aving proper genteel folk for friends. You mark my words,' she said, and resumed her work.

Margaret pondered their exchange as she began pressing the wrinkled sheet in front of her. Could Dixon be correct? She had wondered what his motive might be for assisting her with Albert, and she had dismissed it as simply a kindness. And yet this new version of Mr Thornton did not sit well with her previous opinion of him and his reputation for being a stern and unyielding businessman. His more recent incarnation was so new to her that she deduced that there must be another reason for his attentiveness. Certainly, it could not be due to any romantic attachment, as she had irrevocably ended any notions there, so perhaps Dixon's view of Mr Thornton's motivation had substance. Margaret had the rest of the afternoon to turn this over in her thoughts, until by the evening she was quite sure that Dixon must be right. If Mr

Thornton could not have her as his wife, then he must wish to use his association with her for his benefit in society.

After the seven o'clock evening whistle blew and all of the hands filed out of the mill back to their homes, John endured a silent and tense dinner with his mother. He was anxious to be away soon, so that he could gift Miss Hale as long a rest as possible. Hannah watched the concern on John's face as he ate his meal. She had no idea what was going on inside his head, but she'd bet a gold sovereign that it was something to do with Miss Hale.

After dinner John readied himself for the Hales', and Hannah stood watching him with her arms folded across her bosom. She noted the presence of cologne again as he gathered his belongings together, and she was surprised to see that, as well as the now familiar cotton bundle, John also had a stack of mill ledgers with him. She refused to ask what the devil he was up to. Mother and son appeared to have reached an impasse regarding Miss Hale, where he would not venture any information, and she would not ask for it. He kissed her cheek and was gone.

John had not received word from Miss Hale that she did not want him to attend that evening, but even so he felt a measure of trepidation as he rang the Hales' doorbell. There was a long pause. He wasn't sure whether he should ring again or knock, wait a little longer or go home. He stood his ground for a moment more, anxiety creeping in, until the door was eventually opened by Dixon with her customary terse greeting, as if opening the door to him of all people was a great inconvenience.

'Mr Hale is indisposed with a pupil,' she said, with her head tipped back so that she could stare down her nose at him.

'And Miss Hale?' he asked.

'Humph,' she said, turning her back to him and marching towards the parlour. 'It's not right if you ask me. Miss Hale is a gentlewoman. She shouldn't be entertaining men.' With that, she opened the parlour door and ushered him through, ensuring that it was left wide open so as not to give the likes of Mr Thornton any ideas regarding improper thoughts or deeds. Miss Hale was standing in the middle of the room with her back towards him as he entered.

'Good evening, Miss Hale. Are you well?' he asked, as he shrugged off his coat, having not been divested of it by Dixon. Miss Hale turned and approached him with an enigmatic expression.

'I must thank you, Mr Thornton, for the kindness you showed to us yesterday,' she said formally.

John assessed her pose. Margaret faced him full on, with her hands clasped in front of her waist. She had her chin at that defiant angle again.

'You are welcome. I need no thanks,' he simply replied, waiting with anticipation for the reason for her annoyance with him.

'I have your handkerchief to return,' she said, passing it to him.

'Thank you. I didn't expect to get it back so quickly, or to put you to any trouble,' he said cautiously, still expecting a storm to descend.

'It is our washing day. It was no trouble to press your handkerchief. Dixon says that my prowess with the flat iron only goes as far as uncomplicated items,' she said, with a small smile, seemingly having forgotten that she was cross with him.

As he was comprehending the fact that Miss Hale had pressed his handkerchief herself, and that she was responsible for ironing the laundry in the Hales' household, the gloom descended back on her countenance.

'You did not have to come tonight,' she said, with her eyes fixed somewhere just below his cravat.

'You didn't send word that I was not welcome,' he parried, his head slightly tilted in question, as his stomach turned over with the dread that she did not want him there again after all. He blinked once or twice. 'Do you want me to go?' he asked, warily.

'Not exactly,' she admitted, and then more firmly stated, 'I don't know what you want from me. What your gain is in helping me with Albert.'

She watched as Mr Thornton's eyebrows first rose sharply with his surprise at her words and then pulled down, nearly meeting together in a deep frown as vexation took hold of him, and the short fuse on his temper was ignited.

'You believe I cannot offer my aid to you without expecting something in return?' he bristled. 'I am not capable of providing a service without getting a reward.

Is that your opinion? I am merely a tradesman, and you cannot separate the man from his occupation,' he spat.

'I simply do not understand your intention and Dixon said—'

'Dixon!' he cut in. 'I have to account for my actions to my mother, you and now Miss Dixon,' he said testily, and Margaret watched as he scratched at his head, forming those troublesome shiny spikes again. 'Must I have an ulterior motive? If Higgins offered his help would you question his reasoning?' He glared at her awaiting her response.

Margaret felt the situation spiralling out of her control. She had not meant to offend, simply to understand, and now she was uncertain about the accuracy of Dixon's argument.

'I see you have brought some work to do,' she said, making an attempt at diverting the conversation.

'I can work as well here as I can at home, if you don't object to me attending to the accounts of my trade in your parlour at a time when polite society is at its leisure,' he said sarcastically, then immediately regretted his harsh words. He pushed at his hair again. 'I have spoken out of turn,' he offered in apology, his flare of anger now past its peak.

'I am sorry to have offended you, Mr Thornton. I can't seem to ever say or do the right thing,' she said, quietly and with remorse.

Through his agitation he sensed that Miss Hale might be near to tears again and he could not be the cause of that, no matter how deeply she had upset him. He took a breath. 'Is Albert all right?'

'Yes. Thank you.'

'Then I'll be on my way. Good evening, Miss Hale.' He gave a curt bow and exited the room, leaving behind him his slightly smoky scent of soap and a hint of cologne.

John let himself out of the front door with a slam, still smarting from her comments that emphasised her low opinion of him. He put down his ledgers on the Hales' residence steps so he could don his overcoat and hat. He still had the wretched cotton bundle with him. He neatened the stack of ledgers on the step. He fiddled with his cravat. He looked at the door knocker. He buttoned his coat and straightened his hat, then sat on the step next to the books and cotton while he regained control of his composure.

Margaret stood in the hallway and touched her hand to the front door, her head bowed. She had injured him again, and hit an exposed nerve so soundly as to have raised his temper and caused his departure. She could hardly believe her own words to him. The fight had completely drained from her, and she wondered why on earth she had given any credence to Dixon's opinions over her own. Her sorrow at Mr Thornton's leaving took her by surprise, although she wasn't sure if it was because she had upset him or simply because he wasn't there.

She walked back to the parlour, picked Albert up from his crate and snuggled the pup into her neck, taking comfort from his soft warmth. She felt like crying again; it was the tiredness, of course. She was not wont to tears, and yet just recently she felt on the very verge of them all of the time. Margaret crossed to the window to catch a glimpse of Mr Thornton before he disappeared from view when he rounded the corner at the bottom of the street, but he wasn't there. Had he reached the turning point already? She watched as two passers-by stopped and looked in the direction of her house. They whispered to each other, then quickly moved on. Intrigued by their behaviour, Margaret leaned forwards into the bay window that overlooked the front door to see what it was that had caused the interest in her home.

John collected his thoughts and picked up his belongings from the Hales' step just as Margaret opened the door. They stood for a moment in silence.

'I'm sorry,' they both said in unison. A hesitant smile crept on her face, and with Albert still clutched to her neck, she opened the door wide for Mr Thornton to come back in. He swallowed, paused, and then walked back up the steps and into the Hales' home.

John put his books on the hall table, took off his hat and absently smoothed the nap with his hand, unsure of the next move. They had fallen out again, and although she was trying to make amends, he still wasn't sure if he should remain or take his leave in a more gentlemanly way, and slink back home to Marlborough House to lick his wounds. His decision was made when she tentatively touched his arm.

'Will you stay? I quite understand the imposition …'

'I'll stay,' he said gruffly, and hung his coat and hat back up. He held his hands out for Albert and Margaret relinquished him to Mr Thornton's care.

'Goodnight,' he said to her hands, blinking.

'Before I made a mess of things this evening, I meant to tell you that I am truly grateful. I wouldn't be able to keep Albert if it wasn't for your assistance. I am certain of it.'

John blocked her words of thanks with a little half-shake of his head. She noticed that he was not proficient at accepting gratitude, and for a second she wondered if it was because he was unfamiliar with it. Margaret proffered her hand to Mr Thornton, not in the feminine way to be bestowed with a kiss as was the custom in the South, but as gentlemen did – palm to palm. He transferred Albert to his left hand, took her hand in his and she shook it firmly.

She was halfway up the stairs when he called out, 'Should I come tomorrow?'

Margaret stilled on the stairs and turned her head so that she could meet his eyes, sparkling blue against his otherwise monochrome figure. She noticed his hair was still in disarray.

'Yes please,' she said, and John nodded in tacit agreement as she turned and continued upstairs, disappearing from his view.

John saw to Albert's needs, even coexisting with Dixon in her kitchen for a time while he heated the milk, much to the maid's displeasure. The pup's eyes and ears were still closed but he was getting sturdier by the day, little scantling that he was. When Albert was settled once more in his bed, John sat at the table and opened his ledgers. He had forgotten his ink and pen, and it was too late now to ask to borrow some from the Hales. Stern mill master that he was, he dared not impose on Dixon at this time. His frayed nerves needed no further battering this evening.

He looked at his palm once or twice where Miss Hale had touched him. He wasn't sure what she had meant by the gesture. He wondered if she was offering her thanks, saying farewell, or even making a bargain with him. But no matter what her reason, it was still welcome. John took the handkerchief out of his pocket to admire Miss Hale's handiwork, then held it to his face, and he realised that it held her rose scent. He put it carefully in his breast pocket for safekeeping with a small, satisfied smile. He closed his eyes and thought about Miss Hale's words to him. Was there a ring of truth to them? Did he want to get something in return for helping her? She had been correct in that he did have a goal, but he couldn't divulge his reason to her. Certainly, he wanted Albert to thrive, he was already firmly attached to the little chap himself, but that was not his prime objective. He wanted Miss Hale's happiness, pure and simple.

Chapter 8

Two weeks had passed, and every evening after finishing work and having dinner with his mother, John had visited the Hale household. Margaret greeted him each time with their new custom of shaking hands, and John took over the care of Albert while she went to bed. Between them they provided the round the clock care that the puppy needed. Hannah watched her son pack up his workbooks or ledgers and stride off towards Crampton with unerring regularity be it rain or shine, and she was unable to stop him. She was powerless to prevent him from making a damned fool of himself over that girl and a dog, and it appeared everyone of note was talking about it.

Hannah had been in Wearing's haberdashers on New Street when she had been accosted by Mrs Slickson, the wife of one of John's fellow mill masters. Usually, the women would merely nod in passing, as the difference in their ages precluded a close friendship. However, on this day, Mrs Slickson approached Mrs Thornton with what Hannah felt was a brazen forwardness, and asked her outright if John was courting Miss Hale.

'We've heard he goes there every evening, regular as clockwork,' the younger woman twittered. 'So there must be an attachment, surely? I know many a young maiden will be sorry to see Mr Thornton spoken for,' she said excitedly, giving Mrs Thornton's arm a most unwelcome pat.

'I don't know who you are referring to as "we", but I will tell you that my son's business, as to whether he is courting or not, is not for me to say. I do not gossip, Mrs Slickson, and I'll thank you not to be tittle-tattling about it either,' said Mrs Thornton sharply, stunning Mrs Slickson who gave a nervous laugh, and excused herself to engage Mr Wearing in a discussion on his current stock of buttons. Hannah was livid. She knew that Miss Hale would not have John, and young women who were more suitable for him might be put off if they thought he was already attached. It seemed to Hannah that Margaret Hale was merely playing with her son's affections, but the foolish boy couldn't see it.

Fanny Watson paid her mother a visit later that day, and had been planning on imparting similar gossip to that which Hannah had already heard from Mrs Slickson. She quickly decided against adding fuel to that fire when Hannah spewed forth such hatred for Miss Hale's influence over John, and exposing the Thorntons to gossip, that Fanny was quite taken aback at the degree of her mother's ire.

Fanny had spent her life playing second fiddle to John, who as far as she could tell, had never disappointed their mother except in his association with Miss Hale. Fanny had tried to exert her presence in the Thornton family by developing her love for colourful fashions and attention seeking mannerisms that were as different from John as she could achieve. When her efforts were dismissed as simply silly, she had eventually given up and decided to marry to get away from the somewhat poisonous environment cultivated by their mother.

Fanny had accepted a marriage proposal from Mr Watson. As a mill master, and a man considerably older than Fanny, it was believed by many that she had married him for his money. But Fanny's reason for accepting Watson was because he had promised to make her the centre of his world, and he had. Fanny was now content, and as she no longer needed to vie for her mother's attention, she had the opportunity to examine the relationship of mother and son with detached interest. She was somewhat ashamed to realise that she had never really attempted to see John's relationship with their mother from his point of view, and now that she saw her mother's rage at John and his apparently unrequited love for Miss Hale, she felt sympathy for him. She knew how it felt to be a disappointment to their mother and was sure that John didn't deserve it. He was a good son and brother, and although she loved him, there had always been a barrier of animosity between them due to their mother's obvious preference for John over her. Fanny acknowledged that that was not his fault, and though she would not have dared to voice her thoughts to her mother, she vowed to be kinder to John. If her mother's assessment regarding Miss Hale was correct, then it appeared that at some time in the near future he might need her comfort. She decided to ask her mother to stay with her for a little while, so that

John might have an interlude from their mother's sharp tongue.

During his evenings at the Hales', John spent his time in relative solitude, with Dixon being the most frequent person he bumped into when he had to venture into the kitchen. He made his own tea, heated Albert's milk, and washed up the crockery he had used for himself and the pup. On Edwin Bailey's advice, Albert had now progressed onto being bottle fed by means of a thick curved glass bottle and rubber teat, which Margaret had purchased on the Milton high street. It was a much simpler and less messy procedure than the waxed paper and muslin method, but the chemist had instructed Margaret that thorough cleaning between feeds was necessary to prevent illnesses in bottle fed babies, and so Margaret and John ensured they applied the same principle to keep Albert from becoming sick.

Mr Hale occasionally made an appearance when John was in the parlour with Albert but mostly kept to his study, using either the excuse of needing to prepare for a lecture or that he was with a pupil. In fact, Mr Hale was embarrassed that John was doing what he should have offered to do. Instead of helping his daughter with the evidently monumental task of hand rearing the puppy, he had wanted to get rid of it and he was ashamed. He acknowledged that John's selflessness had led to Margaret's happiness.

John found working at Crampton Terrace to be very constructive as he had no distractions, save tending to Albert every two hours. Each evening, John brought with him a long, wide piece of cotton that he folded lengthways to form a pocket. He tied it around his waist and then tucked Albert into the pouch. This arrangement meant that he could keep Albert on his lap without the puppy falling off. Albert benefitted from John's body heat, and John had both hands free so that he could work at the same time.

As his ledgers were now up to date, John was able to divert his attention to a project that he had been considering for some time. He had been wanting to experiment on a fabric printing method that he had read about. Orders were slow and raw cotton was increasing in price by the day, so he was considering how he might diversify by investigating dying the cotton at Marlborough Mills. Printed cotton attracted a higher price and might set him apart from his local competitors. He currently didn't have the means to expand his business, far from it. However, should the mill survive, he felt as though this would be a way to help ensure the longevity of his business, and secure the living this provided for himself and his workers.

John had taken the time whilst at the Hales' to do some research on block, screen and roller printing methods, and was preparing to make an attempt. In the longer term, roller printing would be much quicker and efficient, and the automated process was developing rapidly. However, the equipment was expensive, so John had decided to experiment with the block printing process first. He had discussed his plans with Edwin Bailey during one of his chats with the weaver about Albert, and the young man had expressed enthusiasm in participating in the trial. John had reserved a bolt of their finest product to practise on, which could not be sold due to a flaw running throughout near the selvedge, and he was keen to see what they could achieve.

Almost three weeks after Albert's dramatic birth, John arrived as usual for his evening stint of looking after the pup. But instead of Dixon answering the door to his now familiar knock, he was both surprised and delighted to be welcomed by Miss Hale. He was no further than crossing the threshold when she spoke.

'Oh, Mr Thornton, come quickly,' she urged him, in a highly excited state.

'What has happened? Is Albert ill?' he said, now equally urgently, as he deduced from her attitude that something was seriously amiss. He practically threw his overcoat at the hall stand and made for the parlour.

'Oh no, no, he is well. Look,' she said triumphantly, and John beamed as he looked at Albert on the hearth rug. The little mite's eyes were open, and he was busy attempting to investigate his surroundings on his tiny wobbly legs.

'Well,' said John softly, dropping to his knees. 'Hello little fellow.'

He picked up Albert and held him to his face so that they could see each other for the first time.

'Isn't it marvellous,' said Margaret. 'I was so anxious for you to arrive so you could see,' and Mr Thornton and Miss Hale shared an honest, happy smile.

❧

By four weeks of age, Albert was much sturdier. His coat was fluffy and soft, and his ears, or rather one ear, was constantly pointed up while the other refused to do so, giving him a perpetually quizzical look. His baby teeth were visible, and Ernest Bailey had informed John that the swabbing for toileting was no longer needed. Albert now required weaning onto solid food, and thankfully would not demand feeding so frequently. John sent word to Miss Hale that he had developmental information regarding Albert to impart to her, and so when he arrived that evening she did not immediately retire. Mr Hale joined them in the parlour to read while John explained the need for changes to their routine. He produced from his pocket a recipe, dictated by Mr Bailey, for a type of gruel suitable for puppies, and Margaret listened carefully to the instructions then took the list from him.

'He will be tired now that he's on his feet so much, Mr Bailey informs me, so he won't disturb you too much in the night,' said John, attempting to keep the regret from his voice.

'I see,' said Margaret, happy that she could resume a more normal schedule. But strangely, at the same time, she felt inexplicably bereft that there was no longer a need for Mr Thornton's daily visits, even though she had spent very little time with him. She realised that she felt comfortable knowing that he was there, which took her quite by surprise. She wondered if he was pleased that he didn't need to come to their house every day, and that his assistance to her was no longer necessary.

Mr Thornton cleared his throat. 'If it is acceptable to you and Mr Hale, I would still like to visit Albert a time or two each week. If you are agreeable?' he said, blinking.

Mr Hale looked up from his book, glasses perched on the end of his nose and bushy grey eyebrows knitted together.

'John, you must come whenever you like. I daresay the puppy will still be running rings around us in months to come,' he said.

Margaret bestowed a grateful smile on her father.

'Thank you,' John said, and meant it more than the two words could convey.

John continued to visit the Hales three times weekly, once for his lesson with Mr Hale, and twice with the sole objective of spending time with Miss Hale and Albert, although her father was always in attendance, as was proper. John was confident in debating during his lessons, but when he simply sat companionably with the Hales, he felt shyness hold his tongue. His contribution to their discussions was less than he would have liked, although neither of the Hales appeared to be concerned by his reserve. He enjoyed the peace and simple pleasure of listening to Mr Hale and his daughter as they chatted, occasionally being drawn into their conversation. Having little experience of the countryside, John was thoroughly taken by the mental picture that Margaret and her father painted of Helstone, when they talked with fondness about their time there.

Albert appeared to alternate between periods of great activity, investigating all that was available to him, and complete exhaustion when he would flop, asleep instantly. During this time John would lift the puppy and place him on his knee, and stroke the young dog while he slept. It was a most enjoyable time for John, sitting on the faded old settee in the Hales' parlour with Albert fast asleep on his lap, though his mother was less pleased with the dog hairs he came home coated in. Sometimes Margaret would make Dutch cocoa for her father, and John was especially pleased to be asked to partake in this special treat. These evenings spent with the Hales and Albert, though simple in entertainment, infused John with a happiness that he could not remember experiencing before, and which fortified him for his continued challenges at the mill.

Chapter 9

May 1855

John looked out over the mill from the elevated position of his office. It was a fine and unseasonably warm spring day, and the courtyard was busy with both activity and chatter as several of his hands enjoyed a moment in the sunshine, taking part in some light-hearted banter. John could see Higgins in conversation with two women that he recognised from the carding shed, although he didn't know their names. His head tilted slightly to one side as he concentrated on Higgins' interaction with the women. John was fairly proficient at lip reading from years working in the clamour of the weaving shed, but Higgins and the women were side on to him and he couldn't make out what was being said. Suddenly all three of them laughed. Then, as their conversation was over, the women headed back to the carding room and Higgins went in the opposite direction, towards a delivery that needed unloading.

A sense of sadness washed over John. What would it be like to be able to converse normally with women? A woman. How wonderful it must be to speak plainly without the constraints of polite society or his own reserve; just to be one's self. To have such freedom was a luxury that the hands were oblivious to, and he was jealous. He could speak with his mother, of course, and Fanny, but not as friends. He wasn't entirely sure either one of them had a sense of humour. He wanted to be able to take part in conversations and laughter, like that shared by Higgins and the women from the carding shed.

Miss Hale and he conversed regularly now, and he wondered if she found any pleasure in his company. His talks with her were generally led by her father, and while their discussions were stimulating and enjoyable, it wasn't the same as casually chatting to someone. Mr Hale had called him a friend, but he didn't know if Miss Hale thought of him in that regard. He always felt so awkward. Stiff. Self-conscious. Shy. He wanted to be himself with her. He wanted to be able to laugh and smile, but he was lost. Some conversations they had had when Albert was born had left him pink with embarrassment like a school boy, wet behind the ears, not a man of over thirty years. More recently she had talked to him about her beloved home in Helstone, and described the countryside to him. She had told him about a particular kind of rose that grew in abundance there, around the vicarage where the Hales had lived. She had spoken of meadows as far as the eye could see, full of cornflowers and buttercups. John always listened intently to her descriptions, and loved to hear the warmth in her voice when she reminisced. But John never felt that he had anything of interest to tell her in return, as he didn't think she would be entertained by advances in machinery or his day at the mill, and so his shyness sometimes prevented him from trying.

John sighed and leant his arm on the window ledge, resting his chin on his hand as he daydreamed about the impossible situation he found himself in – incurably and irrevocably in love with a woman who did not like him and found his passion for her offensive. Perhaps she might be beginning to like him a bit, he mused. Then the most extraordinary thing happened. John started, jerking his head up off his hand. As if his mind had willed her there, in through the gates of Marlborough Mills stepped Margaret Hale. She walked slowly carrying a large basket. Higgins pulled at his hat peak as she passed him, and she smiled and nodded at him and exchanged a few words, but never stopped. John watched to see if she approached the house, and he reached behind him to grab his jacket off the chair but it wasn't there. *Damn.* He'd come back to work this afternoon in his shirt sleeves as the weather was so warm. He hadn't anticipated an encounter with Miss Hale. Of all the days to not have his coat!

Never taking his eyes off her, he started rolling his sleeves down. He saw her put the basket down, rub her back and heave it up again. It was heavy. John clattered down his office steps then strode out into the yard to meet Miss Hale, and to offer his assistance.

'Mr Thornton. Thank goodness,' said Margaret, putting the basket down again. 'I wasn't sure if I would make it up the steps to your office,' she said, and blessed him with one of her teasing smiles. John frowned slightly. Margaret looked hot, even a little sweaty.

'Can I offer you some refreshment?' he asked, reaching down for the basket. It was surprisingly heavy, and he wondered what was inside. 'You have carried this all the way from Crampton?' he said, with eyebrows raised.

'I have! He has become heavier with every step,' she said, rubbing her arms to ease the aching.

'He?' said John, and just then the weight in the basket moved. 'Albert?' he said, looking from her to the basket.

Margaret looked a little unsure. 'I need to ask a favour of you.'

'Of course. Come into the house. Please.'

John and Margaret entered Marlborough House and John requested tea to be brought into the drawing room. He explained that his mother was staying with Fanny for a few days, and that she would be sorry to have missed Miss Hale's visit. Margaret doubted it.

John lifted the lid on the basket and reached in for Albert, a gentle smile softening his features as he gave the puppy a little cuddle and sat him on his knee, the customary dog hairs immediately adhering to his black work trousers. Despite being the guest, Margaret was happy to see to pouring the tea, as John had his hands full, and John enjoyed the simple pleasure of watching her perform the ritual as he had done now on many an occasion.

Margaret took a deep breath. 'Mr Thornton, would it be possible for you to have Albert for a few days? A week at the most. I know it will be most inconvenient for you. You are so busy I know, and now that I find Mrs Thornton is also away—'

'Yes,' he interrupted.

'Sorry?'

'Yes,' he laughed. John's eyebrows lifted a fraction as he thought back to his earlier musing. The laugh had escaped him without thinking. Perhaps he wasn't a hopeless case after all.

'Of course I will have him. I would be pleased to have him,' he said, looking warmly into the dog's eyes, and ruffling his soft ears.

'Really? Oh, thank you. I hoped you would. Father and I must travel to London at short notice, and Dixon will have the house to look after, and—'

'Miss Hale, I am honoured,' he said gently. And he was.

Margaret explained that she and her father had been summoned to her aunt's house in Harley Street, where she had spent much of her youth. Aunt Shaw was due back from a protracted trip to the continent, and Edith had arranged a surprise party for her. Margaret was unsure if her aunt would appreciate such an occasion being thrust upon her, and that the attendance of Margaret and her father was not likely to make any impression on the festivities. However, Mr Hale was anxious that Margaret maintain family links with the Shaws and Lennoxes, as with no husband, Margaret may need their support in the coming years. He had been firm that they should go and Margaret had no choice but to comply.

Margaret had supplied John with the necessary ingredients to make the puppy food, and a list of instructions, which she had insisted on going through with him as if he couldn't read it by himself. John listened to Margaret's every word, although apart from Albert's bedtime routine, he was already familiar with the puppy's feeding and sleeping regime. Albert was not fully house trained, and John was glad that his mother was away, as he had no doubt she would have some caustic remarks to share on the topic. He didn't want his mother to spoil the enjoyment of having Albert to stay, nor to criticise Miss Hale for asking for his help.

When Margaret had gone, John tucked Albert under his arm and went into the mill in search of a suitable box for a bed, and a supply of cotton for Albert's mattress. John felt he had never been as popular with his workers, as all that he passed either looked with curiosity or even reached out to pat and fuss over Albert as he went by.

Albert spent the afternoon asleep in his cosy new bed beside John's desk. As the seven o'clock whistle sounded, and the steam engine powering the looms was allowed to slow, John considered how much work he had accomplished. What with first daydreaming about Miss Hale, the subsequent visit from her, and then having Albert with him for the rest of the day, he had achieved precious little in the way of work. But John was happy, and he allowed himself to sit relaxed and smiling. Against the backdrop of the precarious state his business was in, on the brink between failure and survival, today had been a good day.

The night, however, was not as good. He had put Albert's bed in his own bedroom to keep a close eye on the pup, but this had been a distraction for the youngster who whined for attention while John pretended he couldn't hear him. He heard the pup's nails lightly tapping on the floorboards when he ventured off the rug, exploring the nooks and crannies of John's chamber into the small hours of the morning.

John's happy mood persisted into the next day, despite his interrupted night's sleep. After both he and the pup had breakfast, he readied himself for work.

'Now then, Bertie, look sharp. We don't want to be setting a bad example by being late,' he said, scooping up the eager puppy who rewarded John with a rasping kiss along his master's jaw.

John Thornton and the puppy were an arresting sight, and several stopped to stare. Both were handsome, and complemented one another with their matching black and white attire. Although Albert followed his master about, John had attached a thin rope about his neck as a lead so that he didn't stray into dangerous territory. He always kept the puppy in his arms when in the weaving shed so as not to put the dog at risk of injury, or endanger the workers by distracting them. John asked Edwin Bailey about training Albert to complete simple commands, and Edwin guided him on starting with instructions such as to sit and stay, advocating rewards when the puppy got it right.

John was overheard speaking to the dog, who would cock his head to the side as he listened. Higgins chuckled at the sight of them, particularly as the master had started using the pet name of 'Bertie' when addressing the puppy. He thought about the transformation in Thornton. But then again, he wondered, had there been a change, or was it that Thornton had not had the opportunity nor inclination to allow the workers to witness his softer side before. No other masters would, that was for certain. The difference was Miss Margaret, and Higgins knew it well. Thornton had rules and you stuck to them or you got the sharp side of his tongue. Do something dangerous and you were out. But Higgins also knew that the master was a fair man and didn't lord it over the workers, unlike some. He wasn't raking in profits and keeping them to himself either. He grafted and sweated like the rest of them. Higgins respected that. He deserved a bit of happiness he supposed, and so did Miss Margaret too.

The week was nearly over, and much as John longed for Margaret to return to Milton, he was sorry that this 'favour' of helping Miss Hale would soon come to an end and Albert would go home. Master and puppy had eased into a routine made simple by the existing bond that they already shared. However, Albert had started a seemingly new habit of rubbing his nose at John's ankle, particularly when he was sitting at his desk. The pup would snuffle until he had managed to work John's trouser leg high enough so that he could reach the skin above his sock, and then would bestow tickling wet kisses upon his master until John eventually pulled his leg away. John wondered if it was a habit that the puppy did at home with Margaret. He frowned. It was probably better not to contemplate Miss Hale's ankles, and he endeavoured to divert his thoughts back to mill matters.

Over the last few days, John's thoughts had strayed to thinking about the events that Miss Hale would have attended while she was in London, and the people she might have met, perhaps old friends and new. She would have people of her class to converse with, and he didn't doubt that they would have the genteel grace that he lacked. Perhaps her friend Henry Lennox would be there. John supposed that it was more than likely. He felt a stab of jealousy and an accompanying emptiness at the thought that one day Miss Hale would marry some unknown gentleman. He must make the most of his happiness now before it ended, and he patted Albert's little head and went back to work.

Margaret had indeed met Henry Lennox. He graced them with his presence at Harley Street every day. At first Margaret had been stilted in her behaviour around him, as she had not seen him since she had refused his marriage proposal over a year and a half ago. However, Henry appeared to have no embarrassment regarding his failed attempt for her hand, and was effusive in both his friendliness and attentiveness towards Margaret and her father. Henry informed them that he had been looking into the circumstances of Frederick's involvement in the mutiny, and asked Mr Hale's permission to visit them when he had firmer details. He raised the possibility that, depending on Frederick's role in the rebellion, he might be awarded a posthumous pardon from the navy, and thereby his honour would be restored.

Margaret was struck by the thoughtfulness of Henry's actions, particularly as neither she nor her father had asked him to pursue a line of inquiry, believing that no further information would be divulged by the navy. Mr

Hale was exceedingly grateful for Mr Lennox's attention on behalf of his son, and provided an open invitation for Henry to visit them in Milton whenever was convenient to him. Henry was delighted. He was anxious to visit Milton to assure himself that Margaret had no prospective suitors who might imminently snatch her from his grasp, while he found a way to her heart. Although he had not lifted a finger to find out any information about the wretched Frederick Hale's demise, Miss Hale and her buffoon of a father need not know that. He had devised a way to make himself welcome in Milton, and to have the Hales in his debt. Miss Hale would look more favourably upon him now, and his plans to secure her hand had begun.

Chapter 10

Miss Hale and her father had been away in London for almost a week, and John was exhilarated at the prospect of her imminent return to Milton. He had greatly enjoyed his time with Albert, who he naturally now always thought of by his pet name of Bertie. The puppy had turned out to be tremendous company for John, especially in his mother's absence. On learning of the dog's temporary residence at Marlborough House, Hannah had extended her stay with Fanny to ensure her habitation at the mill house and that of Miss Hale's dog did not overlap. Without the Hales or his mother for company, John had taken to walking to the thin strip of grass by the canal each evening to exercise Bertie, and to unwind from the gruelling hours he worked each day. It was deserted at that time, save for a few waterfowl that lived there. Bertie was a constant source of amusement as he chased the ducks along the bank until they escaped into the water, making John curtail the puppy's play for fear that he would follow them into the canal too. John enjoyed the solitude of his evening walks, but contemplated the joy it would be to share the simple pleasure with another.

John sat at his desk with Bertie by his feet, while the thrum of the steam engine beat a regular rhythm in the background, and the noise of the general commotion of mill life seeped into the office from the yard below. He inspected his post, eager to find any correspondence which might provide balance payment for goods provided. One letter in the pile of missives piqued John's interest due to its singularity. It was from Mr Bell, his landlord, informing him of his plans to visit the mill in the next few weeks. That Mr Bell was visiting was quite out of the ordinary, as he was usually satisfied with John's rent submissions without the need for question or comment. John had never missed a payment, and he frowned at the thought that perhaps Mr Bell had heard of the possible demise of Marlborough Mills. He could understand his landlord's interest if that were the case. John deduced that Mr Bell was probably coming to question him about his viability as a tenant.

John thought that Mr Bell would be sure to visit the Hales while he was in Milton, as John knew that Mr Bell and Mr Hale had been friends for many years. In fact, the Hales had relocated to Milton at Mr Bell's suggestion. In all honesty, John would admit to himself that he did not care for Mr Bell. The older gentleman had a predilection for devilment that John generally found annoying and not compatible with his more straightforward character. However, John mused that the Hales' introduction to Milton had been advantageous, and he made a mental note to be kindlier to Mr Bell, simply for the fact that he had been responsible for Margaret Hale being part of his life.

Mr and Miss Hale had been glad to return to Milton and the quiet, comfortable surroundings of their cosy house in Crampton Terrace. Neither one of them was completely at ease when thrust into London society, although they had both acquitted themselves tolerably well. Margaret had called at Marlborough Mills to collect Albert, and proceeded straight to the master's office in eager anticipation of being reunited with the puppy. She knocked briskly on the door and entered at Mr Thornton's behest.

John was sitting at his desk when Miss Hale entered, and Albert was fast asleep curled up in a ball in his bed, evidently undisturbed by her arrival. On seeing the identity of his visitor, John immediately rose. He was momentarily lost for words at her sheer loveliness that seemed to have increased, if that were possible, in the week since he had last seen her.

'Miss Hale,' he said. 'You are returned.'

'Indeed,' she laughed prettily. 'I see Albert has settled in well! I hope he has been well behaved for you?'

John rounded the desk to the dog's bed, slightly embarrassed that Miss Hale had not had a better welcome home from the puppy.

'Now then, Bertie,' he said softly, ruffling the pup's ears to gently wake him. 'Look who is here to see you?'

Margaret was amused to hear Mr Thornton's pet name for Albert and immediately liked it, but she decided to tease him a little bit about it first.

'Bertie, is it? Goodness, I have only been gone for a few days and you have made changes already!' she said, with mock reproach.

It came as a revelation to John that he could tell that Miss Hale was being playful, which inspired a smile to lighten his face for an instant before it was replaced with a frown.

'Umm, there are a couple of other changes,' he said, tousling his own hair in that way that Margaret found utterly appealing. She also knew it signified some kind of inner turmoil. 'I hope you don't think I have overstepped. I asked Mr Bailey about training methods, and we've made a start on sit and stay. It's early days but he's getting the hang of it.'

'That's marvellous! How clever,' she said, crouching down and fussing Albert.

'And there is another thing. Mr Hartley the saddler visited earlier in the week. Just routine maintenance of the horses' tack,' he faltered, suddenly unsure if Miss Hale would be receptive to the gift he had procured for Bertie. He blinked twice, then went on, 'I asked him to manufacture a collar and lead for Bertie ... I mean Albert. Of course you don't need to use them. I hope you don't mind ... that is, if I have presumed too much then please do say.' He closed his eyes briefly and shook his head, almost as if to reset his words to her.

Margaret smiled brightly at him. 'May I see?'

John withdrew a coil of leather from his desk drawer, held it for a moment and then firmly passed it to Margaret. She unfurled the objects and identified a dog's collar of tan leather, beautifully stitched along both edges and with a gleaming brass buckle. As she examined the collar she noted that it had a brass disk hanging from a chain loop with 'Albert' engraved in copperplate script. Along with the collar was a matching lead that clipped onto a fastening ring.

'Oh, Mr Thornton. You shouldn't have,' she said.

'You like them?' he asked, with his rare, bashful half-smile.

'They are perfect. Simply perfect. Albert, or should I call you Bertie as it is not Sunday,' she said, glancing at Mr Thornton as she addressed the dog. 'Come and see what Mr Thornton has bought for you. What a lucky boy you are.' And Bertie, as he now was, duly sniffed his approval of the leather items, while Margaret placed the collar around his neck and fastened the buckle.

'He looks marvellous. Thank you,' she said again, and John's heart swelled a little bit more with his love for this woman.

He had bought many gifts for Fanny over the years, from ribbons when he was still a boy himself working in the drapers shop after their father died, to much grander items prior to her wedding, including articles as extravagant as a piano. She had always thanked him, as it was polite to do so, and he thought she had genuinely liked his gifts. But he lacked a connection with Fanny which he regretted bitterly. He wished he had tried harder to understand her, and had taken an interest in the pastimes that she favoured. It was a sorry excuse to say that his neglect of his sister had been due to being occupied by work. He was busy now but found time for Miss Hale. He judged that it was too late now to form a bond with his sister, and he was saddened that he would never have the relationship with Fanny that she deserved.

So, although he had been thanked by Fanny for the gifts he had given to her in the past, he didn't think he had ever been as pleased by a reaction to a present as he was that afternoon. Miss Hale had looked him directly in the eye and thanked him as if he had given her the crown jewels. He had to admit that Mr Hartley had done a fine job, and Bertie did indeed look very smart.

John knelt on the floor near to Margaret, their heads together as he showed her how to attach the lead, and he was treated to her lovely rose scent that was now so familiar to him. She could easily have worked out the lead's clip herself, and John was aware of that too, but they both chose to ignore that fact and enjoyed the excuse to be close.

Margaret and Bertie took their leave from Mr Thornton, and he watched them from his office as they crossed the yard. As she was about to depart through the gate, Margaret turned to glance up to his office window, and seeing him there she raised her hand in farewell and he responded in kind, happier than he could say that she had looked back at him.

Chapter 11

June 1855

Mr Hale shouted to Margaret to come quickly. He was in quite a state of excited agitation. 'Margaret my dear, we will have a visitor! Nay two!' he said, wafting an opened letter in his hand.

Margaret laughed indulgently. She had not fully appreciated how lonely her father was. She berated herself for focusing on her own solitude, and apart from Dixon, the only company that she or her father regularly conversed with was Nicholas Higgins or Mr Thornton.

'Who, Father? Do tell me. You are so excited I would worry that it is the Queen herself that you expect to come to tea,' she teased, and fondly kissed his cheek.

'It is Mr Bell and Mr Lennox, dear,' he said, and Margaret was as delighted as her father. She held Mr Bell in the highest esteem, although he could be a mischief maker, and Henry had been a friend to her. During her recent trip to London he had been good company, having evidently put behind him any awkwardness regarding the occasion when he had misread her friendship for something more.

'We, well you, my dear, must arrange a dinner for our guests. I know it will not be easy,' Mr Hale said, worry troubling his face as he pondered the extra work this visit would cause Margaret with only Dixon for help.

'We will manage, Father,' she said, squeezing his arm. 'Both gentlemen know we are not of grand means. I'm sure Dixon and I can concoct a presentable meal and not poison anyone.'

'Yes, indeed,' Mr Hale agreed, with a happy countenance again, looking forward to the entertainment their friends' visit would bring.

The next day, Margaret was required to visit Mr Thornton at Marlborough Mills. As Mr Bell and Henry's visit coincided with the usual night for Mr Thornton's weekly lesson with her father, she needed to rearrange the appointment. She could have sent a note, but it was easier and quicker to walk there herself, and it would provide a purpose for Bertie's exercise that day. Marlborough Mills was one of their favourite and most frequent destinations for Bertie's daily walk, and they were now a familiar sight in the mill courtyard. The mill was not too far for Bertie, and they always received a warm welcome. The bench in the yard was suitable for a rest before they walked back home, and many a hand would stop for a quick word or two with her and fuss over the dog. Margaret would ask them about their families, and should they mention any extra hardship or illness, she would ensure that she paid them a visit.

There was not a single worker who didn't wonder why the master had not put a ring on her finger yet. She had tamed him, that was for sure. He still had a fearful temper, but it appeared infrequently these days. Thanks to Nicholas Higgins, the majority of the hands were aware that Thornton's exacting standards, and need to fulfil contracts on time, were due to the master and the mill clinging onto the cliff edge of solvency. If he failed they all would suffer, and every man and woman was grateful that he put his heart and soul into keeping the mill alive, even if they were on the receiving end of a tongue lashing on occasion.

News of Miss Hale's arrival always spread quickly through the mill. The message easily passed from one to another, despite the tremendous noise in the sheds, by way of lip reading. John was usually apprised of her presence by the women's eyes landing on him in a wave, as the information swept through them. He was thus alerted that they were talking about him, and he could spot Miss Hale or Bertie's name on their lips easily. He didn't pretend to conceal his delight, and always hurried to the mill yard to see them.

On this particular day, he found Margaret to be in conversation with Mary and Nicholas Higgins. Nicholas had noticed the master's stiffness and reserve in Miss Margaret's company, although the puppy had the power to soften him considerably. He wished Thornton would just get on with it and propose to her, but he was not aware of the history that Margaret and the master shared on that subject. He wondered if they might need a little push to get them together.

John was pleased to see Bertie looking first-rate wearing his leather collar and lead. The puppy sat obediently at Margaret's feet, his nose pressing into her hand which moments before had bestowed a biscuit treat on him.

'Miss Hale, Bertie,' said John in greeting, crouching down to ruffle the dog's ears. As Margaret looked down on the two dark heads, she had a sudden urge to put her hand through Mr Thornton's hair, like she was wont to do with Bertie, and her cheeks flushed pink. Hannah spied the exchange from her vantage point in the front parlour window. She wondered what might have brought a blush to Miss Hale's countenance. It had been a while now since she, along with all at the mill, believed it to be only a matter of time before Miss Hale shared her name. She had counselled John on the impropriety of his frequent and lengthy visits to the Hales' residence in Crampton, especially since Miss Hale had shown herself to not know the worth of her son, though he had not heeded her words. But she had to admit that the girl made John happy, and there was no doubt in her mind that an affection for her son had now blossomed in Miss Hale too.

'Are you well, Miss Hale?' enquired John, noticing Margaret's flushed features. 'Can I offer you some refreshment?'

'I am quite well, thank you. I don't wish to interrupt your busy day. I just needed to tell you that Father must postpone your lesson this week as Mr Bell is visiting. He is coming with Edith's brother-in-law, Henry Lennox. Henry is Mr Bell's lawyer.'

It had been many months since John had heard Miss Hale refer to Henry Lennox. *Henry.* He had assumed that they would have met during her trip to London, and he was perturbed that Lennox should be visiting her so soon after their last meeting. It still maddened him that she called this man by his first name. It was an intimacy that he was not afforded. With disappointment he thought that she must not think of him as a friend, and that she must not view him as favourably as she did this *Henry* fellow. While John had known about Mr Bell's planned visit, it troubled him to receive the additional intelligence that he was bringing his attorney with him.

Margaret misconstrued John's scowl. 'Father does apologise. It is only this one time,' she said gently, coaxing a smile back onto his face.

'Of course. I understand. I will miss it, that's all,' he said, and meant it. 'I hope you have a pleasant evening.'

As John made his way back to the mill, he glanced behind him to have another look at Margaret, and coincidentally she did the same. The two of them shared a shy smile, each realising they had been caught out by the other.

Later that afternoon, after Nicholas Higgins' shift had finished, he and Margaret stood by the back door at Crampton Terrace watching his children throw a stick for Bertie to fetch back, although Bertie appeared to have other ideas. The pup collected the stick but then preferred that the children chase him to try to get it back, which produced squeals of delight from them as they raced after him.

'The master enjoyed having Bertie to stay,' said Higgins, casually, not taking his eyes off the children at play. 'I think 'is trips over 'ere and that pup bring him a lot of enjoyment, even wi' the struggle he's 'avin' wi' the mill.'

Margaret frowned. 'I hope so. But, Nicholas, is the mill really in trouble? I thought the mill masters were amassing great wealth and kept it to themselves instead of raising wages? Can he not use his own money to save the business?'

'I'm sorry to say that the only result from t'strike was to bring down the one master worth 'is salt. I 'eard he'd put 'is money in the mill. Safety measures, an' the canteen an' the like. He's tryin' 'ard to keep it goin', an' we're all tryin' with 'im. Mind you, I'm not sayin' the man's a saint. Bringin' in them Irish workers for example. I don't think I can forgive 'im that. But I speak as I find. He's been good to me, an' he works 'arder than anyone I know. That'll do in my book.'

'I see,' said Margaret quietly, though she needed more time to consider Nicholas' words. He appeared to be inferring that Mr Thornton was different from the other masters that she had heard about, and while she was pleased to hear it, she was also unsettled to think that she had done him an injustice. She had not thought of Mr Thornton 'the mill master' as an individual, but had grouped him with men of his occupation in general. That Nicholas should think him to be a good man was high praise indeed, and she could easily agree that in her heart she thought of him with a similar regard.

The dinner party at the Hale's residence for Mr Bell and Mr Lennox was a jolly affair, mainly due to the diverting conversation and Mr Bell's outrageous anecdotes. Mr Bell raised the prospect of taking Mr Hale to Oxford for a holiday, and with encouragement from Margaret, her father accepted. Henry was attentive to her throughout the meal, freely bestowing compliments upon Margaret about anything and everything that she might have been responsible for. In fact, his accolades were so effusive that even Mr Bell, who was adept at such flattering remarks himself, was alerted to Mr Lennox's singular focus on Margaret. Bertie had been relegated to the kitchen where he aggravated Dixon by persistently getting under her feet. If he could have been trusted with their provisions she would have locked him in the pantry until the dinner was over.

As Margaret was the only female at the dinner, the men did not retire for port and cigars, and the whole group removed to the sitting room. Henry had been quite dismayed when he first laid eyes on the Hales' home, as it was very modest indeed. However, he deemed that Margaret's current reduced circumstances might make him more desirable to her, and provide her with a way to extricate herself from this situation. Henry was not averse to being used by Margaret to improve her lot, after all, he was planning to do the same thing to her.

Bertie was allowed into the room with them, and Margaret let him show off his full repertoire of commands to the audience. Throughout the evening, on several occasions, the name of Mr Thornton came up in conversation. Henry feigned indifference to this man's role in the Hales' lives. He was relieved to find that this man, for a gentleman he was not, was a manufacturer and tenant of Mr Bell. He determined to pay close attention to the tradesman named Thornton. It appeared he had found favour with the Hales by way of lessons in the classics, and then had become involved in the care of Margaret's dog. Henry thought Bertie was entertaining enough but was inappropriate. The hairy beast was a working dog, not a genteel lap dog that would be more suited to Margaret's station when she was his wife.

Mr Hale and Margaret had been anxious to hear any news that Henry had discovered regarding Frederick, which in turn might lead to a pardon from the navy. Indeed, Margaret knew the immense solace that her father in particular would gain from such a gesture of forgiveness for Frederick's alleged crime. It was unclear what his role in the mutiny had been, and Margaret and her father struggled to understand how a man as sweet as Frederick could have been involved in such a seemingly despicable and illegal act. They felt certain that there was an explanation, but no witness testimony had previously been forthcoming to suggest an acquittal for Frederick.

Henry had not conducted an investigation into Frederick Hale's participation in the mutiny. He saw no value in it, and of course he would not be paid for his efforts. His offer of assistance to the Hales on this matter was purely to get closer to Margaret, and it had worked. He apologised with the appearance of deepest sympathy. He told the father and daughter that, alas, there was no evidence that would clear Frederick Hale's name, although he would be sure to remain alert for any further intelligence. It was a blow to Mr Hale and Margaret to hear Henry's report. Having become accustomed to the devastating news of Frederick's disgrace, it was especially hard to hear that the flicker of hope that Henry had reignited, had come to nought. Even though they were disappointed with the outcome, Mr Hale and Margaret expressed their thanks, and were indebted to Henry for the trouble that they believed he had taken on their behalf.

The next day, Henry Lennox and John Thornton's curiosity regarding each other was satisfied, and neither one of them was happy about it. Henry accompanied Mr Bell on his visit to Marlborough Mills. As far as John could see, the only good thing about Henry Lennox was that he showed some interest in the manufacturing of cotton, showing more enthusiasm for the subject than Mr Bell ever had. Little did John know that Lennox was appraising the investment that would be his, if his plans to marry Margaret came to fruition.

What really needled John was that Lennox continually referred to Margaret by her Christian name. Of course, she had similarly referred to Lennox as 'Henry', although not as frequently. It felt to John as if Lennox was staking his claim on Margaret by enforcing his familiarity with her.

Henry understood from his excursion and subsequent tour of Marlborough Mills, that the business was in some financial bother after the upheaval following a riot several months ago. It appeared that the pecuniary difficulty would be a temporary problem should a short term, if large, injection of capital be invested to get it back on its feet. Mr Thornton appeared well respected by Mr Bell, and Henry could see the benefit of the continuation of the lease to this man. The fly in the ointment was Thornton himself. He was striking in the exact opposite way to Henry's own brother. Where Sholto was blonde, bright in his captain's uniform and of a continually happy disposition, Thornton was the polar opposite. He was dark where Sholto was fair, and wore black austere clothes. His Darkshire accent was unrefined, and cemented Henry's opinion of his inferiority. Where Sholto was attractive to women on a level Henry was incapable of reaching, he suspected Mr Thornton was as impressive to the fairer sex for being quite the antithesis. Thornton and Margaret also had a connection through the dog that Margaret had championed the previous evening. Henry discerned that Thornton was a threat to his plans, and the sooner Margaret and this mill master were separated the better it would be.

Mr Bell requested a further, private meeting with Mr Thornton the following day, and Henry was annoyed at being excluded. He was desperate to know what information Mr Bell might be withholding from him that might help in his plans to secure Margaret, and in turn, Mr Bell's fortune. Henry had argued that as Mr Bell's lawyer it would be advisable to accompany him, but Mr Bell was adamant. He would see Thornton alone.

As Mr Bell would be absent due to his visit to the mill, Henry decided to use the time wisely and spend it with Margaret, displaying his gentlemanly ways. In doing so he hoped to highlight the chasm between local men and himself, allowing Margaret a glimpse at her mistake in refusing him. His refined manners would attract her to him, and his plans to win her over would progress further. For a brief moment, Henry considered contriving a situation in which Margaret would be compromised, and thereby force a marital union between the two of them, but he soon dismissed the idea. He would not stoop so low, and judging by the coarse society that Margaret was currently subjected to, he felt certain that she would soon realise that her affections had changed in his favour without the need for such an unscrupulous scheme. All things considered, Henry felt that this trip to Milton had been a success. He believed he had the measure of Thornton, had ingratiated himself with Mr Hale over the ghastly business of Frederick Hale, and had made strides forwards in securing Margaret with his southern manners.

It was dawning on Mr Bell that he may have made an error in engaging Mr Lennox as his lawyer. He had been somewhat surprised when Lennox had asked to accompany him on his visit to Milton but saw no reason to object. However, he noticed that Lennox was fawning over Margaret, and he had a worrying suspicion that she had become Lennox's quarry, most likely because he knew that she would inherit his fortune. Mr Bell gave some thought to changing his legal agent, but rejected that idea as Lennox already knew the details of his will, so it appeared pointless to make changes now.

Despite his flattery of her, Margaret appeared to have no romantic fondness for Lennox, therefore Mr Bell deduced that no harm would be done. The business of settling the particulars of his will had become most urgent to Mr Bell. Though he had kept the information to himself, he had received distressing news from his physician, and his departure from life appeared to be imminent. In fact, Mr Bell's death would be sooner than he could ever have comprehended.

Mr Bell was a perceptive and somewhat romantic fellow. He held an undisclosed admiration for John Thornton, as although he was a gruff and somewhat prickly man, Mr Bell also knew him to be a hard worker and, most importantly, an honest man. It was as clear as day on observing Margaret when she spoke of him, that she and Thornton had formed a fondness for one another, albeit an unofficial one which Mr Hale appeared to be oblivious to. She had been radiant last evening when conversing about Thornton, and her reports of his steadfast commitment and assistance to the Hales spoke to Mr Bell of a mutual feeling. It amused him to think of the future that Margaret and Thornton might enjoy with the benefit of his fortune, and it gave him a measure of comfort to think that it would be put to good use, and in his hometown too.

However, Mr Bell had a niggling, troublesome notion that lurked in the recesses of his brain that he could not clearly identify, and it would not go away. He fancied that it was linked to Henry Lennox and his recent overt interest in Margaret. Mr Bell felt the need to divulge a little of Margaret's inheritance to Thornton, though he could not pinpoint why. It almost felt like an insurance policy, that with an external person knowing a little of what was to come to Margaret, she would be protected. He knew that news of Margaret's inheritance would be no inducement to make her attractive to Thornton, as a romantic attachment appeared already in place, and he would not insult the man with the concept.

It occurred to Mr Bell that it was a ridiculous state of affairs that he did not trust his own lawyer, and berated himself for not settling his affairs sooner and without the haste which had become necessary. If he did not trust Henry Lennox, then he should simply discharge his services, but he was aware that he was running out of time. He was dying, and if his doctor was to be believed, he would be gone in a matter of a few months. Due to his impending trip to Oxford with Richard Hale, he had no opportunity now to engage a new lawyer. The logical step would be to inform Mr Hale of the contents of his will, but this visit to Milton had highlighted to him how frail his friend had also become, and he didn't want to burden him with the knowledge or associated sorrow. He was being cowardly he knew, but he wished to avoid witnessing his friend contemplate further grief. Mr Bell also considered telling Margaret herself, but rejected this too, as he didn't want to upset her with talk of his death. He was entertained to think of the lovely surprise Margaret would get on finding herself to be an heiress after he had died. That news might lighten her sadness at his passing, for he was sure that she would grieve for him. So Mr Bell had decided to tell John Thornton. Of course, there was no guarantee that Margaret would choose to marry Thornton. She might choose Lennox or another fellow, but Mr Bell decided that he would feel happier knowing that Thornton was aware all the same. Margaret would inherit his fortune, and as she was a sensible girl, he must trust in her to choose her life partner wisely.

The sharp rap of a walking cane on John's office door heralded the arrival of Mr Bell. John welcomed his landlord with his usual handshake, and offered the older man the seat opposite his desk. John considered Mr Bell to be a debonair man, who was opinionated and flamboyant in his manner, although he had noticed yesterday that Mr Bell looked older, more lined and greyer than the last time they had met, perhaps nine or ten months ago.

'Mr Bell, this is an unexpected pleasure, seeing you two days in a row. I hope there is nothing amiss that has made you feel the need to come to talk to me personally,' said John.

'Well, well, straight to the point, Thornton, as ever,' the older man chuckled. 'I will answer as directly as you have asked. There is a matter that brings me here. I shan't beat around the bush. I will be going away in the next month or two and will not be returning,' said Mr Bell.

John's black brows drew down in consternation.

'I am dying, Thornton, if my doctor is to be believed, and I have no reason to doubt him. So, I shall be having a holiday with Richard Hale for old times' sake and then … well, then, we shall see.'

'Mr Bell, I am sorry—' began John.

'Yes, yes,' interjected Bell. 'I felt it prudent to let you know, confidentially of course, as it will impact upon Marlborough Mills.'

'I am sorry to hear of your ill health. Is there nothing that can be done?' asked John, his thoughts immediately going to Margaret, and the additional sorrow that she would be required to bear in the forthcoming months.

'Indeed no. But worry not. I am reconciled with it, after all, none of us can live forever. I look favourably on the chance to set my affairs in order and spend time with those I care for. As you know, Henry Lennox is my lawyer, and he will act on my behalf and be executor of my will.'

John's mind was whirring, taking in all of this fresh and quite shocking information. Mr Bell was dying, Mr Hale would be leaving Margaret to go on a trip, and the spectre that was Henry Lennox, Margaret's 'Henry', would resurface to manage Mr Bell's will.

'May I ask, if it is not too impertinent, to whom you will bequeath Marlborough Mills? If I am to have a new landlord, it would be beneficial to know if I am familiar with them,' asked John, ordering his thoughts. At this Mr Bell's eyes twinkled.

'I shall tell you. Indeed, it is the reason I wanted to speak to you in person and privately. Do I have your word as a gentleman that you will not divulge the information to any other soul until I have shuffled off this mortal coil?' said Mr Bell, who was thoroughly enjoying the drama.

'We both know that I am no gentleman Mr Bell, but I give you my word if you feel that it is of merit.'

'My goddaughter is the heir to Marlborough Mills, Thornton,' said Bell, sitting back in his chair and watching the news sink in.

'Miss Hale?' said John, surprise evident in his features.

'Indeed. I thought perhaps you might need a little further incentive to keep the mill afloat,' laughed Mr Bell, who winked at John and rose from his chair abruptly. 'Good day, Thornton,' he said, extending his hand.

'Good day, Mr Bell,' said John, shaking his hand. With that, Mr Bell strode from the office, never to be seen by John again.

John sat back down, stunned, his mind brimming with Mr Bell's news and its implications. Miss Hale would be bereaved again, and unless he could turn the tide on the waning fortunes of his business, she would inherit the vacant mill buildings and land with no means to do anything with it. John had to commend Mr Bell, the wily old fox, he certainly knew how to stir the pot. But he had been correct. It was another reason why John needed Marlborough Mills to succeed.

✍

Chapter 12

The information that nothing further could be done to clear Frederick's name regarding the mutiny had hit Mr Hale very hard. The case being brought up by Mr Lennox had in itself been unsettling for the older man, and yet he had been persuaded that there might be hope for a pardon for his son. So he had allowed his hopes to be raised, only to have them dashed again. Mr Hale took to his room after Mr Bell and Mr Lennox had left to return to the South, and Margaret was concerned for her father's low mood. Mr Hale had no wish to go to Oxford with Mr Bell when he felt so dispirited, but was unable to change the plans.

John arrived to see Bertie and the Hales after work as was usual. On entering the parlour, he was surprised to find only Miss Hale and Bertie present, and she looked worried.

'Good evening, Miss Hale, Bertie,' John said, as the puppy sprang over to him in welcome.

'Good evening, Mr Thornton. I do apologise, but I should have sent word that it is not convenient for you to call tonight,' she replied. She felt so sorry to have to ask him to leave and yet she could not entertain him alone, and her father was in no state for visitors. 'I am sorry, but we received some bad news and Father is upset you see,' she explained, and worried that she had said too much.

'Oh, I see. I'm sorry to hear that. Can I be of any help?' he said. John suspected that Mr Bell had informed them of his ill health.

Margaret was anxious and restless as she struggled to decide whether to tell Mr Thornton about Frederick or not. It seemed somehow dishonest to keep the tale from him now that he was so familiar with them, and she believed him to be their friend.

'It is a secret you see,' she said nervously. 'But if you wished to listen, then I think I would feel better to have told you.'

John sat down on the old green settee and waited for Margaret to speak.

'I have, or should I say had, a brother. Frederick,' she said, and was immediately glad that she had spoken the words.

'A brother?' he said, shocked.

Margaret began to recount the upsetting and tragic story about her previously undisclosed brother and his part in the mutiny. She explained how it had been a hard cross for them to bear. They had not only lost a dear son and brother, but had felt compelled to be secretive about Frederick in their grief.

'Father and I will always love Frederick as the good person that he was. It is hard to reconcile what we know of him with that person described in the navy's reports, but there is nothing to be done. We can only remember him ourselves as he was to us. It is a comfort to be able to speak his name when ordinarily I cannot,' Margaret said. 'Henry has investigated trying to obtain a pardon for Frederick, but told us on his visit that it is impossible. So Father's hopes have once again been shattered and he is not himself. You do understand? It is the shame which is so hard to abide,' she said bravely, keeping her tears at bay.

John knew all about the shadow that disrepute could cast over a family due to his father's perceived act of cowardice and equally untimely death, and he wanted nothing more than to take her in his arms to console her, but it was simply not permitted. It was bad enough that they were alone, and he would not bring disgrace upon her. So instead, he tried to soothe her with his understanding.

'I know how it is to feel blighted by the actions of another. My father brought humiliation upon my family, and it is hard to endure the censure when you are already distressed by their loss. My father's disgrace is well known, so it's not the same I suppose. I don't for one minute blame you for keeping the information about your brother private, and I don't think many of those who know you, if any, would hold you in lesser esteem should they find out. I for one am glad to have been taken into your confidence. When I consider how my father's actions may affect people's opinion of me, I remind myself that I am not him. I am my own man, just as you are an independent person from your brother. You know what your brother was like, and you should keep your fond memories of him in your heart, untainted by these reports.'

John's words of understanding were a great comfort to Margaret, and by the time he left shortly after, she was certain that she had done the right thing in confiding in him. Unconsciously, in each of them sharing their difficult pasts, they had become closer still.

∽

Margaret and Bertie walked purposefully through the great open gates of Marlborough Mills. He had been particularly good on his walk that morning and had sat on command at every road that they needed to cross to reach the mill. Margaret was not about to let Bertie end the same way as his mother by wandering across roads unattended. She wanted to see Mr Thornton to assure him that all was well after her revelations to him about Frederick the previous evening, and that her father was also gladdened that she had shared their secret with him. She was considering telling Mr Thornton about Bertie's exemplary behaviour on their journey to the mill when the mill master's voice, raised to a tremendous degree, cut through her reverie. He was standing outside what she knew to be the entrance to the weaving room. In front of him was a young woman, a girl really, who was crying and desperately trying to wrap a scarf around her head but failing, her hands clumsy due to Mr Thornton's scrutiny and ire which was fully directed at her.

Margaret's indignation flared, and she marched up to the pair with Bertie, his tail wagging at the sight of his master, oblivious to the storm he was about to enter. Margaret lifted her chin ready to do battle with this version of Mr Thornton who had receded in her memory, and who had been replaced with the kind man she now understood him to be. Apparently, she had been mistaken in her fresh opinion of him, as here he was severely berating one of his young workers.

'Mr Thornton,' she said crossly, immediately diverting his attention from the girl. He had not seen Margaret arrive at the mill and was momentarily startled by her sudden appearance.

'Miss Hale,' he spat back, not in control of his temper as yet.

'How dare you speak to this young woman in that way? Shouting and demeaning her?' Margaret replied hotly, championing the girl, although she knew no details of what had occurred to cause the scene that she had happened upon. However, finding Mr Thornton acting in a most ungentlemanly way to one of his subordinates was all the reason she needed.

Bertie took this moment to stand on his hind legs with his front paws braced on Mr Thornton's leg, while he tried to insert his nose in his master's pocket in search of treats that he knew were kept there, and that so far had been omitted from his usual greeting.

'Get back to work,' John said gruffly to the girl. As she turned and fled back into the building he shouted angrily after her, 'Your hair!' She stopped, and this time successfully wrapped the scarf around her head and disappeared through the doorway.

Without a word to Margaret, John stalked back to his office and shut the door by kicking it hard, making the glass panes in it rattle. A moment later, she entered the room, eyes blazing with vexation.

'I ask you again, Mr Thornton. How dare you speak to a young woman in that way, exerting your authority over her like some … like some—'

John leant forward towards Margaret and interrupted her diatribe. 'And what would you rather, Miss Hale? See her screaming, strung up by her own hair, mangled in the machinery and have to cut her down? Or perhaps you'd rather her hair be ripped from her scalp? I've seen it before and I won't see it again, Miss Hale,' he shouted, almost nose to nose with her.

John and Margaret stared at each other in silence, panting a little, as their joint anger slowly ebbed. He looked at her lips that were slightly parted. She looked at his, and moved an imperceptibly bit closer.

John became aware of Bertie attempting to get in his pocket again, and the moment was broken. He stood up straight and turned to Bertie, ruffling the dog's ears and reaching for the biscuit that he wanted.

Still turned away from her, he said quietly, 'Your visit today. Did you want something?'

'No,' she said, and left the room.

Since his altercation with Miss Hale, John had struggled to lift his mood, and was desolate that she had witnessed a display of his temper which would surely relegate his standing in her eyes. He attempted to divert his thoughts from his internal distress by completing the project of learning to dye the cotton produced at his mill. His research, which had commenced during his stints looking after Bertie when he was born, had taken several weeks to accomplish. What had started as an idea to diversify his business, should funding allow it, had become an even greater prospect, as John had learnt that synthetic dyes were in an experimental stage of development. Should they be found to be effective they would revolutionise printed fabric production. He deduced that being ready for the advent of this innovation would be highly beneficial to the long-term prospects of Marlborough Mills.

'Don't you have enough to be contending with?' his mother had queried, as he explained his experiments to her over dinner.

'Fanny and her contemporaries wear colourful clothing, Mother. I don't pretend to be familiar with fashion, but bright, patterned fabrics are popular and commercial,' he reasoned.

'But Fanny doesn't wear cotton, John. And neither do her silly friends. It's too common for them in their silks and linens.'

'I know, Mother, but with the roller printing methods and the possibility of chemical dyes, printed fabrics will become more affordable to those of lower means. We are experts in mechanised industry, so expanding to include roller printing machines shouldn't be a problem once we know what we're about.'

'Humph. Seems to me there are plenty of ifs and buts to a scheme you have no time or money for,' Hannah grumbled, and the conversation ended.

John sighed, frustrated that his mother could not simply be interested in his investigations, but he had to concede that she was at least partly right. He felt that prior to their recent falling out, Miss Hale would have been intrigued by his experimentation, but he had decided to keep the project a secret so as to surprise her if the venture was a success.

John had enlisted Edwin Bailey's help in conducting the tests. It was a lengthy process as they endeavoured to attain a specific shade of yellow that John was particularly interested in seeing on his fabric. John had researched dyes available that didn't need to be imported, and eventually fixed upon weld due to its favourable affinity with cotton for the yellow dye, and woad for a blue pattern to be printed upon it. John and Edwin tried several batches of cotton, all immersed in an enamel pot, and made notes on the quantities of weld and the alum mordant used to fix the pigment to the fabric. Eventually the hue of yellow that met with John's approval was finally achieved. The blue dye for the pattern was somewhat easier to accomplish, using woad that didn't require a mordant, and John was not as exacting on the precise shade.

Nicholas Higgins was enlisted to identify one of the hands with a talent for wood carving, and the man, named Ashworth, was tasked with creating a wooden printing block depicting tiny sprigs of flowers. It took an afternoon to block print the pattern with precision onto the last remaining portion of the cotton bolt. When it was done, Higgins joined both John and Edwin in admiring their handiwork, with John clapping Edwin on the back in a gesture of camaraderie which brought a flush of pride to the young weaver.

What should have been a surprise for Miss Hale had now become a peace offering, and John wrapped up the length of material into a brown paper parcel and took it with him to the Hales' that evening. He had not received word that he wouldn't be welcome, following the incident that Miss Hale had witnessed and berated him for. On arrival at the Hales', he was relieved to find Mr Hale his usual self, seemingly recovered from the distress regarding news that his deceased son's name would not be cleared. Miss Hale, however, was somewhat subdued. He hoped his gift would make amends for his behaviour.

'John, John, come and sit down,' welcomed Mr Hale, with his usual friendliness. 'Margaret was just reading a letter to me that has arrived from Edith. Carry on, dear,' he said, nodding to Margaret. Bertie presented himself for John to stroke, and set to work trying to reach the skin above his right sock.

Margaret resumed reading Edith's letter aloud. It gave information regarding new decorations to a room at their home which was being transformed into a nursery, as Edith was expecting her first child. The letter went on to explain her need for larger dresses to accommodate her expanding girth, which Margaret would have found amusing if she had read it to herself, but she found it uncomfortable to read in present company. She was pleased to see that Mr

Thornton didn't appear to be embarrassed by the missive, as he was not exhibiting his familiar symptoms of distress. She recognised his mannerisms easily these days, the most engaging being that of his tousled hair. However, when Margaret went onto a passage regarding fabric, she was mortified by Edith's caustic opinion regarding the inferiority of cotton. Edith referred to an exchange she had once had with Margaret's mother, in which they had agreed on the point that there was no value in the manufacturing of the cloth in the North, as no one she knew wore it, and that women in their society preferred linen or silk.

Margaret had wished she had read the letter first, before making its contents public. She knew that Mr Thornton would be offended, and upsetting him was the last thing she had wanted to do that evening, as she was anxious to put their quarrel from the other day behind them. Margaret had reflected on the circumstances of their disagreement, and had deduced that Mr Thornton's actions were based on his concern for the safety of the young labourer. Margaret understood the reason for his behaviour, and while he had been overly harsh in his manner towards the woman, Margaret had forgiven him for the misdemeanour.

Attempting to lighten the atmosphere when the letter was finished, Margaret asked Mr Thornton about the parcel he had brought with him, as no doubt it would be for Bertie, and she would be able to tease a smile from him. However, Mr Thornton, who had been especially quiet after the reading of Edith's letter, would not be drawn on the parcel.

'It is a mistake,' he said quietly, looking at his hands with a frown. 'I mean, I was mistaken. I shouldn't have brought it here.'

Although she thought his words were strange, Margaret didn't question him further. Their easy manner with one another was not yet restored, and she resolved to try to mend what she considered to be their friendship. She would walk Bertie to Marlborough Mills tomorrow, as that always seemed to have the effect of bringing Mr Thornton cheer.

Nicholas Higgins sat down next to Margaret on the bench in the mill courtyard where she watched as Edwin played with Bertie. The young man was encouraging the little scamp to chase his own tail and making everyone around laugh. Nicholas bumped shoulders with Margaret to attract her attention.

'So? Did you like it then?' he said quietly, so that only she could hear.

Margaret was not fully listening as she observed Bertie's antics. 'Like it?' she repeated.

'Master's present?' he said, with an impish smile.

'Present?' she said, absently.

'Aye. Master were like a dog wi' two tails over it. He says to me, "Higgins, do you think Miss Hale will like this?" An' I says, "She'd look pretty as a picture in it." An' he went bright red as a beetroot,' Nicholas laughed. 'So? Did you?'

Margaret stilled, her full attention now on Nicholas. She frowned, perplexed at his words, and then she remembered Mr Thornton's mysterious parcel from the previous evening.

'Excuse me, Nicholas,' she said. Margaret stood, brushed the creases from her skirt, and walked in the direction of Mr Thornton's office, oblivious to the wide grin now firmly plastered on Nicholas Higgins' face.

John's office door opened, and in swept Miss Hale with no precursory knock. He looked up in surprise from the roller printing machine diagram that he was attempting to give his attention to. Miss Hale stood in front of his desk with her hands on her hips and her chin at the defiant angle that he had encountered several times before.

After a second's pause, Mr Thornton remembered his manners, and in a fluster he got to his feet, 'Miss Hale?'

'I have come for my present,' she said firmly. She watched him as he frowned, and his eyes involuntarily flicked to the brown paper packet that was sitting on a cupboard to her right and his left. She followed his glance and recognised the bundle from the previous night. After a momentary hesitation, they both moved at the same time, but Margaret reached it first as John had to contend with his chair, which clattered to the floor in his haste. They both put their hand out onto the parcel with his landing upon hers. Neither of them moved.

'Is this for me?' she asked primly.

'No.'

'I think it is.'

'No, it's not.'

'Nicholas Higgins says it is.'

'I'll be having words with Mr Higgins,' he said crossly.

'Mr Thornton, I have accused you of being several things, but I didn't think you were accustomed to fibbing,' she said, a small playful smile creeping onto her face. She had him beaten and he knew it. John removed his hand from hers, drew it over his face, and ruffled his hair creating Margaret's favourite spikes.

'It was a mistake,' he said, repeating his statement from the night before. 'I was going to give it to you, but I realised that it's not suitable for you at all. It reminded me of something you once told me and … I foolishly thought for a moment that you might like it. But you won't, so I'd rather you didn't have it,' and he finished the sentence in his head – *because I don't want you to think less of me.*

'Surely, I should be the judge of whether I will like it or not? You may be surprised to learn that I seldom get presents, infinitely fewer than Bertie, so I am not easily persuaded into surrendering this one,' and she finished the sentence in her head – *and most especially because it's from you.*

She watched him swallow and run his finger around and inside his collar. He was blinking furiously, and she understood that he was fighting an internal battle. She decided to push him a little further.

'May I?' she said, picking up the parcel and putting it on his desk.

She slowly pulled the string bow that held the wrapping together, but he didn't stop her. She parted the paper to reveal his gift to her, a material of pale buttery yellow, decorated with tiny mid blue sprigs of flowers. Margaret was rendered speechless. She lifted the fabric and admired the fine texture as it softly cascaded in her hands. John watched transfixed as she held the finest cotton Marlborough Mills could make to her cheek.

'There's a flaw in it. Along the edge,' he said gruffly. 'I know cotton is not fashionable, not good enough for you, and to even think of giving it to you when there is a fault—'

'I love it,' she interrupted, suddenly realising that what she really wanted to say was – *I love you*. 'It's beautiful. Truly. You made this?'

John gave her his small bashful smile. 'I had help, of course. Young Edwin Bailey and Mr Ashworth. It's a right fiddly process, but Edwin has a talent for it I think. It's only cotton. But I thought ...' he stopped and fluffed his hair again.

'Yes?'

'You'll think it's daft. That I'm daft.'

'No, I won't. I promise. Tell me,' she whispered.

John was not a gambling man, but he knew that he must take the chance and make himself vulnerable to her laughter.

'I thought it might remind you of a summer meadow,' he said, so softly she almost missed it.

'Yes, that is exactly so! It does.' She smiled her heavenly beaming smile at him, her eyes sparkling with tears. 'Thank you, Mr Thornton. Thank you so much,' she said, unwilling to hide the joy from her face as she held the material against herself, imagining a summer dress. 'If you weren't so tall,' she said, stopping abruptly, realising how inappropriate her thoughts and words were. But he had understood her meaning. John leant down slightly so that his face was nearer to hers, and held his breath. Margaret stepped forwards and raised herself onto her tiptoes, her delicate rosewater scent tickling his senses, and she placed a firm but gentle kiss upon his cheek.

Nicholas Higgins stopped his work in the courtyard as he looked up to the master's office.

'About bloody time,' he said, chuckling and rubbing his hands together.

Chapter 13

July 1855

Other than opening the door to him, Dixon no longer bothered with the pleasantries of welcoming Mr Thornton when he visited the Hales, and she left him to his own devices. In fact, no one in the small Hale household stood on ceremony with him these days, and John loved it. He felt like one of them, and embraced the friendship that this familiarity manifested. Mr Hale was due to visit Mr Bell in Oxford the following day, so John would be unable to visit Miss Hale again until her father's return. John hoped Mr Hale would not be gone long, but he consoled himself that Margaret had said she would visit Marlborough Mills once or twice during his absence on her daily walks with Bertie, so he would not be starved of her company altogether.

'Mr Thornton! Bertie and I are so pleased to see you,' beamed Margaret, as she intercepted him in the hallway where he was taking off his hat to leave it on the hall table.

'Indeed,' he said, silently noting how Miss Hale appeared to be in especially high spirits this evening. 'I must apologise that I have not had the opportunity to call for a few days. The mill has been very busy, and by the time I could get away it was too late in the day to visit.'

'Is all well at the mill?' asked Margaret, as she, Mr Thornton and Bertie filed into the sitting room.

Mr Hale sat in his customary easy chair, and the men greeted each other with a firm handshake. John sat in his favourite place on the worn velvet settee. He sighed. He wished he could deliver some encouraging news, some information that would provide evidence of his security and his ability to be a successful bread winner, but he could not, and he wouldn't deceive her.

'Things at the mill remain in a tight spot. We may yet prevail,' he said, with one of his charming, though artless, boyish smiles.

Margaret noticed that he appeared less self-conscious these days, even when he spoke about more personal matters with her, and she was glad of it.

'I truly hope so. Nicholas tells me that you and all your labourers are trying your best. I hope you will succeed.' She reached out and fleetingly touched his arm.

John brightened, keen to divert the mood to one less sombre.

'While I am glad that you welcome my visit this evening, was there a particular reason why?'

'Yes!' said Margaret, clasping her hands together in front of her chest in excitement. John observed Mr Hale roll his eyes, not in a dissimilar way to how his own mother would have done.

'Indeed?' laughed John, softly.

'Bertie has learnt a new command. He is such a clever boy, and I know that you in particular will find it most enchanting,' she said, her eyes sparkling.

'Me in particular?' he asked with surprise.

'Yes! We, that is Bertie and I, have perfected this instruction with you specifically in mind. You could say that you inspired it,' she confirmed, to Mr Thornton's delight.

John leant forward in anticipation looking expectantly at the puppy who sat up with one ear pricked, seemingly ready for his performance.

'You must kneel down, Mr Thornton, so that he can reach you,' she directed, and John did as he was bid. 'Now, ask him to shake hands,' she said, scarcely controlling her glee.

John frowned and looked up at her.

'Go on,' she encouraged.

'Shake hands,' John said, uncertainly. Bertie cocked his head slightly in response.

Margaret tutted. 'No, with command! Well, not your usual command. Perhaps tone it down slightly.'

John let a little smile amuse his lips. 'Very well. Bertie, shake hands,' he said firmly, and Bertie lifted his right paw to John. John's little smile grew into a deep, soft rumbling chuckle.

'Oh, Mr Thornton,' Margaret tutted again, shaking her head in mild exasperation. 'You are doing it wrong. You must shake his hand. I am teaching him how one greets friends in Milton,' she said.

John tried again, hardly able to contain his pleasure, 'Bertie, shake hands,' and when the pup offered his paw again John shook it and laughed. 'Good boy,' he said, fluffing the dog's ears with his free hand, and then reached into his pocket and gave the dog a treat that he now always carried with him precisely for such an occasion.

Conversation between Mr Hale, Margaret and John had flowed so naturally that evening that he had not wanted to depart. Seldom, if ever, had he enjoyed an evening as much. They had talked about Mr Hale's impending trip and the plans Mr Bell had made for their entertainment, though John noted that neither Margaret nor her father seemed to be aware of Mr Bell's severe illness. Their light-hearted discussions, mainly centred on Bertie who revelled in being the focus of the attention, gave him such happiness. Margaret had explained that she and Bertie were working on a more elaborate command which they hoped to have perfected and ready to demonstrate to him soon.

John lay in bed that night staring blindly up at the ceiling, turning tonight's visit with the Hales over in his mind. She liked him. Surely, she did. She had been pleased to see him. She had teased him, and it had warmed his heart. She had rejected him so thoroughly when he had declared his feelings for her those many months ago, but she had not known him then and now … now. They had fallen out and she had seen him at his worst with his temper flaring, but they had navigated past it and she still appeared to welcome his company. She had even thought of him whilst training Bertie. Dare he ask her again? He must. Should he ask to court her? Lord knows he visited as often as a courting gentleman would, and his mother had already insinuated, on more than one occasion, that he was engendering 'talk'. John reached for the handkerchief that he had lent to Margaret months ago, and that she had laundered for him. It had not held her scent of rosewater for a long time now, but he still held it to his face with the memory of it.

When she had given him his handkerchief back it had been at the beginning of their fledgling friendship. Since then, over the last weeks and months, she had shared her thoughts with him, matters that were close to her heart, and he in turn had talked to her about his concerns for the mill, as well as his hopes and plans for its future. She had told him about Helstone and confided in him the sad tale of her brother Frederick's apparent disgrace and untimely death. He was honoured that she would share that secret, which some would deem brought disgrace to their family, and that she had faith in him that he would not think less of them for it.

He decided that he could not propose marriage yet, and that he must take things much more slowly so as not to frighten her with the strength of his love. And yet it was so dangerous, for if he asked and she refused him again, he would lose everything of importance in his heart. He would not be able to continue to see the Hales if she turned him down again. Not for a second time. Like the mill, balanced on the edge of success or failure, it felt like a minuscule tilt in either direction would irrevocably end their current relationship in either the greatest joy or utter despair. He could leave things as they were, simply carry on enjoying the visits with Margaret and Mr Hale as friends, but hiding his feelings from her any longer seemed a Herculean task.

John considered what courting Margaret Hale might be like. He would be able to sit with her alone, for a little while at least. He would be able to go for walks with her, and they would take Bertie with them, of course. He smiled at the thought. He would offer her his arm and she would place her hand in the crook of his elbow, and they would walk and talk together. As their familiarity grew, he might then know if another attempt at a proposal would be welcomed. He tried to imagine Margaret accepting him, agreeing to be his wife. His heart ached with longing at the mere thought of it. John was not a coward, he never had been and now was not the time to start. He resolved to do it. When he next saw Miss Hale, he would ask for the honour of courting her.

John didn't have long to wait before his opportunity to speak to Miss Hale arrived. He happened to be in the mill yard on a sunny July afternoon three days later, inspecting the inventory of an order ready for dispatch with Nicholas Higgins, when Miss Hale and Bertie paid him a visit. He was momentarily caught off guard without his coat and with his shirt sleeves rolled up, as the weather for once was glorious. Although Margaret had seen him thus attired before, in view of his planned conversation with her he had wanted to create a good impression on their next meeting and not appear so coarse. Mr Hale had been away on his excursion to Oxford for a few days now, and John had been unable to visit Margaret as it would be deemed improper, so he was delighted that she had visited him at the mill. Perhaps she wanted to see him as much as he needed to see her.

'Miss Hale, Bertie,' he said, welcoming them and hastily returning his sleeves to their intended position.

'Good afternoon. Have we arrived at an inopportune moment?' she asked, looking at the stacked bundles of cotton.

'Not at all. If you could just give me five minutes to finish this order?' he asked.

'Of course,' she said, and walked over to the bench in the sunshine which was currently vacant as it was not a break time for the workers. She had brought a basket with her which she put it next to her on the seat, and Bertie lay down under the bench in the shade by her feet. The din from the mill rattled noisily away in the vast building across the yard from her, and many of the workers nodded in greeting as they passed by. Margaret was happy to watch the comings and goings of the hands as they went about their work, though her eyes often found themselves wandering back to settle their focus upon Mr Thornton in his shirt sleeves and waistcoat. She remembered Nicholas' description of Mr Thornton as being a hardworking man, and as she watched him with his labourers, she knew that she liked that about him. She found that his prowess at his occupation was more attractive to her than, for example, one who had wealth and chose to do nothing. It somehow made him more vital and dynamic.

John had found it unsettling to know that Miss Hale was a few feet away from him as he finished processing the order. In fact, Higgins had noticed with some amusement that he had made an error once or twice, and that they had to begin counting the batches again. A short while later, Margaret watched as Mr Thornton passed his list to Higgins, the checking of the shipment completed, and Higgins gave Margaret a mischievous wink as he departed into one of the warehouses. Mr Thornton approached Margaret and sat on the bench beside her, but for propriety's sake, with as much room between them as the seat would allow.

'It is very pleasant to sit here in the sunshine and admire the energy and industriousness around me. Though perhaps it might annoy those who work so hard to have another watch them in idleness,' she said.

'You are welcome here any time. I am pleased to see you and I know many of my workers are.'

'When one sits here observing, the organisation of the factory becomes apparent. Everyone has their individual tasks, but it's only when you put them all together that you get the end results. Perhaps one could compare it to being like an orchestra,' she said, her appreciative words warming his soul. 'However, the noise cannot be compared to music. I don't know how you can hear when you have been in the weaving shed for a while. I am surprised that it doesn't make you quite deaf.'

'Pardon?' said John, cupping his hand to his ear. A smile crept as high as his eyes that crinkled as Margaret perceived his little joke, and she giggled prettily but genuinely with him. He recalled that afternoon when he had been jealous of Nicholas Higgins chatting and laughing with women from the carding shed, and he realised that he had finally succeeded; he was able to be himself at last.

'Are you shopping this afternoon?' he said, eyeing her basket.

'Oh, no. Would it be possible to speak with you inside?' she asked, remembering the reason for her visit. John got up from the bench and gestured for her to precede him towards his office. As Margaret carried the basket, John divested her of Bertie's lead, unclipped him and allowed the pup to bound over to Edwin for a little play time.

Margaret placed her basket on John's desk and turned to speak to him. She noticed that he seemed suddenly anxious, with his tell-tale mannerisms giving him away.

'Is there something wrong?' she asked gently.

John realised that this was the moment. He was alone with her and so it was the ideal time to speak to her about his wishes. He had promised himself that he would.

'No, no, not wrong.' He tried to maintain his calm composure as he prepared to speak the words that would decide his future happiness. 'Miss Hale, I did want to speak to you about a matter today, if I may?' At her nod, he began slowly and gravely. 'I quite understand if you don't feel the same, that is, if you don't wish to,' he hesitated, trying to find the right words. 'You see, I thought we had become friends,' and his eyes searched hers for some kind of acknowledgement that she felt the same. Margaret reached for his hand and held it between hers, wishing to give him the support that she perceived he needed at that moment.

Buoyed by her encouraging touch, John continued, 'I wondered if you might like to sometimes walk Bertie with me. That is, in my company. That we might get to know each other better.' He took a deep breath, acutely conscious of the importance of her reaction to his next words. 'And that you would allow me to court you.'

There, it was said. He couldn't take it back now, and her delicate fingers still held his large work roughened hand, which he took as a good sign.

Margaret's heart was in her mouth as she heard him say those words which were so dear to her. Words that she had hoped and prayed that he would speak. John's tender and respectful request for a courtship was completely opposite to his previous proposal. Yet she knew now that his feelings had been genuine, and she again regretted her brutal rejection of him on that occasion.

'I would like that, Mr Thornton,' she said smiling, and with absolute certainty.

'Really?' he said, incredulously.

'Oh! Do you want me to reconsider?' she teased.

'No! No. Thank you.' He took her hands in his and lifted them to his lips where he placed a kiss to the top of each one with such reverence as to bring a sparkle to Margaret's eyes.

'Then I will ask for your father's permission when he returns from Oxford … Margaret,' he said, testing the feel of her name on his lips. And he loved it.

'Very well … John,' she replied, following his lead.

Margaret slipped her hands from his, although truthfully she didn't want to. Slightly flustered at the magnitude of Mr Thornton's words she remembered the basket she had brought for him.

'I realised that I didn't reciprocate when you favoured me with the beautiful material,' she said. 'So I brought a small gift for you.'

John blinked a couple of times, gathering his thoughts before he spoke. This was dangerous ground, as he had a bad feeling that she felt she owed him something for his gift. Although he didn't wish to provoke her, he needed to know if she still thought of him as a man only able to comprehend trade.

'Margaret,' he began quietly, and she admired the way her name sounded when spoken in his deep, rich velvety voice. 'If I give you a gift, and I hope to give you many, it is just that. A gift. I don't view it as a transaction or require something in its stead.'

Margaret looked at him in earnest, understanding his meaning, and that she had touched on that exposed nerve again. However, she was not willing to allow pride, and the memory of her tactless words to him in their past, to spoil the tentative steps they were taking towards their future.

'Well, that is fortunate, as my paltry offering does not compare!' she laughed, lightening the mood. 'And I will promise you that when I give you a present, I shall not want anything in return either.' She gave his arm a reassuring squeeze, hoping that they had managed to circumnavigate around that thorny subject once and for all.

'Let me show you what I have for you,' she said, as she opened the basket and withdrew a small rectangular tin. 'I have made you some lemon shortbread biscuits for when you have your tea. I must confess that it is one of the only recipes that I have any proficiency with at all! If you like you could share them with Mrs Thornton, if you thought she might enjoy them too?'

John was momentarily lost for words. Not only had she brought him a present, but she had thought enough of him to make it herself. Especially for him. He opened the box to find a dozen biscuits dusted with fine grains of sugar.

'May I try one?' he asked.

She laughed, saying, 'They are yours! You may eat them when you please.'

John took a biscuit from the box and broke it in two, giving half to Margaret while he ate the other portion. It melted in his mouth and was fragrant with lemon, although he was honest enough with himself to know that had it the taste and texture of leather he would have been just as charmed.

'I think this is the most pleasing gift I have ever received. Thank you, Margaret,' he said, and meant it. 'I have a mind to be selfish and hide this batch here, in my desk drawer, so that I might keep my present all to myself. Would you be cross with me?' He took a step towards her, spying a tiny speck of sugar upon her lip. It mesmerised him and drew him closer to her.

'No,' she said, eyes fixed now on his mouth as he leant down to her.

His hands found her waist where he held her tightly, and hers reached to cradle his beautiful, prickly jaw. She felt his eyelashes flutter against her cheek before he touched his lips to hers, to sample that speck of sugar and the perfect sweetness of Margaret Hale, and they tasted each other for the first time. For all his imposing features, stern moods and boyish shyness, John Thornton could kiss. His mouth was the perplexing yet heavenly mixture of utter softness and possessive firmness, much like the man himself, and Margaret found his delicious kisses were a heady, tantalising drug that she needed him to repeat countless times. Stirred by Margaret's hands that drifted from his face to roam in his hair, John instinctively gathered her closer, deepening their embrace. Margaret's mouth willingly obeyed his unspoken command, first allowing him to lavish his adoring kisses upon her, and then repaying him with her own tentative responses that became bolder with each press of her lips to his.

Eventually John and Margaret separated, a little breathless and pink with passion.

'Actually, I think I have changed my mind,' said John, with a mock sternness to his face. 'I think I do want to reimburse you for your presents, and be paid back in turn for those I give to you. I believe that we have discovered the payment mechanism.' Margaret giggled at his teasing suggestion.

'Well,' she said, smoothing his hair which she had taken great delight in disturbing. 'I will have to bake biscuits more often.' She gave him a playful smile and then left him to attempt to collect his thoughts.

John placed the tin of lemon biscuits in his desk drawer, almost in a daze. He had not meant to kiss her and he had acted most improperly. He hoped that when she had a chance to reflect on their conversation, and her agreement to him courting her, that she would not have second thoughts due to his unrefined forwardness. He wondered if he should wait before telling his mother, in case Margaret changed her mind. Perhaps it was written plainly across his face and could not be denied. He allowed himself to admit that Margaret had been receptive to his kisses, encouraging him with her lovely fingers combing through his hair and her body pressed against his as he held her in his arms. John concluded that this had been the most wonderful and extraordinary afternoon of his life, and he was brimming with joyfulness which spilled over into thoughts of a positive future for himself and Margaret, together. A lifetime of happiness was surely within his grasp.

Chapter 14

It was almost two weeks since Henry Lennox and Mr Bell had parted company on the journey from Milton towards London. They had both boarded the train at Milton-Northern but Mr Bell had disembarked first at Oxford, in order to prepare for an extended visit from Richard Hale. Henry had continued on to London to resume his tedious but necessary work at the law firm. The more he thought about it, the more Henry was perturbed following his first experience of the industrial town. While Milton itself was as gloomy as he had expected, in fact its sooty dreariness was far worse than Mr Bell had led him to believe, Henry was increasingly disturbed by what he had discovered there.

Henry's agitation was twofold. Firstly, it appeared that Margaret was happily settled there, which was a curiosity, but he concluded that she must have thrown herself into embracing the dirty town as she had no alternative. The second issue was the unexpected threat of the commanding John Thornton. Henry decided that he must redouble his charm to attract Margaret and win her with an abundance of the attributes that Thornton obviously lacked. Though Henry suspected that some, including Margaret, might find Thornton's black and brooding countenance attractive, he was completely unsuitable for her. Margaret and her fortune deserved better than Marlborough Mills' master. Henry just had to find a way to prove that he was what would make Margaret's life complete, and soon.

~

Mr Bell was feeling rather giddy with excitement at the prospect of spending some time with Richard Hale. As he had perhaps a few months to live, he hoped to enjoy one last joyous holiday with his long-time friend. He planned that the two of them would revisit old haunts, and enjoy the warmer weather and soot-free skies of Oxford where they had studied in their younger days. Margaret had encouraged her father to go on the excursion with Mr Bell, delighted that he should have a distraction from his grief, and to brighten his lonely soul. And so it was that early one morning in July, before the chimneys had dulled the blue from the sky, Mr Hale bade his daughter goodbye with a kiss to her cheek and a cheery wave from the carriage taking him to the station, and travelled to Oxford to meet up with Mr Bell.

On their first full day together, the old friends had agreed to meet later in the morning. Mr Hale was tired from the journey and Mr Bell was bothered by niggling, troublesome pains in his chest that advanced up into his jaw, and a creeping tingling sensation to his left hand; symptoms which had informed his doctor's poor prognosis. However, Mr Bell was an optimist and was determined not to let his state of health spoil their enjoyment. They were blessed with fine weather and walked to the river to enjoy some refreshment in the Boat House Tavern. A little later, they watched the rowing boats glide by, and reminisced about similar amusement they had shared in years long past.

'Do you remember when we were young men, Richard? We would spend many an afternoon out here on the Isis showing off to the pretty girls on the bank, taking in the sunshine and the devil to our studies!' said Mr Bell, clapping Mr Hale on the back and emitting a raucous roar.

'I think that may have been your pastime and not mine,' chuckled Mr Hale gently, although his thoughts did return to the days when Maria Beresford had allowed him to accompany her down to the river and watch the likes of Mr Bell at their sport. What a blissful time that had been. Mr Hale was quite overcome with the fond memories of his time as a young scholar and Mr Bell persuaded him that, for one last time together, they should go boating.

The attendant at King's Barge was quite surprised to be asked to rent out a boat to two older gentlemen. They were an odd-looking pair, with Mr Bell dressed finely and exuding a confident air, while Mr Hale ambled beside him, wrapped warmly in his old overcoat despite the summer sunshine, in case he might encounter a chill in the air. Several young men rowing by Christ Church Meadow that afternoon nudged one another and smirked to see Mr Bell and Mr Hale embarking on their river adventure. Mr Hale sat as a passenger in the boat while Mr Bell took the oars, both men quite exhilarated by the escapade and frivolity of the occasion. It took a little while for Mr Bell to get into his rhythm, but eventually he propelled himself and his friend towards Iffley Lock. They had gone no more than five hundred yards when Mr Bell was suddenly gripped by a smothering vice-like hold across his chest, and he gasped for a fortifying breath at the severity and unrelenting pressure of it. Nausea engulfed him and beads of sweat sprang onto his greying countenance.

Seeing his friend's sudden distress, Mr Hale moved forwards to offer him some aid. The boat wobbled, rocking from side to side, and with neither man able to steady the craft it tipped them into the water. Both men spluttered and splashed, immediately shocked to have been unseated, but then the water engulfed their garments making them leaden weights, and the brisk current clawed and clutched at Mr Hale's heavy coat, pulling him into the river's shadowy depths. Mr Bell managed to hold onto the side of the boat. Seeing his friend disappear beneath the surface of the water he reached out and grabbed Mr Hale's coat collar dragging him back up, but a further sudden pain seized his chest and prevented further rescue. Richard Hale floundered helplessly in the murky water. He reached, straining, stretching to grasp something, anything, but his efforts were futile. Paralysed by the excruciating pain in his chest, Mr Bell had to let go of his dear friend who was swept from his grasp and his sight, like a leaf tossing and turning in the current until he disappeared from view into the gloomy void. As the water swallowed him whole, Richard Hale's last thoughts were of Margaret. He had failed her, again.

Young fellows rowing along the Isis, and some upon the shore, had been watching the peculiar spectacle of the two older men chuckling together in their boat, and they had laughed along with them. But when the initial hilarity of the pair being unceremoniously toppled into the water had abated, it became apparent that neither was safe, and three strong lads jumped in to save them. Despite their best efforts, the rescue party was only able to reach one, the grey dapper fellow, whom they hauled to the bank. Whether it be the trauma of his near drowning, or the fault of his diseased heart, Mr Bell succumbed to the ordeal and died on the riverbank in the arms of strangers.

As Henry Lennox was Mr Bell's lawyer and executor of his estate, he learnt of the tragedy involving Mr Bell and Mr Hale quickly, and the shock of the death of the two men that he had been conversing with only weeks before felt quite surreal. Sitting at his magnificent desk, Henry pondered the ramifications of this most unexpected and unhappy event. Margaret would now inherit Mr Bell's fortune and he was powerless to prevent her becoming the prey of every unattached gentleman in the capital. He wouldn't stand a chance in securing her affections although, he considered, Margaret might gain comfort from a friendly face. She had lost her father and was not by nature one to covet the excesses that could be afforded by immense wealth. Henry surmised he was fooling himself. Margaret's grief would eventually wane and then she would find herself having the pick of available men for a husband. That Mr Bell could die so infuriatingly soon was too much to bear. Henry wished he could have had a month or two more to weave himself into Margaret's life before her benefactor died.

Henry mused that there was an advantage to Mr Hale's death, as this would force Margaret back under the roof of Mrs Shaw and the Lennoxes, and would enable him to see her daily. It might help his cause in winning her. At the very least, Margaret would now be saved from dwelling in Milton and would be removed from the danger that was Mr Thornton.

Henry had to think, and he sat tapping his fingers on the desktop as his mind turned over the possibilities. He had to work out if there was still a way for him to manipulate matters for his gain, and to win both Margaret and her fortune. Yet how could there be? Margaret would inherit and he would be a bystander as he watched some handsome rake, not unlike Sholto he supposed, sweep Margaret and her fortune off her feet and away from him. He would not give that money up easily. He considered that he had precious little time to think, as the reading of Mr Bell's will would ordinarily come at the time of his funeral. Margaret, as Mr Bell's only heir, would be invited to the reading of the will. Henry stilled as a wicked thought crept cunningly into his mind. What if he didn't invite Margaret to the reading of the will? What if no one ever knew what was in Mr Bell's will until it was too late? Until Margaret was his. Could he excuse the omission by saying it was to save her feelings during her distressed and grieving state? Perhaps. Could he even say that he himself had been Bell's beneficiary? There were possibilities, and he would need to consider the merits of each one before acting. The primary concern was to get Margaret within his reach.

Henry called into ninety-six Harley Street and relayed the tragic events. Edith and Mrs Shaw were immediately concerned for Margaret. Her mother had passed away so recently and now, to lose her father as well, and so unexpectedly, was cruel indeed. Due to Edith's impending confinement, it was decided that Mrs Shaw would travel to Milton with Henry to break the terrible news. It was a job that the older woman dreaded, but she would not shirk from her duty to her dear sister's daughter. Margaret must come back to London, into the care of her remaining family.

Margaret was sitting by the window in the parlour mending one of her father's shirts where the cuff had frayed, and Bertie was asleep on the hearth rug near her feet. They had been on their daily walk this morning, but she had avoided Marlborough Mills. After her somewhat wanton behaviour kissing Mr Thornton, *John*, the day before, she didn't want him to get the wrong impression of her. She didn't want to appear too keen on him, although she would willingly admit to herself that she was smitten, and had struggled to keep the silly grin from her face since she had left him yesterday. She would go to the mill tomorrow instead, and her mind wandered to any small token that she might take for his delight.

Margaret occasionally glanced out of the window, watching the townsfolk go about their business. She was alerted to visitors to the house when she saw not one, but two figures approaching. The doorbell chimed in the kitchen and Dixon huffed as she went to see who was causing the interruption, but Margaret was already lost in grief. Her skin paled and she closed her eyes, grasping the window ledge for support. There was only one reason why Aunt Shaw would be here with Henry Lennox. *Father.*

Margaret and Dixon sat on the small settee in the parlour, and Margaret's jumbled thoughts reminded her that she was sitting in Mr Thornton's seat. They gripped one another's hands as Henry told them about the sorry demise of both Mr Hale and Mr Bell. He omitted that Mr Hale had been swept away, his body recovered some time later, so as not to cause more distress than was necessary. Later, Margaret would take comfort from the fact that her father and Mr Bell had been having a jolly time, and that their end had been quick. But just now nothing seemed to help, and all she could think of was her lovely father and how she would never see him again. Never kiss his cheek. Never hold his hand. Never laugh with him or talk to him. It was overwhelming. Bertie was aware that something was amiss. He clambered up onto his mistress's knee, despite the objections from Mrs Shaw and Mr Lennox, but Margaret held him fast against her while her tears flowed, and Bertie kissed them away.

Nicholas Higgins knocked on the master's office door. John looked up wearily from his ledger. He was disappointed that Margaret had not visited him that day and hoped that she had not changed her mind about their courtship following their perfect, though extremely forward, kisses.

'Come,' he called.

'Master,' said Higgins, cap twisted in his hands. 'I've bad news.'

Higgins was uncommonly pale and clearly anxious. John's mind immediately flew to the mill, and he was seized by the thought that one of his labourers was injured. John stood, and rounding the desk he held Higgins by the shoulders and sat him in the chair.

'What is it man?' John asked. Higgins was white as a sheet.

'Our Mary's been up to Crampton to 'elp Miss Dixon. She's come back wi' a tale,' explained Higgins solemnly. He knew Mr Hale was a great friend to the master but, more than that, he knew that Miss Margaret would want him to know.

'It's Mr Hale. I'm sorry to tell you, Master. He's dead.'

'Dead?' said John, shocked, as he sat numbly back in his chair. 'Mr Hale is dead? What happened?' he said, shaking his head slightly in disbelief.

'Miss Margaret's aunt an' that fancy fella from a few weeks ago … some kind of a cousin?' said Higgins, and John nodded knowing exactly who he meant.

'Lennox.'

'Aye, that's the fella,' said Higgins. 'They come up to tell Miss Margaret that Mr Hale an' Mr Bell died. A drownin' of all things. Both killed outright. An' now she's gone.'

John had just been hit with the revelation that not only was his cherished friend and mentor dead, but also Mr Bell, when he registered Higgins' last words.

'Gone,' he said, getting to his feet, the chair screeching on the floor as it slid back. 'What do you mean, "she's gone"?'

'Our Mary says 'er aunt an' that Lennox bloke bundled up Miss Margaret and Miss Dixon before they hardly knew what was even goin' on, an' set them off on the train, the three women, this afternoon.'

John grabbed his coat and started for the door.

Higgins got up and halted him with a beefy arm on the younger man's shoulder, stilling him.

'It's too late. They're already gone, Master.'

John ran his hand through his hair and stood looking blankly, hopelessly at the door. Poor Mr Hale. And Mr Bell. *Oh, Margaret*, he thought, and his heart ached at the sorrow that she must be enduring, and that he was unable to alleviate.

'She will be missed,' he said, looking squarely at Higgins, not embarrassed to show the sheen of tears in his eyes. Higgins patted the master on the arm in a gesture of fellowship. It was a signal between the two men that was only possible because of Margaret and the unifying bond that she created between them. In truth, Higgins was devastated too. She was a good friend to him and his family, and as the master had said, she would be missed by them dearly.

Just as the sudden death of Mr Bell had severely affected Henry Lennox's plans to gradually slip himself into Margaret's life, Mr Hale's similarly unexpected death caused such an emotional wrench in John Thornton's heart that he was not sure if it would recover. Losing Mr Hale was shocking enough, but to lose Margaret too was almost unbearable. She had agreed to a courtship but now he was unsure of what to do. She had no father to ask, and anyway it would be completely inappropriate to even broach the subject in her grieving state. Mr Hale would have granted him permission to court Margaret, he was sure of it. But now that Mr Hale was gone he might never be granted approval, and she was so far away.

Before his friendship with Margaret had blossomed, John had given a great deal of thought to his life without her in it. He had imagined watching her fall in love with some young man whom she would eventually marry. It would be a gradual twist of the knife, but he would have had some time to adjust to her being finally and irrevocably out of his reach. But this sudden loss gave him a catastrophic emptiness. He was disgusted in himself for his selfish thoughts; it was Margaret that he should focus his pity on, not himself. It should have been a consolation that she was with her family now, with people that loved her and that she loved in return, but he was devastated to realise that any comfort that he could provide would not be required. She was in her rightful place and all he could do was to accept it. Yet she had agreed to be courted by him; she had feelings for him just as he had for her.

John walked the short distance home in something of a daze. Hannah Thornton looked at the clock as she heard him enter.

'You're too late for tea,' she grumbled. 'But Jane can get you something. What on earth has happened?' she asked, as soon as he came into her view. She rested her needlework on her knee. 'John, speak up! You're frightening me,' she urged.

John recounted the dreadful tale of Mr Hale and Mr Bell, and the hasty removal of Margaret to London. Hannah was understandably shocked. She was a notably strong woman, but this tragic event called for mother and son to partake in a sherry to calm their nerves. Of course, she knew that although her son was fond of Mr Hale, even perhaps seeing him as a father figure, Mr Hale's death was not the main issue upsetting John. The major problem for him was that Margaret Hale, whom he had given his heart to, was now out of his reach. She felt for him and his heartache. She wanted to soothe it away, but she could not. Not because she was unfeeling but because she was glad. She was relieved that Miss Hale would no longer hold dominion over her son's life, and she would not be false. Hannah reverted to more practical matters so as not to show her true feelings to John.

'How will Mr Bell's passing affect the mill?' she asked.

'I don't know, Mother,' he said, automatically. But, he remembered, he did know.

'Margaret,' he said, numbly. Hannah looked at her son as if he'd taken leave of his senses.

'What about Miss Hale,' she said, ignoring the slip of John using Miss Hale's Christian name in his stupor. It was extenuating circumstances to be sure, and she poured him another sherry.

'The mill, Mother. Mr Bell told me that he was leaving the mill to Mar— Miss Hale. He said it was a secret. He had been settling his affairs because he was ill. Neither Miss Hale nor her father were informed as he thought they would make a fuss about it.'

'Why did he tell you?' Hannah asked in surprise.

'I'm not sure. Perhaps because my tenancy is due up for renewal soon, though he never really gave a reason. He knew he was dying, although he couldn't have imagined it would have been so soon. Poor fellow,' he said, taking a fortifying sip of his drink.

John and his mother were still discussing the terrible news when the doorbell chimed.

'Good heavens I hope that's not Fanny,' muttered Hannah. 'I can't face her hysterics at this moment in time,' she said, and John had to smile. In a way he was relieved that his mother appreciated the gravity of the situation, and that she was not dismissing it merely as a sorry tale. He was glad that she didn't suggest that, after the initial shock, things would settle down and normality would return. That life would go on. Because he felt like his life, as he knew it at any rate, could not go on. Not without *her*. She had invaded his soul and even breathing currently hurt without her. He knew he was being selfish and needed to keep perspective on his own sorrow. Margaret was not dead, she was only in London, being cared for by her family as was right.

Bertie leapt into the parlour closely followed by the Thorntons' visitor, Henry Lennox. Lennox was flustered, attempting to brush some errant dog hairs off his morning suit trouser legs. John scooped up Bertie and hugged the puppy as if his life depended upon it.

'Mr Lennox,' he said. 'May I introduce my mother, Mrs Thornton.' Hannah and Henry nodded to one another. 'We have heard the dreadful news. We are greatly saddened, and would express our deepest sympathies to Miss Hale and her extended family.'

'Margaret is safe now,' said Lennox, and Hannah involuntarily raised her eyebrows at Mr Lennox's use of Miss Hale's first name.

The fact that she was now considered 'safe' jarred with John. What did he mean? Had she been unsafe in Milton?

'Margaret tells me that you are acquainted with the animal,' Henry said, nodding at Bertie in John's arms.

'He's a dog,' said Hannah dryly, her own hackles rising at the impertinence of the man.

'Indeed, yes, the dog,' he said, with a sly smile. 'There is no place for a working dog like this in Harley Street,' said Lennox. 'So Margaret had to concede that you would be the most likely to take him in. Oh, here,' he said, handing Bertie's lead to John.

'Yes. Of course. Of course, we will look after him for her. Anything,' he said quietly, and Henry knew then for certain that John Thornton was in love with Margaret. But did she feel the same way? That was the important question.

'How is Miss Hale? This must have been a terrible shock. Is she well?' asked John.

'She will be well now that she is back where she belongs. And she knows that. I bid you good day,' said Lennox imperiously, and then made to take his leave.

John quickly addressed the retreating form, 'Mr Lennox, please tell Miss Hale not to worry about the mill. I know she will have more things on her mind right now, but when everything settles and she becomes aware of her continuing connection with Milton, I would be grateful if you would make it known that I will endeavour to keep the mill afloat and thereby safeguard her property.'

Henry froze. He was glad he had his back to the Thorntons so that he had time to compose his facial expression into one of nonchalance before turning around.

'And what do you know of Margaret's involvement with the mill?'

'Mr Bell told me that he was leaving it to Miss Hale. He informed me just recently due to his illness.'

Henry was fuming. Bell, the old fool, had given the game away. Still, it was likely that Thornton would have needed to be informed anyway soon due to the due legal process. At least knowing that Thornton was apprised of the facts meant Henry was aware of the cards in Thornton's hand. He calmed himself, reasoning that knowledge is power. This information meant that, until he had decided how to handle Margaret's inheritance, he must prevent any communication between Margaret and Thornton.

'I see,' he said. 'Well, one thing at a time. I will be constantly at hand to assist Margaret with business dealings, so I thank you for your assurance. You will understand that Margaret is exceedingly stricken with grief. I would insist that any correspondence to her is directed through me at my office, and I in turn shall liaise with her family, so that she is only given news when she is well enough to receive it. Do you understand, Thornton?'

'Of course. I have no wish to upset Miss Hale. Far from it,' John replied, shocked by Lennox's description of Margaret's suffering.

Henry Lennox left Marlborough House, and John and Hannah sat back in their places in the drawing room, both still stunned by the afternoon's news. John still held Bertie in his arms and thought now about the further blow to Miss Hale. She had lost Bertie as well. He calmed himself, repeating the thought that she would be well cared for. But it troubled him to think that Lennox might be right; it was possible that Margaret was now where she truly belonged, not in smoky, dirty Milton with working men like him. He hoped to find a way to renew his request to court her, but if all he could do for her was to look after Bertie and her property, then he would put his all into it. He would love the dog as she did. As for Marlborough Mills, he would do his damnedest to keep it alive. And so the next part of John's life was mapped out for him and he would not stray from it.

Hannah was less pleased at the prospect of now having a dog living under her roof, but appreciated that there was no point whatsoever in challenging it. There were some battles that were impossible to win, and this was one of them. Hannah knew that nothing would prise that animal from John's grasp, so she decided at that moment to embrace it. She wouldn't take this one bit of happiness from him.

'Well, we'd best get him settled then,' Hannah said, rising from her chair. 'Do you know what he eats?'

'Yes, Mother.'

'Good,' she said, and John's heart melted a little for his mother. She was a hard and formidable woman but at this moment, when he needed her, she was there to support him, and he was thankful that she did not fight him on this matter.

～

Margaret, Mrs Shaw, and Dixon alighted at London Euston station. Henry had sent a telegram ahead to Sholto, and he duly met the party at the station to transfer them back to Harley Street, while Dixon secured a porter to retrieve their luggage, meagre as it was. Margaret had walked away from her home in Milton with only a few trunks of hastily gathered belongings.

The death of Margaret's father was so unexpected that it was hardly believable. She felt as though she might suddenly wake to find it all a dream or more accurately a nightmare, but it was true, and the sheer shock of it had affected her quite profoundly. She felt hollow and brittle as though she might snap under the weight of her sadness. Aunt Shaw and Henry had been so determined, so forceful, that she had acquiesced to their instructions and had walked away from Milton with her clothes and nothing more. They sneered at Milton and the life her father had provided for them there. She wanted to shout at them that they didn't understand, but she hadn't. She let their words wash over her and did as she was told.

Margaret had left Milton assuming that Henry would bring Bertie with him when he finished his business

177

dealings there. It now dawned on her that this was not the case and that she had lost him. How stupid she had been. She had let him go, let them take him from her. But she was distraught, and while her mind was scattered, Aunt Shaw, though well-meaning enough, had dismissed all of her fondness for Milton as folly. Now she felt more isolated in London with her aunt and the Lennoxes than she ever had with just her father in their small house in Crampton. She wanted to go home. She was alone again, displaced at the will of those with power over her, those who had her best interests at heart, but would not allow her any say in the plans which affected her so soundly.

Margaret realised that she was once again beholden to Aunt Shaw for her very survival, providing her with protection and a home. Of course, she had no other option but to accept Aunt Shaw's kind and generous offer, as she had no father, brother or husband to take care of her. Margaret thought back to Mr Thornton's proposal. If she had accepted him then she would be safe in Milton now. She chided herself. It was no use thinking of those days as there was no going back. She missed her father terribly and the cosy surroundings of their house. She missed dear Bertie. She even missed the familiarity of Milton that, after such a short time, she now considered to be the place where she belonged. She missed John. She took comfort that Bertie would be happy with him. She was certain that John would look after him as well as she could. He would give Bertie the home that she was unable to.

ᔐ

Chapter 15

John was struggling to comprehend the colossal changes that had occurred in his life since he had awoken this morning. The pendulum of fate had swung from the indescribably happy promise of a courtship with Margaret, to the despair of her now being two hundred miles away and in mourning for her beloved father. It was quite incredible to think that so much had happened in such a short period of time, and his heart ached to be able to offer her his support.

After Mr Lennox's departure that afternoon, John had returned to his office at the mill with Bertie at his feet and worked until the whistle signified the end of the day, though his mind was understandably occupied elsewhere. John and Hannah were both still in a daze that evening and went through the motions of eating dinner together, although neither one had the heart nor the appetite for it. John was attempting to maintain his customary behaviour so that his mother was not alerted to the fact that his world had just fallen apart, and Hannah, knowing her son suffered deeply, adopted her usual brusque manner so that he had the anchor of normality to cling to.

They retired to the drawing room under the pretence of relaxing after their meal and took their usual seats; Hannah concentrated on her embroidery and John found solace in hiding behind his newspaper rather than reading it. This evening they had the added benefit of Bertie, who was also slightly bewildered as to where his mistress had gone. He sat close by John's feet, looking alternately between his master and 'Mother' for some instruction on what to do, eventually lying down with his head resting on his soft white paws.

John was formulating a reason why he needed to retire early that would be acceptable to his mother, when the mantle clock chimed eight. Neither John nor Hannah noticed as Bertie quietly padded from the room, nor did they hear the pitter-pat of his feet on the stairs as he disappeared up to the bedroom and then returned, placing the object of his task at John's feet. John put down his paper as he felt something land on his foot and Hannah glanced up from her sewing at the rustle of the newspaper.

John's slippers, slightly slippery with saliva, were at his feet, with Bertie sitting expectantly behind them. Hannah looked at John. He swallowed a couple of times, then a smile warmed his face and grew into a soft rumbling laugh as he reached forward to pat Bertie's soft fur, but he couldn't quite manage the accompanying words of thanks or praise. Bertie responded by closing his eyes in delight and wagging his tail furiously. John realised that Bertie had shown him the new command that Margaret had alluded to when he was last at the Hales'. It struck him with a pang of immense regret that he would never experience the friendship and hospitality that was extended to him at their home ever again, and a lump of emotion lodged thickly in his throat. So that Bertie was not offended, John put the slippers on and then excused himself for a few moments to gather his composure. He stood alone in the hallway and wept.

The following day John sat at his desk to write to Margaret, as was only proper, in order to offer his condolences. However, he wrestled with the dilemma of whether to add any inference to their recent plans of a courtship. It seemed too insensitive when she was no doubt distraught over the loss of her father. He decided to add a little about Bertie instead so that she would know that he was well, and it might lift her spirits.

It took several attempts to achieve what he hoped was a suitable note. He sealed it and put it in an envelope addressed to Henry Lennox to forward on as was agreed. He wondered how she was coping and if she would be deemed well enough to receive his letter soon. He wondered if he had been too brief or too impersonal. Should he have been clearer in his affections? When would she receive his letter? How soon, if at all, would she reply? He prayed it wouldn't be long, and yet he also dreaded getting her letter in case she told him she had changed her mind. At least at this moment he had hope that she cared for him. He wished he had not been so forward, so ungentlemanly in his advances that last afternoon when they had met right here in his office. He closed his eyes and remembered her sugar dusted lips; the memory was so vivid he could almost taste them.

John took the letter to the post office himself with Bertie for company, then the two of them ascended the hill to the Milton graveyard where John paid his respects at Maria Hale's resting place both for himself and on behalf of Margaret, as he presumed to think that she would have wanted him to. Looking out across the city at the multitude of chimneys now dormant for the night, he felt utterly alone in the quietude of the hilltop, and he tried to imagine what Margaret might be doing at that moment. Might she be thinking of him, or could it be that he would now be relegated to a corner of her past. He must have courage. She had been happy in her agreement to them courting only a short while ago, and they had become friends. If she wanted him, he would find a way to be with her.

Not twenty-four hours after arriving in London, Margaret was firmly established in her aunt's household. In a way she found it quite comforting that the regime was as she remembered it. Far from being allowed to wallow in her grief, Aunt Shaw recommended assuming the countenance of reserved stoicism, even if it did not reflect one's inner turmoil. Her opinion was that if one gave the outward appearance of calm then the internal feeling would follow suit. The desolation Margaret felt at the loss of her father was hard to bear, and yet she understood Aunt Shaw's recipe for coping with the upset. Margaret determinedly went through the motions of the daily routine, yet her grief was decidedly intense, and she succumbed to tears throughout the day.

Henry had called to report the particulars of the funerals for Mr Hale and Mr Bell. Mr Bell had entrusted him with making the arrangements that were stipulated within the details of his will, and Henry made himself worthy of Margaret's gratitude by arranging Mr Hale's funeral at the same time. She thanked him with true sincerity for the kindness he showed her. Aunt Shaw was adamant that neither Margaret nor any of the women in the family would be present at the funerals, not least as they were to be held in Oxford, making their attendance more problematic if not impossible. Margaret wondered if John would go to pay his respects; she thought it very likely that he would, and she took comfort from it.

Aunt Shaw and Edith had appraised Margaret's meagre wardrobe, and much to her chagrin, Dixon had been commandeered to help. Margaret found that she resented the maid and her derogatory comments about Milton more than when they had been living there. Dixon now had allies and was free with her opinions, knowing that she had the support of Mrs Shaw and Mrs Lennox. It had driven an immovable wedge between Margaret and her mother's maid, and she was brought low by the notion that she could not forgive Dixon for gloating over what she perceived as the inferiority of Milton and its inhabitants. The bond between Margaret and Dixon was now broken, and Margaret was further saddened by it.

Margaret's taste in fashion was somewhat plain compared to that of her aunt and cousin, but even she had to agree that some of her dresses were rather shabby and worn. Aunt Shaw had tutted at Margaret's clothes and arranged for the modiste to call and provide an ensemble of appropriate mourning attire to see Margaret through the next six months of her deep mourning period. Aunt Shaw spotted a large neatly folded piece of patterned material in Margaret's trunk, and although a fine example, because it was cotton she earmarked it for donation to the poor. Margaret was horrified and snatched it back, holding it to her breast.

'No, Aunt, this is special to me. I will make a summer dress from it for when my mourning has passed.'

Aunt Shaw huffed. 'It is a pretty design to be sure, but it is more suited to a country girl than one living in London society, Margaret.'

'I think that may be a reason why I like it so much. Well, one of the reasons,' she said, and as she touched the softness to her cheek she realised that there was a slight scent of Milton on the fabric. It smelled of smoke and soap and cologne, and Margaret knew that it wasn't Milton she could identify from the slight aroma from the material, it was *him*.

It was hard to believe that their agreement for a courtship, though not a formal arrangement due to her father passing before he could give his consent, was only a few days ago. Yet she was starting to feel as though it wasn't real, a part of a life that was no longer hers. Already she dared not think of him as John, as that had been such a new novelty, but he became Mr Thornton again in her mind. Although it was not as intimate, she felt strangely reassured by it.

She was sure that he would write to her soon to offer his condolences, and she would be able to judge from his words whether he still wished for their blossoming affection to continue. She surmised that it would not be an easy courtship, as Aunt Shaw was likely to raise objections to him. She felt an unease creep into her soul. Mr Thornton would have to fight to be granted permission to court her. Fight for her. That bulldog spirit would have to prevail and show Aunt Shaw his worth and his sincerity. Propriety would not allow her to write to him, so she must be patient, and hope that he felt she was worth the battle that lay ahead.

Henry received an envelope addressed with large bold black handwriting, and without even opening the accompanying note, Henry instinctively knew who it was from. He held the letter addressed to Margaret in his hand, weighing up the implications of his next move. If he opened the letter, broke the seal, there would be no going back. Yet if he gave it to Margaret unopened he wouldn't know if Thornton had alerted her to the fact that she was now the legal owner of Marlborough Mills.

Ultimately there could only be one decision. He simply could not take the risk of the truth being discovered, so he ripped open the seal and dispassionately read Thornton's letter to Margaret.

Dear Margaret,

Words cannot express my sadness at the untimely passing of your dear father. He was a treasured friend to me, and I shall miss him and always think of him with great fondness.

I know very well that my own sorrow is nothing compared to the pain which you now endure. Would that I could shoulder some of your burden and that I could offer you some measure of comfort. I take solace in the fact that I know you are well cared for by your family.

I also send you my deepest condolences on the death of your godfather, Mr Bell. He was a gentleman whom I respected, and I appreciated his advocacy of Milton, not least for introducing both yourself and Mr Hale to our town.

I hope you are well. Mr Lennox has advised me to direct my letters to you via his office and I shall continue to do so until informed otherwise. I hope that meets with your approval, Margaret.

Bertie has settled in at Marlborough House. I must tell you that Mother and I have been charmed by his new command which he performed perfectly last evening.

I know he misses you.

I will continue to write to you if you would like to receive letters from me.

Sincerely yours,

John

Henry analysed the letter and noted that it didn't divulge any secrets about Margaret's ownership of the mill. Thornton had used both of their Christian names, inferring the intimacy of a close friendship, and his affection for Margaret was clear. Henry had been correct in his assumption that there was a bond, a fondness of sorts, between Margaret and Thornton, although he was thankful that it had not escalated to being a formal attachment. He considered that the unexpected death of Richard Hale was a most welcome act of providence indeed.

Henry smirked, screwed up the letter and aimed it at the wastepaper bin, his missile missing its mark. Henry tutted but made no move to place it in the bin. Margaret would never receive Thornton's attempt at a tender missive, and he would stew over never receiving a reply from her. Both would eventually give up on their mismatched relationship and leave the door open for another to comfort Margaret. He gathered his coat and hat, and without a second thought to Thornton, he departed for an afternoon's diversion at his club.

Later that afternoon, in the offices of Johnson, Wiley and Lennox, a maid by the name of Josephine went about her daily chores of cleaning the rooms, as she did every day except Sundays. She had only been working at the attorneys for a matter of months, having left her previous position as a housemaid in a splendid house near Hyde Park, where she had been in their employ for nigh on twenty-five years. Her main reason for leaving her long-standing position was to move back home to be with her parents, although one had followed the other to their graves not long after. But quite apart from her daughterly responsibility, she had been beginning to feel out of place at the great house. Fellow maids came to work there and then left when they married, and yet she had never met the right man, or any man for that matter. Somehow, her great love had never happened, and now at forty-five she felt a little embarrassed to be a housemaid amongst girls young enough to be her daughters, which seemed to accentuate her peculiarity in not being found marriageable.

She had often wondered why she had been left on the shelf. It wasn't that she was particularly unattractive. She was small and a little mousey perhaps, with a sprinkling of freckles across her nose and cheeks, but she had a trim figure and was kind and hard-working. The irony was that for as long as she could remember she had longed for romance, and she spent the few pennies that were left over from her wages each week on the publication

'Household Words'. Her favourite articles in the magazine being both serialised and short stories that alluded to love.

Josephine was a neat and tidy woman, well suited to her job, and took great pride in ensuring that the offices she was in charge of cleaning were always spick and span. It was her responsibility to clean all three partners' rooms, the clerks' room, and the entrance vestibule and hallway. It wasn't easy either, as some of the gentlemen lawyers were uncommonly untidy, with great piles of papers heaped up all around their desks. She endeavoured always to leave these important documents where she found them, although she did straighten the stacks so they looked uniform.

Josephine already knew the peculiarities of each of the attorneys that she worked for. Mr Wiley, for instance, smoked cigars and left large mounds of ash on the carpet, along with a few burns, despite her leaving him two ashtrays within easy reach. Mr Johnson appeared to be the most learned fellow, if the mountain of documents in his room was anything to go by. She saw this gentleman most often as he worked long hours, and she always left his room till last. She sometimes had to dust around him to get her work done, but he didn't seem to mind, and he just made little grunting noises as he pored over tiny writing in gigantic books. His room always had a musty smell, more than likely due to the vast array of ancient tomes lining three walls of the office. She had brought in a pomander of lavender to combat the odour, though it had not appeared to help. Mr Lennox was always the first to leave, generally by lunchtime each day, and had the most orderly room, seemingly to either work very tidily or not to work much at all. Josephine surmised it must be due to his junior standing and lack of experience compared to the others. She suspected that in a few years he too would be leaving ash deposits for her to clean up and towers of papers for her to work around.

Josephine knocked, and finding Mr Lennox had already left for the day, as she had anticipated, she entered his office to carry out her duties. Once she had cleaned the grate, she made up the fire ready for the following day. She dusted the furniture and applied some beeswax polish to Mr Lennox's beautiful desk. She had only seen Mr Lennox one time and had been somewhat disappointed. She expected the type of man to sit behind this desk would be commanding and grand, whereas he turned out to be rather insignificant looking in her view. She chided herself as she knew that she was nothing special to look at either, mediocre at best. Deciding to keep her mind on her task, she polished a bit harder to make up for her unkind thoughts.

Josephine knelt down to empty the wastepaper bin into a large sack she had brought with her for just this purpose. She picked up a screwed-up letter from beside the bin, and was attracted to the big bold writing covering one half of the paper with just two words – 'Miss Hale'. Josephine, quite unconsciously, turned over the paper fully expecting it to be some legal document that would mean nothing to her. Instead, she found it not to be an official missive at all, and she sat back on her heels, reading it slowly to give it her full appreciation. The handwriting was beautifully elegant, and she thought it was the loveliest she had seen. She read the address. *Marlborough Mills. Sounds grand*, she thought. *Darkshire*. Josephine had never heard of Darkshire but it sounded mysterious, even dangerous. The secret of the terrible event causing the death of this Miss Hale's father and godfather, and which had parted her from John (who was sincerely hers) whirled in her mind. And who was Bertie? A child? A brother? Josephine knew a love letter when she saw one, and as Mr Lennox had thrown it away she saw no problem in folding it neatly and placing it in her apron pocket. She would take it home with her and save it. She would be able to read it whenever she liked, again and again. This was not just a story, it was real life. These were genuine star-crossed lovers that could inhabit her imagination, and she would lose herself in making up stories to mend their tragic separation.

Mr Bell and Mr Hale were laid to rest, side by side, five days after they had died. Margaret was thankful that they were united in death, as they were so far away in Oxford that she would not be able to visit their graves with any regularity. Despite being the height of summer, the day was grey and drizzling, and John thought it appropriate for such a sombre occasion as he stood by the graveside sheltering from the rain under his umbrella next to fellow mourners that he didn't know. The service had been fitting for the two learned men respected in the city. The church bells had chimed their mournful toll, and John had prayed along with the congregation for Mr Hale and Mr Bell's eternal rest in the joy of heaven.

Henry had not been surprised to see Thornton at the funeral, after all the man had had a close association with both Hale and Bell. But having read the letter that was intended for Margaret's eyes, Henry had reappraised Thornton. He was no longer simply a vague annoyance due to his apparent fondness for Margaret. The implied intimacy in Thornton's letter indicated that they shared a mutual regard, and so he had become a tangible threat to Henry's long-term plans for Margaret and her fortune, and Henry now despised him. As well as securing Margaret and her inheritance, Henry now was of a mind to also bring down Thornton, to crush the man who deigned to have designs on Margaret, a gentlewoman above his station. His predicament was that it was of benefit to Margaret, and therefore himself, to have Thornton in the mill paying rent, as tenants needing the size of the facilities of Marlborough Mills would not be easy to find. Henry just wasn't sure how he would reduce Thornton to a nothing, a nobody that Margaret would not favour with her friendship let alone her affection, but he would do it. As luck would have it, Thornton himself would provide the solution to his problem within days, and Henry would be able to set his plans in motion.

After Mr Hale and Mr Bell's bodies had been interred and the final prayers said, John approached Henry Lennox in the churchyard. Lennox was accompanied by a tall, pale complexioned man wearing a captain's uniform, and Lennox introduced him to John as his brother, Sholto. John remembered that he was married to Margaret's cousin, Edith. It seemed odd to him that he could now put a face to the person he had heard Margaret and her father mention from time to time, and yet she was not there to share in the occasion. John had been anxious to speak to Lennox, primarily to enquire about Margaret, but also to inform him of the severe difficulties the mill continued to endure. If they could not be addressed the mill would close, and this in turn would affect the value of Margaret's inheritance. John wondered if Lennox, via his contacts, might know of a potential investor to alleviate the situation.

'Please will you pass on my regards to Miss Hale?' John asked Henry. 'Has she received my letter yet?'

'She has been understandably distressed, but it is likely that she will be well enough soon. I thought it prudent to get the funeral out of the way first as she is so fragile.'

Fragile? John was filled with concern for Margaret. How selfish he was, longing for a reply to his letter to allay his fears when she was suffering such sorrow.

'Of course. Whatever you think best. May I ask, Mr Lennox, will you be returning to Milton soon. I need to speak with you about a pressing issue regarding the mill.' Henry moved Thornton away from Sholto to keep their conversation private. 'You are still planning to assist Miss Hale with business matters?' John enquired, when they were apart from the group of mourners.

'Indeed. I will come up next week and you may apprise me of the details then.' John extended his hand towards Henry who merely looked at it and raised his eyebrows, gave a curt nod to Thornton, and left him standing in the churchyard feeling like a pariah.

Chapter 16

August 1855

Margaret felt like a prisoner, stifled and penned in like a caged bird at Aunt Shaw's house on Harley Street. After the freedom she had experienced in Milton, she now felt like she had had her wings clipped, and she was frustrated and smothered by the confines now imposed upon her. She found it curious that she hadn't seen the subtle changes in herself until, faced with the life she now lived with Aunt Shaw and Edith, Margaret barely recognised herself as the woman who had spent so much of her time growing up in this house. No longer was she allowed to voice her opinion or go for a walk by herself. The fact that she was now entirely dependent upon her aunt brought her spirits low. She wished she had valued her independence in Milton more at the time, but she had taken it for granted. Her dear father's trust in her that she would do the right thing no longer applied, and she must conform. She didn't blame her aunt or Edith, as she well knew that it was what society demanded. She had been a part of this world before Milton, but now it seemed so foreign, so divorced from what she had come to love.

She was utterly sad, homesick for Milton and its people. She missed them and Bertie, and above all she missed him. Mr Thornton. She had not heard a word from him since she had been removed to London so swiftly on that terrible day when Henry and Aunt Shaw had come to deliver their heart-breaking news. Decency dictated that she could not write to him unless he wrote to her first, and she now found herself in the ridiculous predicament of not being able to contact him. If she had been in Milton, she would have walked up to Marlborough Mills to see him. How she wished she could simply get on the next train to Milton and seek him out. She imagined him sitting at his desk or in their parlour at Crampton, or greeting her and Bertie in the mill yard. She yearned for her life to be what it once was. She longed to turn the clock back, to cherish what she had had. To appreciate him sooner.

Henry arrived at Harley Street in time for dinner, as he did most evenings. As he passed by the hall table, having been divested of his hat and coat by the footman, Henry spied an envelope on a silver tray awaiting delivery to the post office the next day. It was addressed to one Mr J Thornton, Marlborough Mills, Marlborough Street, Milton, Darkshire. Henry's mouth went dry and he flicked his eyes nervously left and right wondering if he should simply snatch it away there and then, but the moment was lost as Sholto emerged from the drawing room to welcome him.

Henry decided to meet the issue head on, and when all were assembled at the dinner table he said coolly, 'I noticed a letter to Mr Thornton in the hallway.' All eyes fell upon Margaret.

'Yes,' she said quietly. 'I have not had an update on Bertie and my friends. That is all,' she said, and forced her eyes onto her meal.

'Your friends!' exclaimed Aunt Shaw, and Edith gave Margaret's knee a little squeeze under the table. She knew what was coming, and while she didn't understand Margaret's fixation with the poor of Milton, she knew that the impending words would cut her to the quick.

'And a good thing too as far as I can tell. I'm glad you have no contact with them. The good Lord only knows what Richard Hale was thinking, dragging you and Maria to that dirty, dismal place. It's good riddance, Margaret.'

'I only wish to enquire, Aunt. Bertie will have grown by now and—'

'If you want a dog Margaret, I will obtain one for you, if you will only end this persistence about some flea ridden mongrel.'

'He is not—'

'Ladies,' interjected Henry, seeing his opportunity to bend this in his favour. 'If I may make a suggestion? I will be regularly corresponding with Mr Thornton. In fact, I am going to Milton tomorrow. I can enquire about the dog if you like, Margaret. Or I could deliver your letter personally. This will enable a level of delicacy and discretion.'

Margaret looked at Aunt Shaw while Edith held her hand under the table.

'Oh, very well. Margaret, you may send your letters if you wish to all and sundry in the North, but only via Henry. If you must,' Aunt Shaw finally agreed, winning a small smile of gratitude from Margaret.

'Thank you, Aunt. I shall rewrite my letter after dinner, Henry, so that Mr Thornton knows that I will direct my correspondence through you.'

Henry was elated. He had gained control again and he congratulated himself on his success, gulping down a goodly swig of Mrs Shaw's best Burgundy.

The following day, Josephine once again started her work in Mr Lennox's room. He had been in the office first thing that day, but she had overheard him complaining about a business trip, so she knew his room was available to clean. She was a little reluctant to apply her usual vigour to her duties as he had only been in the office for a few minutes, so she couldn't see the need to clean it again. Still, she reasoned, it was her job and she was paid to do it, so she had better get on with it.

Josephine had checked the papers in Mr Lennox's wastepaper bin every day since she found the letter from John to Miss Margaret Hale, but no further letters had been discarded. Josephine kept John's letter in an old cigar box by her bed, and she took it out each night to re-read it and daydreamed about him and his lost love.

She was dusting the non-existent dirt from Mr Lennox's desk when her eyes fell onto the strangest thing. It was an envelope addressed to Mr J Thornton of Marlborough Mills. Josephine thought that it was too much of a coincidence that Mr Lennox would be conversing with another person with the initial J at a place called Marlborough Mills, so it must be the mysterious 'John'. Josephine instinctively looked around, yet she knew very well that she was alone and would not be interrupted. She picked up the letter. The seal was broken. She took a steadying breath and read the letter.

Dear Mr Thornton,

I hope this letter finds you and your mother in good health.

Please excuse my impertinence in contacting you. Aunt Shaw is not in favour of my writing to you as it is not seemly, however she has agreed with Henry that he will forward my letters.

I had hoped that you might write to me, though I am sure that you must be very busy at the mill, especially now that poor Mr Bell is gone. Henry has been busy with the settlement of his estate. I hope that my godfather's untimely demise has not had a detrimental effect on the mill and that the new owner, whomever that may be, will be a reasonable one.

Aunt Shaw has welcomed me back into her house and I am grateful to be able to help Edith. The baby is expected soon, and I will assist both Edith and the baby on his or her arrival. I am glad to be of use but confess that I do feel rather a burden to my family.

I would be so grateful if you could send word about dear Bertie. Has he grown? I wondered if he had performed his little trick for you at eight o'clock. If so, I'm sure he has warmed your heart.

Also, I would be glad if you would pass on my best regards to Nicholas, Mary and the children. It would be so lovely to hear from my friends in Milton.

I look forward to your reply.

Yours sincerely,

Margaret Hale

Josephine considered the wording of the letter. His name was John Thornton and Margaret had been waiting for his letter. The letter that Mr Lennox had thrown away! Josephine rifled through the small pile of papers on Mr Lennox's desk and there she found his Christian name. *Henry*. Mr Lennox had agreed to be Miss Hale and Mr Thornton's go-between, but he had deceived them. He had read their letters and not passed them on. *But why?* The identity of Bertie remained a mystery, and now Miss Hale also mentioned friends. She wanted to hear from her friends and him. She was waiting for a reply from him, but it would never come. Mr Lennox surely would not give her letter to him now with the seal broken. Josephine wanted the note, but she couldn't take it as Mr Lennox would notice its disappearance. So, she took a pencil from the desk drawer and a blank piece of paper and copied Miss Hale's letter word for word. Then she noted the day she had found it, folded it neatly and placed it in her pocket, ready for transport home to her cigar box of treasures.

While Josephine was uncovering Henry's latest deception, he was on the train, travelling north to meet with Mr Thornton at Marlborough Mills as planned. Henry thought it a tedious journey, however it was a necessary one, as he also needed to speak with Mr Bell's property agent and arrange the closure of the Hales' residence in Crampton Terrace. The house needed emptying, but for now it could simply remain locked up until Margaret was safely his, and then she could come to choose one or two items she would like to keep. As Margaret owned all of Mr Bell's properties, Henry would allow the loss of rental income on the Crampton home while it was vacant and housing the Hales' possessions, for a little while at least.

On Henry's arrival at the mill, both men sat in John's office with Bertie obediently sitting close to his master.

'Miss Hale has appointed me as her lawyer and, as she has no business experience, I have also agreed to her request to manage her financial affairs.'

'Of course,' said John sombrely. 'And is Miss Hale well? Has she received my letter? Is she now well enough to receive correspondence?' He picked up an envelope off his desk and Henry eyed it warily.

'She is tolerably well. But she is delicate and is best left in peace, though I must say that she is enjoying being back in London. When she was having a good day, we gave her your letter. Her father's death has been a dreadful blow and I would not want you, or anyone else, to cause her distress were she unfit to receive reminders from Milton. I therefore insist that any correspondence remains through my office. Am I quite clear?'

'Of course,' said John, a troubled frown on his face as he pictured Margaret overcome with grief. He would not wish to cause her any further sorrow for the world. 'And she had no reply? For me?'

'None,' said Lennox dispassionately, and he watched as Thornton put the envelope back down on his desk.

John and Henry discussed the business matters which were the reason for the lawyer's visit. John explained the accounts to Lennox, who appeared to have little business acumen himself, and John wondered if Margaret had been given the right advice in putting Lennox in charge of her finances. John's mother had a much sounder grip of the ledgers than this lawyer.

Several hours later, Henry Lennox was bored almost to tears by the intricate details Thornton was going into as he revealed ledger after ledger explaining orders in, orders out, taxes, wages, rent, loans, income and expenditure, and the effect of the strike. Eventually, finally, Thornton got to the crux of the matter – the potential for substantial profit.

'If I may summarise, Thornton,' said Henry, squeezing the bridge of his nose, attempting to alleviate the almighty headache brought on by the incessant drone of Thornton's Darkshire accent. 'Through your most thorough, and may I say transparent explanation of your cotton manufacturing business, the bottom line I believe is this. Unless there is a change in fortunes the mill will close imminently due to global economic reasons and a local further destructive occurrence, by which I refer to the strike.'

'Yes,' said John simply. If that was all Lennox had wanted to know then he would not have wasted the past two hours expounding on the particulars.

'However, correct me if I am wrong,' said Lennox, his small beady eyes fixed on Thornton. 'If you had an injection of capital, you would remain in business.'

'Yes.'

'It would be in Miss Hale's favour if Marlborough Mills continued to trade. An empty mill does not pay the rent,' said Lennox, laughing at his own joke.

'Indeed. Miss Hale would also see the merit in the living that the mill provides to hundreds of families in Milton. She holds the poorer people of this town close to her heart,' said John impassioned.

'Do not presume to tell me about Margaret, Mr Thornton. Margaret and I are ...' Henry paused, taking his time to pick the right words. Both men looked at each other and a heavy silence fell upon them. Henry had John's heart in his hand, and he knew it. John waited for the hammer blow. 'Shall we say … close friends. Very. Close.'

A sickness boiled in the pit of John's stomach. How had Margaret entrusted this 'gentleman' with her business affairs and perhaps even her heart? He could scarcely believe it. Though it felt like an age ago, it was just over two weeks since she had stood with him in this office and kissed him. She had agreed to be courted by him. Surely it couldn't be that after such a short time she had transferred her affections to Mr Lennox.

'Then you will already know of her generosity of spirit. I beg your pardon for being so bold,' John said, drawing on his years of self-control to offer a composed view to Lennox.

'I will take a selection of your ledgers if I might, Thornton, so that I can peruse them at my leisure, and I will see if an arrangement can be reached for a loan.'

'Of course,' agreed John. 'I would welcome such an arrangement. I look forward to hearing from you.' Both men stood and John held his hand out, but Henry simply picked up the pile of ledgers and left.

'Well Bertie, what do you make of that, lad?' Bertie sat up straight and tilted his head, appearing to give some thought to the question. It drew a smile from John who ruffled the dog's ears, rolled up his sleeves and set off towards the weaving room. If the mill might be saved, then there was work to do.

The delight in being eagerly met in the hallway by Margaret soon dissipated when Henry realised that her animation was to find out the news he had brought back from Milton.

'Did you see Mr Thornton, Henry. And Bertie?' she asked impatiently.

'Of course, Margaret. That was the main purpose of my visit,' he said, and chuckled as if indulging her whim. He reached out and held her chin with his thumb and forefinger in a gesture that she found both inappropriately familiar and repulsive at the same time. She stepped away from him.

'And were they well, Henry? Did you give him my letter?'

'Indeed, tolerably well.' He searched his mind for a titbit to satisfy her request for information. 'He said to tell you that the dog is well. I'm sorry Margaret, but that was all he had to say,' said Henry, and he left her standing numbly in the hall.

In need of more information from Henry, Margaret raised the subject again during dinner.

'I should like to come with you when you next travel to Milton,' she said, with a mixture of hope and confidence.

Aunt Shaw came unknowingly to Henry's aid. 'You may not, Margaret. You live under this roof and my guardianship. I for one am gratified that your links with that town and their unsuitable people are breaking. Your place is here now,' she said, with a firmness that Margaret knew brooked no argument.

Margaret found her feeling of powerlessness and the unfairness of her situation at being once again at the command of others to be all consuming. She excused herself so as not to embarrass herself or those present. In the solitude of her room, Margaret went over and over again in her mind her last meeting with Mr Thornton. Had she been too forward in kissing him? He cared for her, she knew he did. So why did he not write to her?

Henry employed the services of an accountant and financial advisor he knew from his club, with Margaret's money, naturally. The accountant took little time to concur with the picture John Thornton had taken pains to explain. The ledgers, meticulously maintained as they were, provided the evidence that with a substantial investment the return would be considerable. This was no 'speculation' assured the accountant, but a solid business deal, and the master of Marlborough Mills appeared to be a credible businessman with vision for increased productivity. He had just endured some catastrophic bad luck.

'And what if a very moderate amount was invested. Say, five hundred pounds?' asked Henry.

'Well, it would be possible for the business to survive, but it would be hard work. I should imagine it's hard work anyway! But I would advise that a sizeable investment would be preferable in order to turn over an equally impressive profit.'

But Henry Lennox did not need nor want Marlborough Mills to make a substantial profit, he just needed it to survive and to pay the rent. A turn around in the fortunes of the mill would take Thornton from under his thumb. It would give Thornton the means to offer for Margaret. As a penniless northern manufacturer on the brink of bankruptcy he could not offer for Margaret's hand. The longer Thornton toiled away to keep his head above the water, the longer it gave Henry to both drive a wedge between Margaret and Thornton, and push her firmly back into his own path. He would win Margaret Hale, and her fortune. And then what of Marlborough Mills? Henry considered his options. He could invest heavily in the business with Margaret's money, which would be legally his once they married, and gloat at Thornton's success putting generous profits in his pocket. Or, he could simply ruin him. He really didn't know which idea he liked the best, as both had their merits. The important thing was that Henry now had a clear plan of how to manage Thornton in a way that would keep Margaret forever out of his reach.

Henry didn't want to endure the tiresome train ride back to Milton, so he decided to write to Mr Thornton with his, or rather Margaret's, business proposition. Margaret would invest five hundred pounds in Marlborough Mills, a sum that he said she had inherited from Mr Hale. Of course, it was an out and out lie. Margaret was immensely wealthy, but no one except Henry knew it.

John sat in his office, shirt sleeves rolled up and elbows on his desk with Henry Lennox's letter in front of him. Miss Hale was saving them. Saving him. Good Lord, it was a lifeline and one that he would not squander. John felt ashamed that he wished it was more. Five hundred pounds was not enough to turn the tide on the fortunes of Marlborough Mills, and it appalled him to be so ungrateful when Margaret was providing him with the means to keep the wolf from the door for hundreds of people in his employ. He would succeed. He would. For her.

Three weeks had passed and still John had received no word from Margaret. Five hundred pounds had been deposited in the bank, as Lennox had said it would, and John had been busy securing further raw materials, and receiving orders for his cotton. Bertie and his master had settled into a routine. Each day Bertie went to the mill with John. He had his own bed in the master's office, right next to his desk so that John could, and did, easily reach down and tickle his ears. However, he was not allowed in the weaving shed. He would follow the master wherever he went around the mill, but once at the weaving shed door, John always said, 'Sit, Bertie. Stay.' And Bertie waited patiently, sometimes for two hours or more, while John was inside the building. When John came out, Bertie would sit up expectantly, and his master would praise him. 'Good boy, Bertie. Shake hands?' and when Bertie complied, he received a biscuit or, his favourite, a piece of dried sausage from John's pocket. The workers at Marlborough Mills all greeted the dog as they went about their business, and although none had food treats for him, he was blessed with pats and strokes and so shook hands with them in return anyway.

After work, when John had had his evening meal with Hannah, he took Bertie walking by the canal nearest the mill, farther on Sundays, whatever the weather. The puppy was still enamoured with scampering after the ducks, but usually John would throw a stick and Bertie would bound along the stretch of grass to dutifully fetch it back. Once they were both tired out they would walk home again. In the evenings, Bertie sat with John and his mother in front of the fire, sometimes on his master's feet which he seemed to like, though he was not permitted to lick his master's ankle when 'Mother' was present.

Bertie's slipper fetching ritual continued every evening and John and Hannah sat in rapt anticipation as to when the novelty would occur. Bertie never did it earlier in the day, even if mother and son were seated as they were in the evening. It had taken a little while for Hannah to identify the trigger for Bertie's actions.

'Good heavens,' she said, with her hand placed over her heart, which John thought was rather theatrical and more akin to Fanny than his mother. 'He can tell the time! It's when the clock chimes eight.'

They looked at one another, not really believing that was the case, but then had to wait another day to test Hannah's theory.

The following night John and Hannah were on tenterhooks awaiting the clock striking at eight o'clock, whilst both tried to act naturally so that they didn't put the young dog off. Finally, the mantle clock softly chimed the hour, and Bertie raised himself from his place at John's feet and silently padded from the room while John and Hannah looked expectantly at one another. Bertie reappeared a moment or two later and deposited John's damp slippers at his feet.

'Well, how extraordinary,' exclaimed Hannah. 'I wouldn't have believed it unless I saw it with my own eyes.'

'I told you he was clever, Mother,' said John beaming, but with a watery sparkle to his eyes.

'Well, I don't want him getting too clever. I don't want dog slaver in my slippers, thank you very much. Are you listening, Albert,' she said, with mock reproach. Bertie merely gave Hannah his quizzical lopsided gaze, with his head cocked to one side as if in concentration, and proceeded to sweep the floor with his tail.

John had waited for a reply from Margaret but nothing had arrived, and he agonised over why she had not replied to him; just a word or two was all he needed. He chastised himself. She was grieving and here he was thinking she would have time to be thinking about him. But John could wait no longer, and he decided that an appropriate time had elapsed since his first letter to Margaret. As time pressed on, he became more concerned that her affections had changed and that she did not care for him. Yet she had loaned him the money she had inherited from her father to save the mill. Of course, her investment would benefit more than him, and it ate away at his confidence that the motive for her investment was solely to benefit the workers. John was in turmoil over Henry Lennox's description of Margaret as being delicate and sometimes not fit to receive correspondence. John would stick to the conditions for his interaction with Margaret as agreed with Mr Lennox as, above all, he did not want to cause her further distress. He and Bertie walked to the post office so that John was sure that his letter was safely posted to Mr Lennox's office, then the master and pup walked back to work.

It had seemed a long four weeks to Josephine since she had seen the letter from Miss Hale to Mr Thornton, and she had felt guilty in inspecting all of the rubbish from Mr Lennox's bin before she disposed of it. However, today her diligence was rewarded as she found another letter in the wastepaper bin. It had been torn in half and then half again and crumpled up before being discarded, but she could easily make out the handwriting. She had seen it so many times now that she knew immediately that it belonged to Mr Thornton. She placed the four pieces of paper flat on Mr Lennox's desk and read the note.

Dear Margaret,

Mr Lennox informs me that you are recovering and that you are happy to have resumed your life in London. It gladdens me that you are finding some contentment.

I wished to extend to you, personally, my heartfelt thanks for your investment and continued support of Marlborough Mills. I know that you hold many in our town in your heart as we hold you in ours.

Bertie is thriving. The hands spoil him, as does Mother when she doesn't think I notice, slipping him treats from the dinner table if you can only imagine it.

You will be pleased to know that Mother and I are transfixed each evening at eight o'clock when Bertie collects and delivers my slippers to me. Mr Hamper held a dinner last evening, but at Mother's request we ensured that we attended after eight so that Bertie was not confused. I wanted you to know that he has not forgotten your lessons and adheres to his training diligently.

I would welcome your response if you had the opportunity to reply.

Sincerely yours,

John

Josephine put her hands to her mouth as her mind raced. He loves her. *You hold many in our town in your heart as we hold you in ours.* And Bertie is a dog! Miss Hale's dog. But why was he not with her? And he delivered Mr Thornton's slippers! What are 'hands'? Men perhaps?

212

And Miss Hale invested in his mill? Surely that was not right? Had she not written to him saying that she had taken up a position as the woman called Edith's companion?

Josephine was more confused than ever with this second letter from Mr Thornton, as although it answered some questions, it now posed new ones. She felt sure that Mr Lennox was at the heart of the mystery.

Chapter 17

December 1855

The sound of the lunchtime whistle and subsequent chatter of voices and clatter of clogs in the yard interrupted John's brooding. He was glad of it, relieved to have some distraction from the dismal subjects that dominated his thoughts – the struggle to maintain his business and not failing Miss Hale, as that is who she had become again since she had withdrawn her affection for him. He must not think of her as Margaret anymore. That luxury was reserved to that fleeting moment in time when she had cared for him. It had been four months since Henry Lennox had first visited him on behalf of Miss Hale, and John had subsequently been loaned five hundred pounds by her in order to save the mill and thereby the livelihoods of his workers.

He had written to her regularly since then. His letters had begun with what he hoped was gentle familiarity from one who cared for the other. He had included information about Bertie and Higgins' family, but not once had he received a reply. With the obvious withdrawal of her regard that this silence signified, he was left to ponder her monetary investment in the mill, and it broke his heart to realise that he had been right all along. She had treated him like the tradesman that he was, and offered him some money that he had been compelled to accept, but she no longer offered him her heart.

Henry Lennox rarely visited Marlborough Mills, and then only when some documentation required his signature. John smirked to think that it was likely that his visits would be more infrequent still, since the last time he had called at the mill. It had been about a month before Christmas, and John had been writing at his desk when Bertie had leapt up from his bed suddenly barking and snarling as Lennox entered the office without knocking. John had never heard Bertie growling before, and the sudden activity had made him jump and knock over his inkwell. The ink had run over the edge of the desk, splattering onto the floor. Bertie had inadvertently run across it, leaving inky paw prints on the floorboards and, unfortunately, onto Mr Lennox's trouser leg, as Bertie investigated the identity of the would-be intruder. The indelible marks on Mr Lennox's clothing had caused him a considerable amount of consternation, while John had put his full attention into maintaining his stern countenance. John suspected that Mr Lennox's impudence at letting himself into his office without permission would not be repeated. He had never considered Bertie's ability as a guard dog, thinking that he was more likely to lick someone to death than attack them, especially if their ankles were available for his ministrations. However, John was pleased with Bertie's performance, and when Lennox had gone he had commended him for his excellent judgement of character. He rewarded Bertie with a treat that he kept in a small container in his desk drawer. It was the same tin that Miss Hale had given him on their last meeting in this very room.

John sent a report every two weeks to Miss Hale via Mr Lennox to apprise her of the situation at the mill, and to pay the interest on her loan. He often wondered if it was her health that had prevented her responses, as Mr Lennox still described her as 'fragile but tolerable', two words that he would never have used to describe Miss Hale during her time in Milton. He wished with all his heart that, even if she no longer held him in her affections, she would regain her previous vigour and fortitude.

John had bought some pencils and had given them, along with some paper, to the Boucher children so that they could draw pictures for Miss Hale and send good wishes to her for Christmas. When buying the drawing materials at the stationers, he had seen a small selection of Christmas cards, and on a whim had bought one to send to Miss Hale. He had been torn between the image of cats pulling a cracker, which the shop assistant assured him was very popular, and a country scene, eventually buying the latter as he thought it more appropriate. He thought it might appeal to her love of the countryside and it reminded him of their conversations about Helstone. Perhaps it would prompt her memory of those times too, when Bertie was tiny, and they had sat with Mr Hale in the cosy sitting room at Crampton. She had talked about Helstone as a most beloved place, while he had absorbed every glorious word from her lips. The shop assistant had been quite amused to see stern Mr Thornton perusing the Christmas cards and two young female customers peering over at his choice, wondering who the lucky recipient might be. Mr Thornton was clearly oblivious to his charm and paid no attention to the fluttering and tittering of the women. He simply settled his bill at the counter and left.

Bertie's inky prints that remained on the office floor, and were likely to do so indefinitely, gave John a frivolous idea. His feelings were real and faithful, and he mused that he had little to lose from further exposure of his heart. It would be worth the risk if it pleased her. It was Christmas, and he would not be embarrassed by a little silliness. He wondered if he might have an underlying familial similarity to Fanny after all.

'Up you come, Bertie,' said John, his breath visible in the starkly cold room, inviting the dog onto his knee. He then proceeded to dab Bertie's paw into some ink and then blotted it onto the card as his signature. John felt sure that it would make Miss Hale smile, as she had surely loved the dog, and he hoped it would bring her some Christmas cheer.

No response ever came to his and Bertie's Christmas card, nor the drawings and letters from the Higginses and Bouchers, and John deduced that her affections for them were over once and for all. He had been surprised that Miss Hale had not replied to Nicholas and the children as, even if she only saw him capable of trade, he had always believed her to have a real affection for them. John didn't blame her for the change in her regard for him, as he had been amazed that she had appeared to have developed a fondness for him in the first place, the rough man that he was. She now associated with finer folk than he, people whom she could respect as equals. But whether she cared for him or not, he still loved her, and would do his utmost to fulfil his vow to protect her property and investment.

In London, Margaret went through the motions of her daily routine, though her desolation was relieved by Edith's darling baby that Margaret helped to care for. In her time alone, Milton was never far from her thoughts. She wondered when she would see her old home or her father's possessions again. Henry had been vague about the reasons why she couldn't have access to the contents of the house Crampton Terrace, saying they were currently unobtainable due to the complexities of Mr Bell's will, and she had neither the vigour nor the inclination to question him further about it. Perhaps she would never see Crampton, or even Milton and its inhabitants again. Not the people like Nicholas and his family, or any of the workers at Marlborough Mills with whom she had become so familiar. Not dear, affectionate Bertie. Not Mr Thornton.

In truth, both Edith and Aunt Shaw had become worried about her. She lacked an appetite, and so her frame that had been pleasingly shapely was now becoming thin, and her skin was pale and lacked its previous lustre. Once, when caught up in her own thoughts, she had looked so forlorn that Aunt Shaw had summoned the doctor to prescribe her a tonic. Edith tried to cheer her by suggesting she wear brighter clothes than her mourning black whilst in the house, but Margaret politely declined; black suited her mood and she didn't care if she looked drab or dour. The only colour to brighten Margaret's appearance was her curious liking for a yellow handkerchief decorated in printed blue flowers that she always kept with her. She had made several of them, and Edith recognised them as coming from the length of material that they had discovered in her trunk when she had arrived several months ago.

Margaret had also taken to avoiding Henry Lennox, which in turn had had the opposite effect on him, in that he sought her out more often. She found his fawning over her to be distasteful. He had touched her face and even put his hand to her waist one time which had troubled her deeply. She didn't entertain any romantic attachment to Henry and hoped her full mourning would shield her from him furthering his attentions towards her. She tried to show him in her manner that she was not attracted to him, but Edith and Sholto both encouraged him. They thought he would be a good match for Margaret once her mourning period was over. Above all things, Margaret did not want Aunt Shaw to think that Henry's new and offensive habit of touching her would cast any suggestion of a lack of propriety on her side that might lead to the requirement to marry.

Aunt Shaw and the Lennoxes were understanding of Margaret's malaise. She was bereaved again so soon after her mother's death, and they appreciated the toll that this had had upon her. Certainly, Margaret was deeply affected by the loss of her parents and not a day went by when she didn't mourn their passing. But it was more than that, and the further details of her despair she kept to herself, as she knew Aunt Shaw would not welcome them. She was heart-sick for Mr Thornton, and struggled to come to terms with the separation from him that had been necessitated by the loss of her father.

Margaret couldn't understand what she had done wrong for Mr Thornton to ignore her so thoroughly. She thought about him throughout every day, how they had reared Bertie together, and the joy they had shared as he grew. Occasionally a smile would creep onto her face as she thought about poor Mr Thornton and his quite surprising shyness that he had had overcome to speak to her about delicate matters for Bertie's care. One time when she was lost in her happy thoughts Edith touched her arm, jolting her from her reverie.

'Is it Milton that you are thinking of, dear?' she asked, and brought a flood of tears to Margaret's eyes, as she nodded and wiped them away with her yellow, flowered handkerchief.

It hurt terribly that she had been removed so quickly from Milton, without even being able to say goodbye to anyone. Perhaps Mr Thornton was angry that she had left so suddenly without a word. But what hurt her the most was that, despite his display of fondness for her, he had not maintained his affections and had let her go without a fight.

Josephine had been unable to locate any further letters from Miss Hale to Mr Thornton. Each day she religiously checked the wastepaper for any discarded notes, but there were none right up until Christmas. In desperation to find out more about Miss Hale and Mr Thornton she had looked through Mr Lennox's – quite shoddy in her opinion – filing system. She would have been dismissed if she had been caught, but she was compelled to investigate further, and instead of cleaning when alone in his room, she went through the papers in every file looking for some information. If Mr Lennox ever noticed that his room was dustier than previously he never said so, so her investigations went unnoticed. She had been all through the files that began with an H for Hale, an M for Marlborough Mills and a T for Thornton, and found nothing. So, she then began reviewing the files in alphabetical order, and quickly identified the information she needed under B for Bell.

In the file for Mr Bell (deceased) there were recent letters from Mr Thornton to Miss Hale. She read them in chronological order and noticed that with each one they became more and more impersonal. In the first letters he addressed her as Margaret and himself as John. He mentioned Bertie and, she presumed, acquaintances including a family called the Higginses who featured regularly in his missives. The letters were dated every two weeks, and eventually the letters were simply an update on the mill and an account balance note which meant little to Josephine. In the more recent letters he always addressed them to Miss Hale, but she noticed he still signed them 'sincerely yours' which brought a tear to her eye.

Josephine felt she had to do something, but could not decide what. She had no one to confide in, and even if she had, surely they would think her mad if she told them she wanted to reunite a pair of lovers whose letters she had found by chance, discarded as rubbish. Equally, if she told anyone at Johnson, Wiley and Lennox, she would be released from her position on the spot.

The need to somehow intervene had come a few days before Christmas, when she was finally rewarded for her daily inspection of the wastepaper. She would have discarded the pencil drawings by children until she saw the Christmas card. It bore a wintry scene of a country cottage with a little snow-covered fence and fields behind, and a lady in a fine red coat holding a muff. Inside he had written 'I wish you a happy Christmas, sincerely yours, John'. But it was not his wording that brought her to tears, it was Bertie's inky paw print that he had added to the card. She wondered if she should write to him herself, but she feared being sacked if he told Mr Lennox what she had done. She even considered getting the train up to Milton on her day off to see him, but she realised the mill would be closed on a Sunday so he would not be there. She felt utterly helpless as she couldn't think what to do other than to carry on gathering the information.

Chapter 18

January 1856

While Miss Hale's five hundred pounds, and John's prudent use of it, had precipitated the immediate survival of the mill, John knew that it was still in a precarious position. The margin between solvency and bankruptcy were tight, and one slight downturn in the market would render them unable to carry on. Therefore, John had been working on a business plan. He had the evidence that a large investment would turn the tide, and take full advantage of his factory's superior equipment and capacity. In time, the increased productivity and the generated profits would also allow him to expand into textile printing that he had experimented with. This plan would result in the mill becoming even more remunerative, and more secure from future volatile external market forces by way of its diversity.

John contacted Mr Lennox stating his case and asked for assistance from him in identifying potential investors. Henry perused Thornton's letter with disdain. His immediate thought was to respond saying that no investors could be identified. Whether Thornton's plans were sound or not, Henry could not take the risk of Thornton becoming successful. Though Margaret still spurned his advances, the best place for Thornton was firmly under Lennox's thumb where he had no power to attract Margaret.

As Henry was considering his response, a wicked thought embedded itself in his brain and would not leave. He contemplated that this request from Thornton could enable him to publicly humiliate Thornton just for the sport of it. How delicious it would be to degrade Thornton in front of his friends from the club; he could expose Thornton as the common uncouth wretch that he was with ideas above his station.

Henry had charged one of the clerks at Johnson, Wiley and Lennox to do a little digging into the particulars of John Thornton's life. Henry had been irritated that Margaret had not warmed to his attempts at flirtatious behaviour, and he suspected that she still harboured feelings for Thornton that stood in his way. He had hoped the clerk would uncover some titbit that would cause Thornton's degradation in Margaret's eyes – an illegitimate child perhaps, or the frequenting of brothels or excessive gambling. However, the clerk was unable to discover any such information. The only little morsel that the clerk had found that would count against Thornton was that his father had died by suicide. It transpired that he had killed himself following his ruin by means of a failed speculation. With no juicier scandal to use against him, Henry surmised that it would have to do. He could still shame Thornton and send him packing back to the grim, smoky place where he belonged. Henry responded to Thornton's letter advising him that he would amass a group of gentlemen with capital and an interest in investing in a business. His friends at the club would enjoy a little fun at this tradesman's expense.

～

John put down his pen and listened. It was unusual to hear voices in his home, and the distant chitter-chatter could only be due to one person. *Fanny.* At the realisation that his sister must be paying them a call a smile touched his lips. He never thought the day would come when he would miss her, but he did. John had found the force of nature that was Fanny Watson utterly irritating when she lived with him and his mother. She was the opposite to him in both appearance and demeanour, and her constant jabber and love for amusement was something he could not understand. Where she was loud and brash, he was quiet and reserved. While she had many friends and enjoyed dances and parties, he had none and preferred to be at home. But was that really true? John had an astounding thought. Fanny was brave. She didn't care about making a fool of herself or being looked at for her sometimes-dubious fashion choices. No, she lived her life as she wished to, and John realised that he should take a leaf out of Fanny's book. He didn't want to be alone. He wanted a partner, and someone to share his life with. He just couldn't have the only one that he wanted.

John had been planning to ask a favour of his sister, so he left the seclusion of his study and headed in the direction of Fanny's voice.

'Hello, Fanny,' he said, smiling.

'Hello, Johnny,' she replied in a sing-song way, as she had done since being a little girl. It amused her to do so knowing that he found the nickname mildly annoying.

'Would you mind stepping into my study for a moment please, Fanny?' he asked cordially.

For John to request a private interview with Fanny was highly unusual, and both she and her mother were immediately intrigued.

Fanny sat in the armchair by the fire in John's study as requested and arranged her crimson striped silk skirts. John pulled up his desk chair to sit facing her, and bent forwards leaning his elbows on his knees with his hands clasped together.

'You are beginning to scare me, John. Whatever is the matter?' she asked.

'Do you know about the difficulty at the mill? Has Watson said anything?'

'No. He doesn't talk to me about his business. Are you ruined, John? Oh John!' she said, and leant forwards so that she could hold his hands.

'I have been unable to recover Marlborough Mills' fortunes since the strike. There are a number of contributing factors, but the main ones being that I had invested heavily in new machinery, and the strike affected me harder than the other masters. I would have had to close months ago but I have had an investor who has given me just enough to keep going. It is hard but I need to carry on, Fanny. I can't explain to you why. It's personal, but believe me I must.'

Fanny was stunned as she had no idea things were so bad. He looked tired and thin, and she wanted to hug him, so she did. Fanny pulled John's hands, encouraging him forwards until he complied and knelt on the floor in front of her, and she wrapped her arms around her stiff, grumpy, sad, kind brother, and he gave himself up into her soothing embrace. After a few moments had passed she pulled away slightly and looked straight into his beautiful clear blue eyes.

'What can I do? Do you want me to ask Watson—'

'No, no. Nothing like that.' He sat back on his heels in front of her. 'I have two requests. I am sorry to ask you,' he said, frowning, his shame there for Fanny to see, and her heart ached for him.

'Firstly, I need to reduce my expenditure further so that I can use that money for supplies and to strengthen my business. I intend to close Marlborough House, perhaps in the next month or so.'

'Then you and Mother must come to live with me and Watson,' she said firmly, taking this revelation in her stride, and he rewarded her with a little smile.

'Thank you, Fan. But I just need a home for Mother. I'll be perfectly all right at the mill.'

She patted his hand. 'I will have a room made up for you as well in case you might need it, and Mother will be most welcome.'

'What about Watson? Won't he mind?'

'You leave Watson to me. He is out all day anyway, so my mother being there will be of no inconvenience to him. Now, you said two things.'

John got up and held his hand out to Fanny, and led her to his desk. Spread across the desktop, along with workbooks and papers, were several large diagrams.

'I have been invited to London to speak to a group of potential investors. I am hoping that this could mark the turning point for the mill's fortunes. These gentlemen will not travel here so, instead of just talking to them, I wanted to show them Marlborough Mills. Make it more real to them. I will take examples of the cloth, of course, and I am making diagrams of the layout, looms per shed, that kind of thing,' he said, pointing to the plans. 'But I also wanted to make it more personal, and I wondered if you might do some sketches? Perhaps some scenes of the hands at work? What do you think?'

Fanny was at first flabbergasted. Not at the project that John had explained to her, but the actual fact that he talked to her about it and asked for her opinion. A little frown marred her pretty face as she searched her memory for a time when he had ever asked for her viewpoint in the past, but no memories were forthcoming.

'I didn't think you liked my drawings,' she said simply, too astonished to elaborate further.

'I did Fan. I should have said. I'm sorry,' he swallowed, knowing that those few words were inadequate for all of the times he could have encouraged her, and had not. He gave her hand a squeeze.

'Will you do it?'

'Of course I will, John,' she said, and pecked him on the cheek. 'I'd do anything for you.'

Hannah Thornton was less than pleased at the prospect of Marlborough House being vacated. She understood her son's reasoning that it was unnecessary expense, but it stung her that all of Milton would know that John's business was in difficulty, a fact that her pride had led her to attempt to conceal. As well as the ignominy of losing her home, on arrival as a permanent guest at the Watsons' she would no longer be the mistress. It was a bitter pill to swallow. Further humiliation was that John had decided to remain at Marlborough Mills, with plans to set up a camp bed and washstand for himself in his office. This really was too much for Hannah to bear, and she insisted that Fanny accommodate John's personal effects when the time came, as she had offered to do, so that his encampment at the mill could be passed off as a temporary measure for convenience's sake should anyone enquire. Hannah dearly hoped that her son's trip to London would be a success, and that there would be no need to close her home after all.

Over the next week, John prepared his speech for the London investors, learning it by heart and practising each night in his office or study to an audience of one; Bertie watched his master intently, head cocked and tail slowly brushing the floor from side to side. Fanny had been true to her word and had attacked her task with vigour. She had spent three days at the mill, and despite ferociously cold weather, she appeared to have enjoyed herself. John wasn't sure how she could feel her fingers while she sat in the yard with her sketch book. Their mother had arranged for some hot cocoa to warm her, though Fanny would have preferred something a little stronger. Not only did Fanny sketch the workers, and John when he wasn't looking, but she also brought her watercolours, and she created what John assessed to be a very proficient painting of the mill buildings and yard. He was especially delighted to see that Fanny had included Bertie in the picture, and decided that he would have it framed when he got back from his trip, and put it up in his office.

Chapter 19

On the morning of the meeting, John took the early morning train from Milton-Northern to London Euston. He carried with him a large leather document folder containing his diagrams, financial forecasts and Fanny's illustrations, and a satchel holding examples of the cloth manufactured at the mill, including the example of printed yellow fabric that he had experimented with during the previous summer. He was ready for any and all questions that might be asked of him, and he was confident in giving a good showing of Marlborough Mills. He was prepared to do his very best to secure some additional funding which would restore his business and maintain Miss Hale's inheritance. He had scarcely allowed himself to consider whether he would see her while he was there. He supposed that Mr Lennox might have told Miss Hale about the meeting, particularly if the success of garnering substantial investment would impact on the security of the income she received from Marlborough Mills in rent, and the repayment of her loan. But then again, he speculated that if Miss Hale knew he would be there, perhaps that would be a greater reason for her to make sure she was absent. He would have liked her to see Fanny's painting at the very least with its tiny depiction of Bertie.

John proceeded directly to the gentlemen's club where Mr Lennox had reserved a room for the presentation. As he was not a member, John waited for several minutes until he was granted entry by the doorman as Lennox's guest.

'This club is reserved for gentlemen, but I suppose we can make an exception this once,' said Henry, with a sharp bark of laughter at his own joke. John appeared to be unaffected by Lennox's barbed comment, save for a couple of blinks that only those who knew him well would have perceived.

John set out his diagrams, illustrations, and cloth on display, as around fifteen men of all ages were ushered into the room by Lennox, carrying with them their glasses of port or malt whiskey and cigars. John was pleased by the number of men that Lennox had managed to interest in his business, and he noticed Lennox's brother, the Captain, also joined the group. It had not been Henry's intention to invite his brother but, as Sholto was at the club that afternoon, it seemed churlish to make a point of excluding him. The Captain and John nodded to each other in greeting and then, when everyone was settled, John began his presentation.

John was completely oblivious to the fact that the amassed group had no interest whatsoever in investing in his, or any, business. Each man had been enticed to attend as Henry had promised them some fun at the expense of a jumped-up northern tradesman down on his luck. Sholto was unaware of his brother's plan to humiliate Thornton.

He had attended without the inducement of sport as he had a mild interest in Thornton, whom he had met at Mr Bell and Mr Hale's funeral. Margaret had spoken of him at one time with some fondness pertaining to his assistance in rearing the dog that she had often mentioned, especially when she had first come to Harley Street six months ago.

Henry had primed every man, bar his brother, to keep silent in order to compound the discomfiture that his prey would endure. John was something of a novelty to these gentlemen who were used to mixing only with their peers. His outward appearance was similar to that of their own, and yet when he spoke, his peculiar northern accent set him apart from them and highlighted his inferior birth. Despite their lack of ambition in making an investment at the beginning of John's talk, several of the gentlemen sat up with interest as he gave a most compelling account of the cotton industry. He also produced the necessary facts and figures to support his business case, which several of the audience found to be a most appealing prospect.

At the end of his talk John invited questions. There was a nervous hush, as a few who genuinely had been engrossed in what John had to say shuffled in their seats, not daring to be the first to break the pact. John kept his chin up and faced the assembly with what he hoped was a confident air.

'Tell us, Thornton,' said Henry, after an uncomfortable silence. 'What do you say to these investors about your mismanagement that nearly brought about the downfall of your mill, to the point where you lacked even five hundred pounds to save yourself?'

All eyes in the room fell on John at Henry's shocking question, which had the power to undermine John's whole presentation. If he was perturbed, the onlookers could not detect it. John raised his chin a little higher, just like Margaret would do, in a sign of defiance.

'The truth,' he replied, with honesty.

'That being?' needled Henry.

'That I expanded my business and over-stretched. The town was affected by a strike, and I had the added expense of hiring unskilled workers and the damage they caused to the orders. These factors, along with the market forces that I have already explained, caused the problem. But I have learnt from it and plan to diversify so that my mill would be largely protected in the future.'

'And is it not true that you are planning to live in one room at your mill? Surely you don't expect gentlemen to invest in a business where the owner has managed his affairs so poorly that he lives in one room?'

John had an almost overwhelming urge to punch the supercilious smirk off Lennox's face. He steadied himself. 'I will do what I can to progress my business, and to protect my landlord and investor. If that means living in one room, then I am not ashamed to do it.'

'Your family and acquaintances must be harmed by association,' stated Lennox.

'I regret any hurt that I may have caused my family, friends or workers. But they know the man I am.'

'And speaking of your investor. You have knowingly taken money from a woman. Is that not so?' said Henry, theatrically gesturing towards John to add emphasis to his words. Henry was rather enjoying himself. He was beginning to understand how colleagues were entertained by the spectacle of the law courts, as opposed to the tedium of wills and probate that were the mainstay of his own legal career.

'Money is money, Mr Lennox. I don't discriminate against those who have a belief in my business or have the wish to help me to safeguard the livelihoods of my workers.' John felt like he was in the dock defending himself against the charge of some reprehensible crime that he had not committed.

'And creditors I dare say! Your father was a failure too was he not? Perhaps it runs in the blood. I heard that he took the coward's way out?'

Murmuring broke out across the spectators, both at the disgrace that Lennox had exposed, and the manner of his questioning. It felt like a courtroom drama rather than the joke that Lennox had promised them. Still, it was diverting nevertheless, and the subject under cross examination held up well to Mr Lennox's scrutiny.

'You may not lay unpaid debts at my door, Mr Lennox. I pay what I owe, as you well know. As for my father, I have never concealed my past. That a man should be brought so low as to see no option but to end his life must be a desperation that I would wish on no one, nor their family. But I have learnt from my father's actions, and I don't participate in risk or speculation as he did. My business plan is a sound investment, and I have shown you the figures to prove it. I am happy to speak to any of you again if you wish me to explain further.'

The tension in the room was palpable, and one or two glanced about nervously.

'Well, gentlemen, if there are no further questions, I will take my leave and wish you a pleasant evening.'

Muttering escalated to chatter which rumbled around the gathering as John quickly collected up his samples of cloth and Fanny's watercolour and left, leaving the rest of the papers for Lennox to dispose of.

Sholto had listened to Henry's attack on Mr Thornton at first with shock, and then something bordering on disgust. Thornton's responses to Henry's savage questioning, that were on a surprisingly personal level, were those of a decent man. He could see how Mr Bell, Mr Hale and Margaret could hold him in their esteem, despite his lower station in society as a manufacturer. However, there was something that was bothering the Captain, pecking away in his mind throughout the presentation until the very last moment as Thornton strode purposefully from the room. It was the material. The example of printed fabric that Thornton had brought with him was the same as that favoured by Margaret, and which she kept with her in the form of handkerchiefs. Sholto instinctively knew that he needed to intervene in some way. Parts in a puzzle were sliding into place.

John exited onto the street and into the cold and densely foggy January afternoon, which was surprisingly comforting. He let out a breath of relief to be free from that dreadfully oppressive room, and was invigorated by the wintry gloom. It felt almost like home. He wondered if he should have collected all of his papers, but he could not have stayed in that room and maintained his composure for a moment longer; he just had to get out. He wasn't sure if he wanted to roar in anger or dissolve into tears. He took a few steadying breaths then decided he may as well return directly to the train station. He heard his name called and he turned to see the Captain rushing down the club's steps behind him.

'Look here, Thornton, I don't know what was going on in there, but I think you gave a rather good account of yourself. If I had any money to invest, I'd give it a go!' said Sholto, a little breathless from rushing.

'Thank you,' John simply replied, unable to muster any further response.

The Captain could see that Henry's attack on Mr Thornton had, in fact, affected him deeply. He knew how that felt having grown up with Henry who could be mean spirited and spiteful.

'May I offer you a cup of tea? You look like you need one.'

It was only as John and Sholto entered the Harley Street residence that John began to emerge from his haze of bewilderment caused by the meeting. He realised that Sholto and Edith Lennox lived under the same roof as Margaret's Aunt Shaw and, of course, Margaret herself. Suddenly alerted to the very real possibility of seeing her, he sharpened his senses to detect any indication that she was near. Sholto called for tea and the two men sat in the drawing room.

'Edith and Mother Shaw will be taking their afternoon rest prior to dinner,' volunteered his host.

'And Miss Hale?' asked John, tentatively.

'Margaret walks with the nanny and my son every afternoon in the gardens of Park Crescent. She is not one to rest. I should say she is much more suited to activity,' said Sholto.

'Yes,' replied John simply, with an enigmatic wistfulness as he remembered Miss Hale's frequent walks to his mill.

The two men conversed about John's earlier presentation and, by and by, he returned more to himself. He was grateful to the Captain for his kindness. John had put off leaving for as long as he could as Margaret had not yet returned, but eventually he had to go for his train. She must surely return soon as it would be starting to get dark. Sholto offered him the use of their carriage to get to the train station, but John politely declined the kind offer saying that he would prefer the walk, and the men shook hands as John took his leave.

Dusk was beginning to fall already, and when mingled with the fog, Margaret felt that the twilight could play tricks with one's eyes. She saw a man walking up Harley Street in the opposite direction to the little party of herself, baby Sholto in his perambulator, and his nanny. The man looked just like Mr Thornton and her heart skipped a beat, but she had had this sensation many times before when she had thought she had caught sight of him in a crowd, only to find that it was not him at all.

The man stopped to cross the road, and as he turned sideways and offered her his profile, she recognised that it *was* him.

'Mr Thornton,' she said, urgently.

In the quiet of the street John heard his name called again for the second time that afternoon. He turned in the direction of her voice, and there she was. He walked steadily back towards her, attempting to control his frayed nerves and galloping heart that had gone through so much already that day.

'Miss Hale,' he said, tipping his hat, suddenly tongue-tied after wanting to see her so badly and for so long. She looked delicate in her black mourning clothes and her face was thinner, but even so, she was more beautiful than he remembered. He thought back to Henry Lennox's description of her as fragile, and it looked to him to be an accurate description of her appearance. He noticed she used a muff like the one in his Christmas card to her and thought to mention it, but then he remembered that they were not friends anymore. At least, she did not view him as a friend.

'Have you had business in London?' she asked, desperate to ask why he was here, now, after no word from him for so long.

'Yes, with Mr Lennox. Perhaps he mentioned it to you? An investment meeting regarding the mill. Unexpectedly Captain Lennox invited me for some refreshment before catching the train back to Milton.'

'No, he didn't,' replied Margaret with a small frown. She could barely take in his words. She forced herself to maintain her calm exterior despite the urge to cling to him and never let him go. She realised that he had not meant to see her, and that his attendance at Harley Street was by chance.

John's thoughts were jumbled. He maintained his outward self-control while he tried to decide what to say and how to say it. He was unsure as to whether she would welcome his conversation.

Margaret broke the silence between them. 'Tell me, Mr Thornton. Is Bertie well? And Nicholas and the children? Would you send them my regards?'

'They are all well, I assure you. I will. And you, Miss Hale? Are you well?'

'Yes, thank you,' she replied. With the cold detachment that Mr Thornton displayed, Margaret felt her emotions begin to overwhelm her. She had to leave before she embarrassed herself and showed him the depth of the feelings she still had for him, and that remained unchanged from when they had last met. 'Goodbye, Mr Thornton,' she said, with her last shred of equanimity, and then quickly turned to hide her face from him as her facade crumbled, and she followed the nanny and baby into the house.

'Goodbye, Miss Hale,' he said to her, tipping his hat again, although she would not see the gesture as she had already turned away from him, and a moment later was gone.

Henry was trying to stay positive. He had succeeded in humiliating Thornton, but the man would not be cowed, and it was vexing that his dominion over Thornton at the meeting had not been absolute. The tradesman had given a steady account of himself, and the pleasure that

Henry had hoped to gain from Thornton's ignominy had been lessened by it. Even his friends at the club had not fully enjoyed the spectacle, as some had come to peruse Thornton's diagrams and illustrations after the infernal man had left. Henry was also highly irritated that he was left to tidy up after Thornton, and had thought to leave the abandoned papers at the club. But he worried that one of his contemporaries might actually contact Thornton and offer him an investment, so he collected them all up and retreated to his office at Johnson, Wiley and Lennox, to consider the consequences of the meeting.

Thornton would know now that he did not wish to help him to expand his business back to its former state. Henry considered that a wounded animal could be dangerous. The only harm that Thornton could do was to alert Margaret to the fact that she was the owner of Marlborough Mills, as he didn't know that she was Mr Bell's heir in toto. As long as Thornton and Margaret were kept apart, then no harm would be done. With each passing week, as Margaret approached her half-mourning period, she mentioned Milton less, so Henry felt he was winning the battle for Margaret's affections.

John settled into his seat on the train. It was quiet in his carriage, and he opened the newspaper he had bought at Euston. He sat with the broadsheet opened in front of him, shielding himself from his fellow travellers as he often did with his mother, so that he could privately lose himself in his thoughts. The gentle motion of the train was comforting, and he closed his eyes, exhausted as he was by the day's events.

He had seen her, for just a moment. She had asked him about his business, which he understood to be natural as she associated him with trade, and of course, because she was his landlord and investor. She had asked about those whom she had previously cared for, of Bertie and Higgins' family, but she had not asked anything about him. This chance meeting in the street underlined what he already knew from her lack of response to any of his letters. He would continue to protect her inheritance, as it was all he had left of her, but he could not fight for someone who did not want him to. He had to give her up because that was what she wanted. Any affection she might have previously had for him was over, and the emptiness of his life stretched before him, devoid of hope or happiness.

John forced his mind to think of something else. The investors meeting had been a complete disaster and he was sure that it would not lead to any capital funding to grow his business. Indeed, the gentlemen had been curiously silent and seemingly had no interest in what he believed was a sound investment.

Lennox had shown his colours. By his severe questioning it was patently clear that not only did he want John to fail, but he had done his best to shame him, though John could not think why. He couldn't comprehend what difference it would make to Lennox on a personal level whether his business prospered or not, and surely Lennox would see that it would benefit his client, Miss Hale, if he succeeded. Perhaps Lennox simply didn't like him, or felt threatened by him in some way. Captain Lennox appeared to be an agreeable sort of chap, and John was glad that Margaret was at least in the company of some pleasant relations. The Captain had been particularly interested in the yellow printed fabric that John had shown to the would-be investors, and it sparked in him the memory of Margaret holding it to her cheek.

It would be late by the time he reached Milton-Northern, and he hoped his mother would be in bed when he got back to the house. He had no wish to recount the day's events to her. Not today. Not when his heart was raw from the sheer desolation he felt at the failure of the business meeting and Miss Hale's hasty retreat from him. He tried to look for plusses but there were few. He had seen her with his own eyes which did nothing more than prove to him that his soul was, and would be forever, hers. They had conversed as polite strangers, not friends, nor lovers who had once shared a sugar speckled kiss.

Margaret was beside herself with emotion. She had seen him, spoken to him. Mr Thornton had travelled to London on business and had been unexpectedly brought to Harley Street, and yet he had not waited to see her. He had not intended to seek her out, even when he was in such close proximity to her. She had been embarrassed to

have called out to him in the street as it transpired he had
had no intention of meeting her. It was clear to Margaret
that she was no longer in his affections, yet she truly
believed that he had cared for her. Twice he had professed
his fondness for her. Once with great passion when she
had refused him, and again six months ago, when their
friendship had developed into an attachment, and he had
asked to court her. She believed him to have been true.
Yet he had let her down. When she was removed from his
life, he let her go, as if she had never been there and not
left even the slightest mark on his heart.

Her deep mourning period was coming to an end and
she would imminently move into half-mourning. Despite
Mr Thornton being finally out of reach, she could not
tolerate the thought of Henry Lennox's advances, and she
wilted at the thought of the determination she would need
to challenge Aunt Shaw if she championed a match with
him. Margaret had no money or any other family to take
her in. Aunt Shaw was her guardian and had considerable
control over Margaret should she wish to exert it. Her life
looked bleak and barren, and tonight she couldn't muster
the inner strength to hide her feelings.

There was a peculiar atmosphere in the house
that evening. Margaret had cried off dinner claiming
a headache, and had requested a tray in her room.
Sholto and Edith had been whispering like a pair of
school children, occasionally glancing at Henry, and had
eventually excused themselves and retired early, and Mrs
Shaw did not like it one bit. Henry had been sullen, and
Mrs Shaw was at a loss as to what the matter was with

everyone, so she retired early too, leaving Henry to see himself out.

～

At Marlborough House, Hannah Thornton was wondering how John had fared that day in London giving his presentation to Mr Lennox's potential investors. She and Bertie sat in the drawing room after dinner, with the absence of John causing some consternation to both of them. As eight o'clock approached, it occurred to Hannah that John being away would upset Bertie's habit of collecting his slippers, and the well-hidden warm vein in Hannah's heart hoped that the dear young dog would not be too confused as to what to do when the clock chimed.

At eight o'clock Bertie roused himself, and trotted off as usual to fetch John's slippers. He re-entered the room with them in his mouth and dropped them at 'Mother's' feet. Hannah looked at Bertie who stared back with his head cocked. Hannah huffed and reached down, taking off her shoes and putting on John's much larger slippers. *Good Lord above*, thought Hannah, astounded at herself for putting on her son's slippers so as not to offend the dog.

'I must be going soft in the head and in the heart. This had better remain our secret, Albert,' said Hannah sternly, thinking she had better remember to put her own shoes back on when she went to bed, or she'd likely break her neck tripping on the stairs.

'Or maybe that's your plan?' she said to the dog, and chuckled to herself.

Happy with performing his task for the evening, Bertie lay back down to snooze, and Hannah's thoughts returned to John and whether he had managed to win over an investor, and in doing so save her home from closure.

Chapter 20

Josephine knocked on Mr Lennox's door. At the expected silence, she entered his room to begin cleaning. Her first task, as always, was to check the Mr Bell (deceased) folder and the wastepaper basket for any further information on either Mr Thornton or Miss Hale. Today in the rubbish she was surprised to find, not merely a discarded letter, but a large pile of drawings, and the title on the very first sketch was 'Weavers at Marlborough Mills'. Josephine put her hand on her heart to steady her excitement. The sketch was of a man and a woman who appeared to be operating large machines. The man was wearing a flat cap and the woman had a scarf tied around her head while she worked. Josephine turned the paper over to look at the next one and she noticed little rough drawings on the back. One was of a young boy, and underneath the depiction the artist had written 'Tom'. The other simple sketch was of a young man with a wide grin and was named 'Edwin'.

The picture on the second page was titled 'Spinners and Piecers at Marlborough Mills', and the next was 'Carding at Marlborough Mills'. Josephine turned the pages quickly, and on the back of one she spotted a drawing of a man standing with his hands on his hips, wearing a waistcoat and a cravat, and with his sleeves rolled up. Underneath the small illustration it said 'John'. It was him. She had finally seen him, and even though it was only a rough study, Josephine thought he more than met her expectations; he was a fine looking fellow indeed. She inspected the rest of the papers looking for a drawing of Higgins or of Bertie, but there were none. As well as the pictures there were large diagrams of rooms and numbers on a page that were beyond her knowledge. She decided to keep the drawings and rolled them up so that she could take them home. To have an image of Mr Thornton was more than she could have ever hoped for.

The master was back from his trip to London and the workers at Marlborough Mills well knew about it. One day with Mrs Thornton in charge, prowling the lines of looms, was almost preferable to having the master back. John had not ventured into the canteen at the noon break. He kept to his office in the afternoon and up to the evening whistle, having spent his vexation that morning on anything and everything that he could find to criticise. His ill temper informed the workers, as well as any words could, that his excursion had not been a success. They knew he was trying to keep the mill in business and they could not fault him for his apparent effort. A subdued sense of reverence had settled over the mill's hands, as they subconsciously let the master come down from his foul mood in solitude.

Nicholas Higgins sat on the bench in the courtyard, long after the other workers had filed home. In the half-light he watched the window of Thornton's office which, if rumour had it, was soon to double as his living quarters. The room was lit by lamplight, but Higgins could see no movement within, no sign of Thornton's activities. Higgins wanted to find out if the master had heard any news about Miss Margaret on his trip to London, but the time had never been right earlier on. It took Higgins by surprise to realise that he was also concerned for the master. Thornton had put his all into preparing for that meeting, and had even persuaded Mrs Watson to help with drawings, so all hands at the mill had sensed its importance. There was no doubt that the master worked hard, he lived and breathed the mill, so the disappointment from his failed business meeting would be a severe blow.

Higgins wondered what on earth he was doing sitting there worrying about a grown man, a master no less, who would likely have told him he was a fool and to be off home to his family. He reasoned that Thornton must be either working at his desk or perhaps he had fallen asleep. There was no other explanation. Higgins snatched his cap off his head and twisted it in his hands as he was suddenly struck with the horror that the master might be dead. He had not been seen since the morning when he had been considerably fired up. By desperation? *God no,* thought Higgins. He had heard that Thornton's own father had killed himself when faced with a hopeless situation, and Higgins knew that Thornton had lost nigh on everything. He ran across the yard and up the steps to the master's office then hesitated, anxious about what he might find behind the door.

He knocked.

Silence.

His heart pounded as he knocked again.

'Who is it?' said John from inside the office, and Higgins closed his eyes and smiled, letting out the breath he didn't know he'd been holding. *Bloody fool*, he thought to himself.

'Me. Higgins, Master.'

'Higgins? Come in.'

Higgins entered the room to find Thornton sitting at his desk, sleeves rolled up and a pen in his hand. The large ink stains on his fingers provided Higgins with the evidence that the master had been working after all.

'I was wonderin' if you 'ad any news on Miss Margaret?' said Higgins, approaching the desk, and following the master's gesture to do so, he sat in the vacant chair opposite him. Bertie stirred from his bed and he nudged his nose into Higgins' hand to coax a few friendly pats from him.

'Did you see 'er? Was she all right?' asked Higgins.

John swallowed. He didn't know what to say, or how to say it. He was frightened that speaking about Margaret when his feelings were so raw might finally tip him over the edge into tears, which he thought once started might never stop. To prevent displaying his heartbreak to Higgins, he reminded himself that he had determined to let her go. It was for the best that he allowed her the freedom from him that she evidently wanted. Best for her, of course, not him. He wasn't her equal and never had been, and her time in London over these last months would have illustrated to her the difference between them. He was a manufacturer, a rough nobody, and although he would love her and protect her till his dying day, he would not stand in the way of her happiness.

'Master?' pressed Higgins.

'Yes, I saw her.' He decided to start with telling Higgins about the business meeting. It was firmer ground for his emotions. 'The presentation to the group of potential investors was a waste of time, Higgins. I keep going over it in my head. It was like they had no interest in investing at all. They didn't ask questions about the set up here or potential revenue. No questioning on the facts and figures. Nothing. They barely looked at the diagrams or illustrations. I'm not telling Fanny,' he said, managing a slight chuckle. 'Their preoccupation appeared to be about me, or more to the point, my failure. It was as if I were some sort of exotic exhibit.'

John put his elbow on the desk, rested his head in his hand, and closed his eyes with a deep sigh.

'I have tried, Higgins. For Miss Hale, for the mill and for the hands,' he admitted softly.

'You're givin' up then, are yer?' asked Higgins, goading the master to show his mettle.

John gave a rueful laugh. 'I can't do that. It's not in my nature, but clinging on by my fingernails month after month is taking its toll I suppose.'

'Tell me about Miss Margaret then. Was she at the meetin'? What did she say?'

'No, not there. It was at a gentlemen's club. They don't let women in. They nearly didn't let me in! Her cousin by marriage, a military captain, took pity on me and gave me a cup of tea after the meeting at their home. I saw her as I was leaving. Just briefly.'

'And?'

'She looked beautiful. Different. Remote I suppose you'd call it. Untouchable. Frosty. Sad.'

Both men sat silently for a moment as they both absorbed John's description of Miss Hale.

'We exchanged superficial pleasantries. She asked about Bertie of course, and the mill. Oh, and the children. Sorry, I should have said. She seemed cross with me. It was a few seconds. That was all.'

Higgins frowned. 'Master, I need you to bear with me now. I'm beggin' pardon in advance if you think I overstep.'

John nodded, allowing Higgins to go on, too emotionally drained to argue.

'When Miss Margaret left Milton you two were in love,' Higgins said, as a statement rather than a question, but John answered him nevertheless.

'Yes. I believe so. We had agreed that I would ask her father's permission for a courtship when he got back from Oxford. But of course, that wasn't to be.'

'And 'ow do you think you were with 'er? In London I mean.'

'I don't know. Probably very similar to her I suppose.'

'And why was that?'

'Sorry?'

'Why were you remote, an' sad, an' frosty, an' whatnot?'

'Because I have not heard a word from her since she left,' John said, a little indignantly.

'Exactly!' said Higgins, beaming triumphantly.

John lifted his head off his hand and stared at Higgins.

'So, you're saying that Miss Hale feels the same way about me as I feel about her, hurt and upset, because she has not heard from me either?' asked John, and Higgins nodded his reply.

John's eyes widened at the epiphany, and ran his hand over his head ruffling his hair into tufts. 'Lennox insisted I send my correspondence through him at his office. He said it was because Miss Hale was so distressed that the family would pass on the letters when she was well enough to receive them.' It was beginning to dawn on John that he, and possibly Margaret, had been taken for fools.

'Let's think about it, Master. What reasons can this Lennox bloke 'ave to keep your letters from Miss Margaret? And drawin's from the children? That's not protecting 'er, is it? But it's more than just keepin' the two of you apart. I mean, he might well want 'er for 'imself, but why would he cut 'er off from us all? Stop 'er findin' out about what's goin' on 'ere? It seems so cruel.'

'To isolate her,' said John, nodding slowly.

'Maybe it's just he doesn't want any of 'er affections goin' elsewhere?' suggested Higgins.

'Perhaps so. But why? What harm can it do for her to hear about the mill and Bertie? When I had not had any replies to my more personal letters, and realised that her affection for me had changed, I wrote about the mill, the workers, Milton and of course Bertie. I made no declarations of affection after I received no warmth in return. I have sent a letter every two weeks with the accounts to Mr Lennox's office. Good God, Higgins. She's never received them has she. She must hate me,' and he returned his head to his hands.

'Well, 'ang on before you get all worked up again. Do you hate 'er?'

'No, of course not.'

'Well then. I can't see Miss Margaret turnin' off 'er feelin's just like that either.'

'Of course, we are only guessing. I need to get to the truth of it, Higgins,' said John with renewed enthusiasm.

'Well, I don't know about you, Master, but I think that this Lennox character might need a visit.'

Margaret thought about her fleeting encounter with Mr Thornton time and time again, searching for any small sign from him that he still held some fondness for her, but she could think of none. Their meeting had been so brief because she had left him standing in the street. She had known that if she stayed any longer, she would shame herself with a sudden display of tears and expose her feelings to him.

She remembered when she had wept, mainly due to exhaustion, when Bertie had been the tiniest pup, and Mr Thornton had comforted and helped her. He had always been calm and kind even when she was blubbering in a most unladylike fashion. They had become friends. He had wanted to court her and yet, when she was forced to leave Milton, he had simply let her go. He clearly didn't care enough for her to object to her departure and had accepted it. She was not worth fighting for after all.

Pining for Mr Thornton would not bring him back, or make him love her enough to need her in his life. She would most likely never see him again and she must come to terms with it. It was time to move on and put him in her history as he did not care for her. But deciding to forget Mr Thornton, when he inhabited her thoughts so thoroughly, felt almost impossible, but she must try. Despite her resolution she could not dispel the aching emptiness in her soul. She sobbed into her pretty yellow and blue handkerchief, a symbol of his previous regard for her, which only made her cry harder.

Chapter 21

Henry was a little apprehensive about retiring to his club that afternoon. He had called in yesterday at lunchtime, as was his wont, but had sensed a strange, unsettling atmosphere. Some of his regular acquaintances appeared to be giving him the cold shoulder, and he deduced that perhaps they had not found the spurious investors meeting he had orchestrated the day before to be as diverting as he had promised. He too had been somewhat disappointed with the outcome, as although he had succeeded in publicly humiliating Thornton, Henry had been quite dismayed that a number of his associates at the club had actually wanted to invest in the mill, citing Thornton's presentation as a viable and attractive investment.

Sholto's appearance had also been a blow, as Henry was concerned that his efforts to humble Thornton might get back to Edith, and thereby also to Margaret. If Margaret found out about his treatment of Thornton, her good opinion of him might be blighted, and could negate all of the tiresome attention he had paid her to win her acceptance of his suit. Henry decided that he must cut short his plans to gradually woo Margaret, and stake his claim upon her. Mrs Shaw must be informed of his aspirations to secure Margaret as his wife. He would forego his afternoon at the club, and pay a visit to Mrs Shaw instead.

∽

The doorbell chimed at Johnson, Wiley and Lennox, signalling the arrival of visitors. Josephine had just started polishing Mr Lennox's room, as that gentleman had left the building not ten minutes before in an unusually agitated state. The maid left her work to see who was at the front door, although she was not expecting any further clients to call that day. Josephine applied her most cordial and welcoming face and opened the door to find two men awaiting entry. She looked at the tall, broad shouldered man dressed in black, and her face became ashen. She put a hand to her lips and whispered, 'Mr Thornton,' and did the one thing that she had never done in her life before and never would again – Josephine fainted. Both men, surprised by the sudden affliction overwhelming the maid, lunged forwards and grabbed her so that she didn't hurt herself by falling onto the mosaic tiled floor of the vestibule.

Higgins lifted the small woman in his arms, and followed Thornton into a vacant room where the door was ajar. The nameplate read 'H Lennox Esq'. Higgins sat the woman on a chair and John poured some water from a carafe on the desk. As Josephine came round, she was at first quite disorientated, and then it came back to her – Mr Thornton was here.

The maid's attention was caught by Higgins, who asked her gently, 'May I ask your name, miss?'

'Josephine,' she replied, shakily taking the glass from Mr Thornton's fingers and sipping some water to calm herself.

Both men were now kneeling on the floor in front of her, and she suddenly felt quite silly for her girlish swoon. John had also poured himself some water, as he was quite perturbed that this woman, a maid in Middle Temple that he had never seen before in his life, had taken one look at him and recognised him.

Higgins broke the silence. 'Well, Miss Josephine, this is Thornton, as you already seem to know, and I'm Higgins.' John nodded his agreement to Higgins' explanation. 'Don't mind 'im,' continued Higgins, attempting to lighten the mood. Inclining his head towards John, he winked at Josephine and said, 'He gets 'is tongue in knots wi' women.'

John froze with his glass halfway to his lips to give Higgins a hard stare.

'Well, his letters are very good,' offered Josephine kindly, directing her words to Higgins.

John's eyebrows nearly disappeared under his hairline at the maid's surprising disclosure, and he coughed having inhaled some of the water, though neither Higgins nor Josephine paid him any attention.

'Higgins? Higgins with the children?' asked Josephine, and now it was Nicholas' turn to be stunned.

Josephine explained to both men how she had come across Mr Thornton's first letter by chance, when she had found it with the waste paper, and that she had been charmed by it. She proceeded to tell them about finding Miss Hale's letter to him, her furtive and clandestine surveillance of the Mr Bell (deceased) folder, and the discarded illustrations where she had seen Mr Thornton's image, so faithfully represented that she had recognised him instantly. Josephine was honest and truthful in her explanation and left no detail unspoken.

'I wanted to tell you, but I didn't know if you would tell Mr Lennox what I've been doing. I'll surely lose my job if he ever knew. You won't tell him, sir, will you?'

'Of course not, Miss Josephine,' said John distractedly. The quantity of information that the maid had to impart was quite overwhelming, but the main issue to be immediately identified was that, as Higgins had suspected, Miss Hale had likely not received a single one of his letters to her, nor his card or the drawings from the children; certainly not the ones Miss Josephine had found discarded in the bin. Of course, he couldn't be sure that she hadn't seen the letters that Miss Josephine said were filed with Mr Bell's documents. And the next, even headier revelation to comprehend, was that Miss Hale had written to him after all.

'Miss Josephine, what did Miss Hale say in her letter to me?' he asked nervously. 'Can you remember?'

'Oh yes, she asked about Bertie and her friends in Milton, and asked that you write to her.'

John sat back, his legs starting to ache from his position on the floor. 'So, when I didn't write to her, I mean, when she didn't receive my letters, she stopped too?'

'It's not right for a lady to write to an unattached gentleman, Mr Thornton. I think she took a risk with the first one. And she might have written more that I didn't find. But she did say that she had to correspond through Mr Lennox, so perhaps there were no more letters. I just don't know.'

'Yes,' agreed John, as he well knew that she was not free to write to him as and when she wished to.

The faint bang of Mr Johnson's door across the hall brought Josephine to her senses.

'I need to get on with my work or I'll get the sack anyway!' she said.

'Miss Josephine, is it possible to look at the documents in Mr Bell's folder?' John asked.

'I don't know, sir. I could get in serious trouble.'

'Of course, Miss Josephine, I apologise. I don't wish to cause you any bother. You have been most helpful already,' said John, not wishing to press her on the matter when she had already been informative and obliging. He reached into his breast pocket and withdrew his card.

'If you ever need anything, you need only ask me. I am most profoundly in your debt,' he said, giving her his calling card. Of course, Josephine knew his address already by heart, but she was delighted to receive it all the same.

John and Nicholas stepped out into the street, both dumbfounded at their incredible luck at meeting with Josephine. John guessed that they had gained more particulars from her than they would have from Lennox if he had been there himself.

'Higgins, I would like to call on Miss Hale. I must make amends,' said John.

'Aye, Master. I'll meet you at t'station. Tell 'er hello from me,' Higgins replied, winking.

~~~

Mrs Shaw was surprised by Henry Lennox's arrival so early in the day, as he was likely to call again for the evening meal. She wondered how he had ever fed himself before Edith had become attached to the Captain, as he was almost always in attendance for dinner. Mrs Shaw was further astonished to be asked to grant him an interview regarding a personal matter. She received Henry in her private sitting room where she had been resting, and invited him to be seated, although she did not offer him some tea. It seemed to her that he partook of their refreshments rather too frequently as it was.

'Mrs Shaw, I will not be coy in my reason for requesting to speak with you in private. Indeed, I don't doubt that without Margaret's deep mourning period you would have expected me sooner,' said Henry, with an air of confidence and fellowship that Mrs Shaw found mildly irritating.

'Go on,' she simply said, denting Henry's resolve slightly.

'I am here to ask your permission to marry Margaret. You must know by my attentiveness towards her that I love her most intensely. I am building my legal practice and gaining some exceedingly influential clients, so I am sure that Margaret and I will benefit from a very comfortable life together.'

Mrs Shaw considered Henry's request which, in retrospect, was not so surprising. Some months ago, she had heard the Captain and Edith discussing the merits of Henry being matched with Margaret and what a delightful time they would have together. However, Mrs Shaw was not convinced that Margaret returned Henry's feelings. It was a fact that the girl needed to marry, and a good match would be difficult in reduced circumstances as she was. The main obstacle, as Mrs Shaw saw it, was that Margaret was still grieving, although her first six months of mourning had now ended and she had entered into her half-mourning period. Mrs Shaw was happy to provide protection to her niece during that time, and beyond if a suitable match could not be secured, but if Margaret did care for Henry, then perhaps he would be the answer to their prayers.

'My niece is in mourning, Henry. It would not be seemly for an engagement or marriage at this time. If Margaret is to marry from my household it will be done properly,' Mrs Shaw declared haughtily.

Henry's disappointment was clear for Mrs Shaw to see, and it bolstered her belief that he held a true affection for her ward and was sincere in his wish to have Margaret as his wife. Henry tried again, desperate as he was to secure Margaret's hand.

'Of course, Mrs Shaw. It is just that I am so eager to know that Margaret will be mine. No one could be more impatient than I to know that your dear niece will be entrusted to me. Would a courtship be acceptable then, if an engagement is not? With a view to marrying when Margaret's half-mourning period is over?' he asked, and he bestowed on her what he thought of as his most winning smile.

'I can't see the need for urgency, however, if Margaret is in agreement then you may have my blessing,' said Mrs Shaw, hoping that this news would lift Margaret's spirits and give her something to look forward to. The poor girl had been crying again, and Mrs Shaw wondered if this might be the tonic that she needed.

Henry left Mrs Shaw's parlour after thanking her profusely, but he admitted to himself that the interview could have gone better. What he had really wanted was for Mrs Shaw to pledge Margaret to him. With that assurance from her guardian, Henry's future would be sealed without needing to get Margaret's agreement. He suspected that an acceptance of his hand at this time was still not guaranteed. He decided to describe Mrs Shaw's assent to a courtship to Margaret as a prelude to their marriage, almost as a fait accompli, as if Mrs Shaw had agreed to their betrothal. But he would omit the necessity for her to add her consent. With a little luck, Margaret would accept the arrangement and his long-term protection without further discussion. She was older than the last time he had proposed to her, and he hoped that, now she had been led to believe that she had been let down by Thornton, she would appreciate that there was more to a successful match than merely love.

John wondered if he had ever been as nervous in his life as he walked up Harley Street, and his thoughts were in a muddle. Margaret may not even be there, or he might not be admitted. It was possible that she wouldn't want to see him and decline his call, but there was a chance that she would. He simply had to try.

Margaret and Edith were in the drawing room instead of pursuing their usual afternoon activities. Edith and Mrs Shaw usually enjoyed a carriage ride after lunch followed by a rest prior to dinner, while Margaret preferred to accompany the nanny and baby Sholto on their afternoon walk instead. Today, however, Aunt Shaw had retired to her room, and Edith had insisted that Margaret join her to do some sewing. Edith was concerned about her cousin. In the past few days, Margaret had been in as distressed a state as when she had first come to London six months ago. Her eyes were constantly puffy from crying, and she had been so miserable that she had excused herself from attending dinner to spend her evenings in solitude. Margaret had just transferred into half-mourning, a state that Edith thought would have brought a measure of cheer, but she wondered if this had precipitated Margaret's distress.

Edith and her husband had discussed the relevance of Margaret's affinity with her patterned cotton handkerchiefs, which the Captain had linked to the charismatic Mr Thornton, whom he was certain had been eager to see Margaret on the afternoon of the investors meeting. Edith and Sholto remembered that Margaret had made a fuss about wanting to write to him when she had first arrived, and now felt sure that Margaret was in love with this man. It had come as a disappointment to the Lennoxes that Margaret was not attracted to Henry, but despite spending considerable time in each other's company, Margaret had shown no inclination towards him.

The realisation that her affections were engaged elsewhere made it now perfectly understandable that Margaret was not interested one bit in poor Henry, who had appeared to be quite agitated at Margaret's absence from dinner for the past two days. Edith was a little upset that Margaret had not confided in her about the love she held for Mr Thornton, and wondered if she may have done so if he had sought her out in London. Edith wanted Margaret's happiness, but without Mr Thornton close at hand there was little that she or Sholto could do to bring the unfortunate pair together.

The two ladies had received a pot of tea, and were engrossed in their pastime when they heard the distant tinkle of the doorbell. A moment later, the butler entered the room.

'Miss Hale, there is a gentleman who wishes to see you,' he said, with his eyes fixed on the middle distance as he addressed the room in general.

'A gentleman?' asked Margaret, and Edith looked up from her sewing too with mild curiosity.

'A … Mr Thornton, miss,' said the servant, reading the name from the calling card on the silver tray in his hand. Margaret and Edith both stilled, stunned into silence as, for an instant, the world seemed to stop.

'Here?' asked Margaret tremulously.

'Indeed, miss.'

Both ladies rose simultaneously.

'Thank you,' said Margaret. 'I should be delighted to receive Mr Thornton's call.'

The butler's eyebrows lifted almost imperceptibly, and he withdrew to bring Mr Thornton to the drawing room. Margaret smoothed her skirt and patted her hair in readiness to receive this most unexpected visitor. Edith clasped her hand for a second, and squeezed her support to Margaret.

He walked into the room with his usual bearing, exhibiting no hint of the anguish he harboured. Even though the Captain had described Mr Thornton to his wife she was still somewhat surprised to see him in the flesh and experience his presence. Margaret was equally awed by his appearance. Against the backdrop of Aunt Shaw's impeccable yet fashionably ornate room, he looked even more impressive than Margaret remembered. Taller. Blacker. He held his gloves and hat in his hands.

John's eyes eagerly fell upon Margaret, and immediately recognised the tell-tale signs on her face; she had been crying. He noticed that she was in half-mourning and was dressed plainly, as was usual, wearing a white muslin blouse, worn with a brooch at the neck and a grey skirt.

'Miss Hale,' he said, bowing respectfully.

'Mr Thornton,' she replied with a small curtsy. 'May I introduce my cousin, Mrs Edith Lennox,' she said, turning to Edith.

'Good afternoon, Mrs Lennox. I have had the pleasure of meeting your husband a time or two. He was most kind to me earlier this week when I found myself quite in need of a friendly face.'

'Indeed, Mr Thornton. How lovely to meet you. Oh dear. I must apologise. Please do excuse me Mr Thornton, Margaret dear, I forgot that I was supposed to … to … be with the baby,' Edith said, and hastily exited the room, leaving Margaret and John to first stare after her then back at each other. She saw his eyelashes flutter as he blinked. He was nervous.

'I hope I am not disturbing you, Miss Hale,' he said. She was indeed disturbed. 'I apologise for attending unexpectedly but I was in the area … and … I thought. Well. I simply wanted to.' He gifted her one of his bashful smiles that she remembered so well from when they had been building their friendship.

'I am pleased that you called. Truly. Please say you will stay for some tea?'

'I will, thank you.' John was elated at the reception Miss Hale had granted him, which was so different from when he had seen her just a few days before.

Margaret and John sat in the drawing room with a small table between them where the tea tray was situated. John quelled the thoughts of taking the seat next to her on the settee.

'Please do tell me about the mill. And your mother and Mrs Watson. Are they well? And dear Nicholas and Mary and the children. I wrote to them but received no reply. Of course, the postal fee may have been too much for them. I do understand that. I wondered if, well, now that I am gone from Milton, that they don't think of me anymore?'

she said, and John's heart swelled. She was so much as he remembered her, and he rushed to answer her questions.

'Mother and Fanny are well. Fanny has been very helpful to me recently, and we have grown closer, which has given me a great deal of pleasure. Mother will be moving to live with my sister and Watson shortly, so perhaps Fanny will not like me quite so much then,' he said with a small hesitant smile, as he attempted to make Miss Hale smile too; it worked quite delightfully.

John decided to test his theory about the letters, and braced himself for the shattering news that she had received them after all.

'The mill is much as I have explained in my letters. We survive,' he said.

Margaret frowned.

John continued, 'Higgins and the children tried hard to write a letter to you that you would like. I believe it took several drafts to concoct a Christmas message that they felt worthy of you. I sent it with the children's drawings and my card. You didn't get them?' he said, and let his words seep into her brain.

Margaret stood up sharply, her knee knocking the small table causing a clattering of the teacups and saucers, and John reached forwards to steady it. Margaret stood staring at him, her heart clamouring beneath her breast.

'Letters?' She said simply. 'How many letters?'

'I have written to you every two weeks, latterly with mainly an update on the mill and Bertie.' He didn't need to search her face to know that she had not received them. It was as clear as day, and his heart soared at the realisation. However, Miss Hale had gone quite white, and he wondered if the revelation was too much for her. He stood and walked around the table, and taking her gently by the shoulders, he guided her back to the sitting position and he took the much longed for seat beside her.

'You have not received any of them? None?' he asked.

She shook her head slowly, her eyes becoming sparkly before a large solitary tear spilled over, and he watched its silvery path down her pale skin until it touched her mouth.

'Have I been deceived?' she whispered, engaging his limpid blue eyes.

'Perhaps there's an explanation?' he tried, though even to him it appeared preposterous. 'Perhaps it was to protect you in your mourning period. Mr Lennox explained—'

Margaret was on her feet again, making the china clatter once more and the tea slop over into the saucers. She swiped at her tears angrily.

'What did Mr Lennox explain? What do my affairs, my well-being, have to do with him?'

John stood. 'Well … the mill,' he answered simply.

'What about the mill?' she replied hotly, though he knew that her anger was not directed at him. Just then, the sound of footsteps coming down the stairs and into the hallway near to the drawing room could be heard followed by a male voice conversing with a member of the staff. Margaret and John immediately discerned its owner to be none other than Henry Lennox.

'Quick,' said Margaret impulsively, and she grabbed John by the hand and pulled him towards another door which led into the adjoining back drawing room, and they crept through, closing the door behind them. John and Margaret stood in silence, so close that he was aware of her evocative delicate rose scent that he had missed so much. They heard Henry enter the drawing room next door, and Margaret, realising she was still holding Mr Thornton's hand, lifted her other hand and put a finger to her lips indicating the need for their continued quiet, and drew him with her as she tiptoed through an adjacent door that connected the back drawing room to the hall. She led him down the rear staircase to the kitchen and let him out into the back street.

'Mr Thornton, I would like to speak with you further about this.' In the cold wintry air, she finally let go of his hand. 'I walk almost every day to Park Crescent gardens with my baby nephew Sholto and his nanny.' And with that she slipped back into the house.

John stood in the alley staring at the door. In a daze he walked towards the train station and once there he found a vacant bench and sat looking at his hand, the hand Margaret had held. He turned their conversation over in his head and waited for Higgins and their train back to Milton.

Chapter 22

The next afternoon was dark with low steel-coloured clouds shedding drizzle across the capital. John sat on a bench in the gardens of Park Crescent under both his umbrella and a tree for protection from the elements, as he envisioned he might be there all afternoon. He had no idea when, or even if, Margaret would come. He suspected that the dismal weather might prevent her daily walk with the nanny, but he could not bear the thought of her coming to the park with hope of seeing him, and being disappointed that he was not there.

John had imparted the events at Harley Street to Higgins on the way home the previous evening, and initially he was heartened by Miss Hale's reception of him. But now that he was sitting alone, the notion nibbled away at his confidence that perhaps she would have second thoughts, and may not wish to see him after all. Although their conversation had been interrupted, Margaret had not seemed to know about her association with the mill. The thought was astonishing, yet it seemed that information about Miss Hale's inheritance may have been kept from her. John and Higgins had discussed the quite unbelievable theory at length and neither man could identify a single credible reason why that may be the case. There was no doubt that his letters had been concealed from Miss Hale, and he wondered if her family had provided a plausible reason for the deception. Their word would be more worthy to her than his. Whether Miss Hale had received an explanation or not, John had no alternative as he was firm in his decision – he would come every day until he could see her. Miss Hale had said she wanted to speak to him and he would help her even if his hopes of regaining her affections came to nought.

Fortunately, the gardens were quite small, and one could see almost across the whole area which had newly planted shrubbery and only small clumps of young trees blocking the view here and there. John sat on the bench from twelve midday until the light faded and it was so dark that he could no longer see the time on his pocket watch. He stood up, stiff from the inactivity, and low in spirits from the gradual realisation as the afternoon had worn on that she would not come. He was positively frozen to the core, and he forced himself into a brisk pace to warm himself up on his way back to the train station.

The following morning, much to his mother's surprise, John stated his intention to travel once again to London. This time he put on an extra pair of socks and his long underwear. He also tucked in a woollen scarf under his coat, and procured some sandwiches from the cook for the journey home.

When John entered the park, just before twelve midday, it was raining lightly again. But in the distance he could see a patch of blue sky, and he prayed that the dark clouds would soon dissipate, and in doing so, perhaps increase the chances of Margaret visiting the gardens that day.

Despite his contingency planning for the freezing conditions, John didn't feel much warmer than the day before. Though the rain had stopped it was still perishingly cold, but he would not leave his post while he waited. His eyes continually surveyed the view for his quarry, and then, finally, his heart skipped a beat – she was there. At the far entrance to the park, a lady, who was unmistakably Margaret, was walking next to a grey uniformed woman pushing a perambulator. As they gradually neared his vantage point John stood up, took a breath, and walked purposefully towards the ladies.

Margaret had spotted him as soon as she had arrived, indeed, he was hard to miss. As he walked towards them, Margaret couldn't hold back her smile of gratitude. He had not let her down. He had understood her and had come. For her.

'Good afternoon, Miss Hale,' John said, tipping his hat and extended his greeting to the nanny with a nod. 'He's a fine fellow,' he said, looking down into the pram where baby Sholto lay sleeping. The nanny and Margaret both smiled fondly at the baby, agreeing that he was.

'Miss Hale, may I walk with you for a moment?' asked John, and he held out his elbow for her to take.

'Certainly,' she replied, and took his arm, then the two of them walked ahead and out of earshot of the nanny.

'Mr Thornton! Thank you for coming. I was not sure that you would, but I am so glad of it. I have gone over and

273

over what you said to me just two days ago and I cannot reconcile it.'

'I too have had our conversation in my thoughts constantly since we met. I hope you won't be angry with me, but I have disclosed it to Higgins. He will keep our confidence.'

'Oh, dear Nicholas. I am glad,' she said, and squeezed his arm, sending little tingles of happiness straight to his heart.

'Miss Hale, Higgins and I can make neither head nor tail of the matter. If Mr Lennox withheld our letters to you, perhaps to protect you from our friendship tainting you in some way, then it seems high-handed indeed. May I ask if there is an understanding between you and Mr Lennox? I know it is ungentlemanly of me to ask, but I wondered if he was taking responsibility for you in advance of a permanent arrangement?'

'Let me assure you, Mr Thornton, there is no understanding between Mr Lennox and I. Never could there be. I have been most explicit on that matter with him long ago, and if I had been considering an attachment to him, which I have not, then this deceit would completely have prevented any chance of that happening,' she said indignantly.

John allowed himself a little smile at Margaret's feistiness, and the pink that it brought to her cheeks. Her admission informed John that he had not been the only recipient of her refusal, and he briefly felt sorry for the man; he could understand the pain that he must have endured. He considered that this extra piece of information might be a clue. Mr Lennox had previously wanted to marry Miss Hale, so perhaps his actions now were driven by his continuing affection for her. It would make sense that if Lennox knew of John's fondness for Margaret, then keeping those letters from her would be to his benefit.

'Miss Hale, if I may approach this at a tangent,' John began. 'What do you know about Mr Bell's heirs? In particular, the new owner of Marlborough Mills?'

'Nothing. I mean, I know that Henry has been dealing with the legalities as Mr Bell's lawyer, but that is all. Mr Bell had no close family that I was ever aware of, so I assumed he had left his estate to charitable organisations or his college. Perhaps that has made it more complex for Henry?' Margaret glanced at John while she was talking. She could see his slightly stubbled jaw tensing. 'But how is this related to Henry not giving me your letters or those from Nicholas. I know it is not usual for single women to receive correspondence from unattached men but,' her chin rose defiantly, 'he is not my father, brother or husband! He has no right to withhold things from me or to decide for me.' Margaret halted. 'Do you think it was my aunt's doing?' she asked.

By now they were close to John's bench. 'If you please, would you sit for a moment?' he asked, and the nanny with baby Sholto passed by and headed in the direction of a small pond. John and Margaret sat side by side on the form, her arm still through his. He placed his gloved hand upon hers gently, not so hard as to make her keep it there, but just to indicate that it was his wish that she did so, and she complied.

'Miss Hale, I think it is becoming clearer why Mr Lennox has manipulated our correspondence,' he said with a deep sigh. 'Mr Bell did leave at least part of his estate to someone. I believe that the identity of this person is the reason why Mr Lennox has concealed our letters and my updates on the mill from you. I think he means to isolate you in case his secret is revealed.'

'His secret? Whatever do you mean?'

John pressed her hand a little more firmly, aware of the shocking news he was about to impart.

'Miss Hale, Mr Bell left Marlborough Mills to you.' John became silent, his eyes searching her beautiful face for signs of distress.

'Me?' she whispered. Cloudy grey eyes fixed onto blue. He nodded once slowly.

'I am the owner of Marlborough Mills?' she said incredulously.

'Yes, he told me the last time he was in Milton. In retrospect I think that, as Mr Lennox knows that Mr Bell made me privy to this information, he must keep us apart.'

'But why? And why did Mr Bell not tell me?' she gasped, clutching now at Mr Thornton's arm.

The nanny then approached. 'Beg pardon, miss, but I must get Master Sholto back now.'

'Yes, of course. You go ahead and I will follow directly,' said Margaret.

Once the nanny was far enough away not to overhear their conversation, John replied, 'I presume Mr Bell didn't want to distress you as he told me in confidence, and I promised him not to speak of it while he lived.

He intimated that he was ill, but of course the accident was unexpected. Why Mr Lennox has concealed your ownership of Marlborough Mills, I just don't know.'

John stood to follow the nanny towards the exit of the park and then back to Harley Street, with the delight of Miss Hale on his arm. They walked in silence while the information that Mr Thornton had told her swam in her head. She wondered if all of the Lennoxes and Aunt Shaw were involved in the deception, and she made a decision.

'I can't go back. Not now. Will you help me? Let me come back to Milton?'

John was shocked and excited in equal measure at her words, but he understood the gravity of her suggestion and the potential for harm it could cause her. However, if she needed him, he would not let her down.

'There is a train in thirty-five minutes,' he said uncertainly, checking his pocket watch. 'You will be compromised travelling back with me. I don't want to injure you.'

Margaret felt sick. In the face of adversity, it appeared that he would not help her.

But a moment later he said, 'I have it! It is still a risk, but it's the best I can think of. I will ensure your safe transfer onto the next train to Milton, and I shall board the following one so that you are not harmed by us travelling together. I will send a telegram to Fanny to meet you at the station and take you to her house. Then tomorrow, when we are rested and able to think clearly, we can discuss this again. Do you agree?'

Margaret took his hands in hers and held on tight. His assistance when she needed it, needed him, meant more than she could put into words. He recognised the sparkling pools in her eyes as the prelude to tears, and quickly retrieved his handkerchief for her.

'You must be strong for now, Miss Hale if you are certain of this plan of action, at least until you get to Fanny's. We must not draw any attention to ourselves so that we evade detection until you are safe in Milton, and we can sort this mess out.'

Margaret lifted her chin, mopped her eyes and thrust his handkerchief into her pocket. She knew he was right, and she summoned up her courage. She would do her best to match Mr Thornton's fighting spirit. The couple then walked sedately out of the park, but instead of turning towards Harley Street, they turned right, and walked towards a stand of hansom cabs to take one to the train station.

On arrival at Harley Street, the nanny, who was quite shaken by Miss Hale's departure with the stranger and also the thought that she might somehow be judged to be complicit, immediately sought out Mrs Lennox and the Captain in their private sitting room.

'I need to speak with you urgently!' exclaimed the nanny, causing instant fear in both of the baby's parents as they assumed some misfortune had befallen their cherished child. 'Oh no, he is well. It's not Master Sholto but Miss Hale that I must speak with you about.'

The nanny was invited into the sitting room where she gave her explanation of encountering a gentleman on arrival at the gardens, whom Miss Hale had appeared to know. She told Captain and Mrs Lennox, who were both enthralled by her tale, that Miss Hale and the man had walked and talked and sat for a little while. Then, when it was time to return home, Miss Hale and the stranger had disappeared.

Edith and the Captain shared a brief glance.

'It is quite all right, nanny,' said Edith with feigned calmness. 'Was he very tall with dark hair? Is that how you would describe him?'

'Oh yes, Mrs Lennox. He was fearfully handsome if I might say.'

Nanny was dismissed, and Edith and Sholto, who were both captivated by the romance of Margaret and Mr Thornton's secret long-standing affection for one another, considered what to do. They wondered if perhaps Mr Thornton and Margaret were on their way to Scotland for an elopement. They decided that while they needed to afford the couple a little time to make their escape, they probably should make an effort to appear to have looked for them. Edith would have liked to find them just to wish them well. However, she knew that her mother would not sanction their match and that Margaret's reputation would suffer, especially if a swift marriage did not take place. Edith speculated that Margaret's half-mourning period could well be given as the reason for a quiet wedding. Edith and Sholto decided that they must at least go to the train station, as that would appease her mother that they had made an attempt to recover Margaret.

On their arrival at Euston, Mr Thornton was easy to spot as he exited the telegraph office and headed to the platform, where he chose an unoccupied bench and sat in solitude.

'Mr Thornton,' said Edith. John stood.

'Mrs Lennox, Captain,' he said, tipping his hat.

'Where is Margaret? Is she safe?'

'Quite safe. I put her on the train to Milton not ten minutes ago. She joined a first-class carriage with a respectable family travelling as far as Milton, so she is not alone. I have telegraphed my sister Fanny, who will receive her at Milton-Northern and keep her in her care. My sister and her husband are trustworthy, and Miss Hale has made their acquaintance several times before. I shall get the next train and go to my own home tonight.'

'Why did you not travel with her?' asked the Captain, somewhat confused.

'I wanted to protect her reputation as best I could. I know it's not ideal, but I could see no alternative on the spur of the moment. She wanted to come with me, home to Milton, and I would not refuse her.'

The Captain held out his hand in a gesture of solidarity, and John shook it. 'Then we shall keep your secret until you are on your way. There will be a commotion for certain, but Mother Shaw will come around eventually. Oh! You are planning to marry?'

'Miss Hale needs some time to think. I have presented her with some troubling information that has been concealed from her, and I shan't impose my wishes on her while she is in distress.'

Margaret had been quite stoic on the train after Mr Thornton had secured her safe passage with a family named Beatwell. After introductions had been exchanged and the journey was in motion, Mr Beatwell explained to her his occupation as a civil engineer designing the new system of sewers for Milton. Mrs Beatwell tutted at her husband for fear of affronting the young gentlewoman with his talk, but Margaret was diverted. She smiled to herself, knowing that Mr Thornton would have been quite fascinated by Mr Beatwell's expertise in the improvements underway in Milton. Before their meeting at the station, Mr Thornton had no knowledge of Mr Beatwell nor his family, but John was a well-known and somewhat formidable figure in the town, and the Beatwells felt most privileged to have been asked by him for their assistance. Of course, they didn't know the strange situation that Margaret found herself in, nor the fact that she travelled without luggage. Margaret was grateful for their kindness in welcoming her into their party, and she was able to ride comfortably without the scrutiny that she might have endured without their companionship.

When they felt an adequate time had elapsed, Edith and Sholto informed Mrs Shaw about Margaret's flight from London, how they had seen Mr Thornton at the station, and that he had given them the reassuring news that Margaret and her reputation were safe. Mrs Shaw had naturally been outraged, but surprisingly not to the same extent as Henry, who had been apoplectic with rage at Mr Thornton's apparent high-handedness in removing his 'betrothed' to Milton. Edith and the Captain were aghast at Henry's announcement of an attachment to Margaret. They wondered if this might be the disturbing information that Mr Thornton had mentioned, and had caused Margaret to ask for his assistance in fleeing.

'Betrothed, Henry? Goodness, I had no idea! Margaret never said a word,' said Edith incredulously.

'I do not believe that is the correct term,' interrupted Mrs Shaw, who was so irritated at the disappearance of her niece with a manufacturer, that Henry's blathering only heightened her ire and gave rise to an urge to put him in his place. 'I have given you my blessing to court Margaret, but a betrothal is not appropriate at this time as I have already told you. She is in mourning, don't forget. And of course, Margaret must agree. By the fact that she has up and left with Mr Thornton I wonder if you are a little presumptuous?'

Henry had been seething and left the house in such a high state of anxiety that Mrs Shaw believed that he was utterly desperate to marry Margaret. This left her feeling both cross with her niece for rebuffing Henry's affections, and vexed with Henry for his manner in approaching Margaret, as he had seemingly pushed her into the path of Mr Thornton. It was decided that Mrs Shaw, Edith and the Captain would travel up to Milton the next day. Much to Mrs Shaw's consternation, Edith had insisted on arranging for Margaret's travel trunks to be packed and taken with them, in case she planned to stay in Milton for some time, if not forever.

John sat in his coach on the train, rattling towards Milton-Northern. Miss Hale, who had set off an hour ahead of him, would already be there. It would be an interesting conversation with his mother, and Fanny for that matter. However, propriety had been maintained as best he could. He mused on the repercussions that must be occurring at Mrs Shaw's house. He wondered how Captain and Mrs Lennox had kept Miss Hale's whereabouts secret until his train was on its way. He was grateful that they were on her side. On their side. He even allowed himself to think that if her feelings for him were renewed, it would be a great comfort to Miss Hale knowing that Mrs Lennox and the Captain were in support of their match.

John suspected that Henry Lennox would not easily accept Miss Hale's departure to the North, and he fully expected him to come to Milton that very night. He would have to recount the events, as far as he knew them, to his mother as soon as he got home. But the main thing was that Margaret was out of Lennox's clutches at Fanny's home. He would not find her, at least not tonight.

It was late when John eventually entered his front door, and the house was dark and silent except for the steady ticking of the grandfather clock in the entrance hall. Bertie padded softly to greet him and bestowed loving kisses on his master. Hannah, oblivious to any of the day's events, except for another curious trip by John to London, had waited up for her son to return home safely, and she called him through into the drawing room.

'You're late, son. I expected you an hour ago at the latest. Is all well?'

'Is all well? Mother, I don't know where to begin.' Mother and son sat together, with Bertie pressed against John's legs and his muzzle upon his master's knee, and illuminated by only the golden glow of a single lamp, John described the events of the last few days as best he could.

Hannah Thornton listened intently to her son's explanation. 'Well!' she said. 'That girl can get in a mess and no mistaking.'

'Mother …' he warned, his voice a low rumble.

Not usually a tactile woman, Hannah reached to pat John's hand to calm him. He wondered fleetingly about the power and diverse reactions that such a simple gesture had on a man's emotions. He had not comprehended before his need to touch and be touched, and his innate desire for physical affection that had for so long been suppressed.

'It's not her doing, I can see that, but you have to admit there is never a dull moment when Miss Hale is involved,' Hannah said, in her usual prickly manner. John found it quite comforting, as though part of the world remained steady, and a slow smile crept its way across his face.

'You do realise that Fanny couldn't keep a secret if her life depended upon it,' Hannah said wryly.

'What secret is there to tell, Mother? Miss Hale is the owner of Marlborough Mills. Everyone should know it, as it's the truth. She is staying with Fanny while she is in Milton. There is nothing wrong with that,' he reasoned.

'She walked away from her family, who have been manipulating her for some unknown reason, and got the train to Milton with no possessions to her name. Tell me that is a titbit that Fanny will not spread by noon tomorrow at the latest,' Hannah responded.

John grimaced. 'I will speak to Fanny. But it's the truth, and while the gossips may be diverted by the information, it will not harm Miss Hale's reputation. Mother, I must tell you. If I were Lennox and my covert plans had been thwarted, I would catch the first available train to Milton. So, he may turn up tonight. We need to be prepared.'

'Go to bed, son. You'll need your wits about you tomorrow,' Hannah said. 'You leave him to me.'

At eleven forty-five that night, pounding on the front door of Marlborough House woke Hannah as she dozed in the drawing room. Bertie, sensing that something was wrong, had decided to stay with her rather than follow his master to bed. He was startled by the knocking at the door and, quite unusually, he growled. *Good,* thought Hannah. *It's about time the beast earned his crust.* Hannah knew that the dog had not a single fierce bone in his body due to the affection that John both lavished on him and received in return, but a would-be intruder was not to know that. *Keep that up my boy.* A wicked glint flickered in her steely eyes, and she struggled to subdue the smirk from her face as she approached the door to open it. She slid the chain bolt into place so that she couldn't be overpowered.

Hannah opened the door a sliver. 'Who goes there, hammering at my front door at this time of night?' she said, in her harshest tone.

'Henry Lennox. I have come for Miss Hale. I know you are holding her against her will and I have come to remove her,' shouted Henry, affecting a tone of authority.

'I have not seen Miss Hale for some six months and can assure you she is not here. Be on your way,' she said, shutting the door. Henry put his foot in the gap preventing Hannah from closing it.

'She is here. I know it,' he insisted. Bertie barked and snarled, baring his teeth to Hannah's aggressor until Henry withdrew his foot.

'I am no liar, Mr Lennox. I have not seen Miss Hale and she is not here. Fetch the constabulary if you wish. I have nothing to hide. Now be on your way,' said Hannah, closing the door firmly shut, and loudly applying the bolts. She knelt down and nuzzled Bertie. 'Good boy,' she said, patting his head while his tail created a draft of cold air as he wagged it furiously at the unexpected attention. 'Let's get you a treat,' Hannah said, and led him to the kitchen.

Henry was not going to lose Margaret now, nor her fortune that had been so close to his grasp. The town was quiet as its workers were long in their beds in preparation for the next working day so, with no alternative to him, Henry Lennox walked the streets of Milton until he found a hotel in which to spend the night.

Chapter 23

John was awake in advance of the early morning whistle. He was shaved and dressed before the maid had finished setting out the breakfast, and he was grateful to see his mother already in the dining room, equally eager to see him. Hannah recounted to him her altercation with Mr Lennox the previous evening, including Bertie's intervention, which earned the dog a piece of bacon from the breakfast table. John went straight to his mill office to get some work done before he could break off to see Miss Hale. He felt invigorated, not only by her proximity, but also with the knowledge that he would see her again shortly.

When the workers started filing in through the great mill gates to begin their daily work, John spotted Higgins and beckoned him to come over to the office. John told him the facts, from meeting Margaret in the park, their journey back, the apparent support of Captain and Mrs Lennox, and Henry Lennox's arrival at Marlborough House late last night. Higgins was not an educated man, but he was not daft either; he grasped the whole of the yarn.

'He'll be back. An' sharpish I'll bet.' he said.

Margaret could hear the sounds of the house coming to life. The faint thud of a door in the distance. Footsteps. Muffled chatter. But these were not the familiar sounds of Harley Street. She was warmly cocooned, lying awake in a guest room at Fanny and John Watson's house, having walked away from her own family's protection the afternoon before. Mr and Mrs Watson had collected her from Milton-Northern station, just as Mr Thornton had told her they would. Both husband and wife had been very kind, particularly Fanny, who had babbled away as if they were old friends, and Margaret was glad. She was relieved that Fanny was attempting to put her at ease when Margaret herself felt quite fragile.

Margaret's room at the Watsons' was lovely; it was both comfortable and modern. Fanny had clearly spared none of Mr Watson's purse on the luxurious bed linens, wallpaper and drapes. Margaret looked over to her clothes, folded neatly on a chair. How dull and drab they looked against Fanny's pretty decorations. She would need to wear them again today, and that brought home to her the gravity of her decision yesterday afternoon, when she had decided to walk away from the shelter of Aunt Shaw's house and return to Milton with literally nothing but the clothes she wore. Although she felt in her heart that it was the right thing to do, she wondered if there was a simple explanation for Henry's apparent deception. According to Mr Thornton, she was the owner of Marlborough Mills, which was curious indeed, and she wondered what Mr Bell had meant by bequeathing her the mill. Had he seen a connection between her and Mr Thornton, or was it merely coincidence?

Being the owner of the mill also meant that she had an income. While she had no idea how much that might be, she pondered that, even if Mr Thornton had no plans to repeat his offer, she now had a measure of independence and would not be solely reliant on her aunt and the Lennoxes. She again wondered what the motive might be for her family to keep this from her. Surely they would see the merit of her not being a burden to them in the future. It was a revelation to realise that the control she had long wished for was no longer as attractive to her as a partnership of affection would be, and she hoped above all else that Mr Thornton might feel the same way.

There was a gentle knock on the door, and the maid brought in a breakfast tray. 'Mrs Watson thought you might prefer breakfast in bed, miss,' she said. 'Then I'll come and help you get ready, as Mrs Watson says you'll be expecting visitors.'

Margaret was touched by Fanny's considerate actions, and she had to agree, it was likely that she would receive several visitors that day. She knew that Mr Thornton, and perhaps Nicholas, would want to meet with her to discuss the peculiar business of Marlborough Mills. She expected Henry might also appear and offer her the explanation that she deserved. Unbeknown to Margaret, her Aunt Shaw, Edith and the Captain were also journeying to see her. It was going to be a trying and eventful day for all of them.

∽

At nine o'clock a telegram was delivered to Marlborough House, and John was summoned home to receive it. He read it aloud to his mother. It informed them that the Lennoxes and Mrs Shaw were even now travelling towards the North to meet with them. Mother and son had only just started discussing how best to manage their influx of visitors when there was a sharp rap on the front door. John and Hannah were in no doubt as to who it would be at this early hour, and having composed themselves, they waited in the drawing room for the maid to introduce their visitor.

Henry Lennox burst into the room. 'Where is she?'

'Good morning, Mr Lennox,' said John calmly, and fluffed Bertie's ears to pacify him.

'I said, where is she? You have absconded with my intended and I must recover her.'

Henry's words all but cleaved John's heart in two and he momentarily faltered. He was still amazed that she had asked to come back to Milton with him, and his insecurity and feelings of inferiority resurfaced. He must remember that she had chosen Milton, not him.

Hannah was not so easily put off. It had taken many months for her to come to terms with the fact that John still harboured a passionate love for Miss Hale. Further mettle had been required to put to one side her own opinion that Miss Hale did not deserve her son. His mysterious trips to London, followed by the revelations from the night before, had cemented her belief that there was nothing to be done other than to accept it. If John could forgive the girl for rejecting him those many months ago, then she must also, or she would lose her own special place in his heart. If her son wanted Miss Hale, then she would do her damnedest to help him to get his true love. If he would fight for Miss Hale, then she would fight for her too.

'I wonder at Miss Hale's commitment to this attachment that you claim Mr Lennox, seeing as she has willingly left London to return to us and our town,' said Hannah icily, with her chest puffed out and hands clasped beneath her bosom.

'Miss Hale's aunt, who is also her guardian, has approved the match. So, I repeat, where is she?'

John responded with controlled civility, 'I have received a telegram from Captain and Mrs Lennox advising that they and Mrs Shaw will arrive at Milton on the one-fifteen. So, I propose that we all meet here, once they have had time for refreshment, at two-thirty.'

'And you will ensure Margaret will be here then?'

He would not force Miss Hale to do anything, nor would he presume to speak for her. 'I will ask Miss Hale to attend,' said John composedly, and Henry flounced out of the house.

John, Hannah and Bertie arrived at the Watsons' at ten-thirty, only because Hannah couldn't keep her son away from Miss Hale any longer. His agitation as the morning had progressed after the departure of Mr Lennox had Hannah completely on edge. John was torn between desperation to see Margaret again and apprehension. He worried that, in the cold light of day, she might regret her decision to return to Milton, and his inflated hopes that she might care for him again would be dashed. Henry Lennox had claimed an attachment to her, and yet she had told him, quite vehemently, the opposite. John resolved to trust Margaret. His frayed nerves were somewhat calmed on entering the Watsons' drawing room to find Miss Hale and Fanny looking relaxed, sitting comfortably and seemingly engaged in conversation.

'Miss Hale, Fanny,' said John, with a small bow. Any further polite discourse was prevented by Bertie who immediately recognised his mistress despite their long separation. He bounded up to her, tail wagging so hard that his whole body writhed. Margaret fell to her knees and accepted Bertie's kisses, and she in turn cuddled the wriggling dog. She was astounded at his growth. He had lost his puppy appearance, and was very handsome in his shiny black and white coat. He still wore his leather collar that Mr Thornton had once presented her with as a gift.

After their reunion was complete, John asked Bertie to sit, which he did, reversing up to Margaret so that he was nestled against her. When sitting with John, Bertie preferred to be very close, and it made him smile to think that Bertie's bond with Margaret had not been diminished by their forced separation. However, Margaret was not acquainted with Bertie's bad habits as yet. John's weakness for the dog had prevented him from dissuading Bertie from his love for ankles, and he prayed that Bertie would not take this opportunity to apply further evidence of affection for his mistress by seeking out his preferred site for bestowing kisses.

John was delighted that Miss Hale was in good spirits this morning. She was buoyed by Fanny's hospitality, and then further heartened by the news that John was able to impart regarding Sholto and Edith's assistance the previous night in temporarily concealing her departure to Milton. He didn't mention that the Lennoxes appeared to be in favour of their match. It seemed too presumptuous to bring it up at this time when he was not sure of her feelings for him.

It was agreed that Fanny would accompany Margaret to Marlborough House in readiness for their meeting with Mrs Shaw and all three Lennoxes. After a little while, and when all of the necessary information had been conveyed, John and his mother took their leave to get ready for their visitors. Fanny saw her mother and John to the door.

'Thank you, Fanny,' said John, kissing her cheek. 'I couldn't have helped her without you. Can you keep this tale to yourself?' he asked, intense brows drawn down in a frown. It felt wrong to find fault with her when she had done so much for him. Fanny slipped her arm through his.

'John, I may like tittle-tattle as much as the next young woman, but I will not harm you and I have no wish to injure Miss Hale. I rather like her. She likes my wallpaper.'

At two-thirty the drawing room at Marlborough House was almost at full capacity. There was a tangible air of anxiety in the room, and nervous chatter permeated the gathering. Mrs Shaw, Edith, Sholto and Fanny were impatient to learn the details of the mystery that had led to Margaret's flight to Milton. All those gathered together, bar one, wished for a happy outcome for Margaret, albeit that Hannah's wish for Margaret's happiness was primarily so that her son's heart would benefit in turn. Only Henry Lennox had a different goal. He wished for his own delectation in the form of possessing Margaret and, crucially, her fortune.

Hannah had arranged for refreshments to be provided for their guests out of courtesy, although none had an appetite. Nevertheless, the Thornton's hospitality would not be found wanting. The assembly chose their seats, unconsciously forming battle lines, with Margaret situated on the settee next to Fanny on her right, and flanked by the Thorntons and Bertie on her left. The Lennoxes and Mrs Shaw took the seats facing them, and Edith had the curious feeling that she and her husband were positioned on the wrong side.

John had also asked Nicholas Higgins to attend, as he could corroborate John's account of them going to Lennox's office and finding out that the correspondence between Margaret and himself had not been forwarded. He would keep his word to Josephine that her name would not be mentioned in the uncovering of the deception. Much to Hannah's relief, Nicholas had declined to participate in the meeting, understanding that his attendance would likely cause a distraction, and he remained in the hallway in case he was required to speak.

John began the discussion. His expression was grave, but he spoke plainly. 'It came to light yesterday that information on Miss Hale's inheritance of Marlborough Mills has been withheld from her,' he said, then paused. A few gasps punctuated the silence.

Mrs Shaw spoke up. 'My niece is the owner of your mill?' she asked, for clarity.

'Yes, Mrs Shaw. The land and the buildings,' John confirmed.

Mrs Shaw looked at her daughter and son-in-law who were equally perplexed. Fanny turned her questioning eyes to Miss Hale for confirmation, and Margaret verified John's claim with a simple nod of her head. Fanny reached for Miss Hale's hand to hold. The reactions of Margaret's family came as a great relief to her, as it was obvious that they were not party to the despicable deceit.

'Furthermore, letters from myself and other friends of Miss Hale's in Milton were concealed from her, discarded, as was her correspondence meant for me. Can you explain, Mr Lennox, how that came to be? And, why was Miss Hale not informed of her inheritance?'

'And I should like to know why you are Margaret's spokesman? Who appointed you? I am her attorney!' said Henry petulantly.

John's eyes narrowed and his countenance became glacial as he addressed his nemesis. 'Because you are the person who has duped Miss Hale. Your omission has led her to seek refuge with my family which, in turn, has led to us all being gathered in my drawing room this afternoon.

I am your host. Now then, Mr Lennox, please enlighten us as to why you have kept Miss Hale's inheritance from her.'

'It's not that simple,' said Henry. 'There are complications with Mr Bell's will, so it was not appropriate to tell Margaret at the time.'

'Complications? What kind of complications would cause a delay in informing her? It's been over six months.'

'Mr Bell's will has been … misplaced,' said Henry, grappling for some contrivance that would afford him more time.

'"Misplaced",' murmured several of those in the room with disbelief.

'Indeed. It is most regrettable,' said Henry.

Nicholas Higgins had moved into the doorway on hearing this latest announcement. John and Nicholas looked at each other. Unless Lennox was a complete idiot, something else was afoot, and both men suspected that Mr Bell's will held the answers. While the rest of the party discussed the astounding news that Henry had lost Mr Bell's will, John met Higgins in the hallway.

'I can't leave as it will raise suspicion, so you must go to the telegraph office now, Higgins. I don't believe for a moment that Mr Bell's will has been lost. It must hold in it some information that Lennox needs to conceal. We must not give him the opportunity to get back and hide it. I will draft a telegram to Mr Johnson, the senior partner at Lennox's law firm, and urge him to locate and safeguard the document. It's the best we can do. There must be something else, a detail we might have missed,' he said ruffling his hair.

With Higgins dispatched, John re-entered the drawing room where the excited conversation was subsiding. Henry appeared to have rallied after his announcement about Mr Bell's will.

'It is of no consequence to Margaret. She need not trouble herself with the details. I will take responsibility for her legal matters when she is my wife,' he said, looking straight at John with authority and triumph. 'Similarly, it was not prudent to allow Margaret to receive letters from a single man.'

John's eyes slid shut. She was engaged to Lennox after all. Yet she had told him that she was not! He pulled himself together just in time to see Margaret's hand as it connected sharply with a stinging smack against Henry's cheek. Not only was Margaret now standing, but Bertie had sprung to his feet, and his low rumbling growl warned Henry of the consequences of upsetting his mistress. Mrs Shaw and Edith gasped in horror at Margaret's unexpected outburst. Hannah on the other hand was delighted; Henry Lennox needed bringing down a peg or two. She was warming to Miss Hale by the second.

'How dare you be so presumptuous. I will not marry you Henry, just as I refused you in the past. Aunt,' she said, turning to Mrs Shaw, who was now dealing with the news that Henry had made a previous unsuccessful offer to Margaret, 'you cannot force me. Have you made arrangements behind my back?'

Mrs Shaw struggled to find the words. It was a situation she was not familiar with.

Margaret seized the opportunity to realise her dream. 'I accepted Mr Thornton's request for courtship immediately prior to my father's death, and I should like that to happen now that my deep mourning period has ended,' she said firmly, her chin lifted boldly.

'You can't be serious!' exclaimed Henry, still holding his hand against his smarting cheek, and glancing warily at the dog. 'You would choose this rough tradesman over a gentleman like me? He has nothing to offer you Margaret. I dare say it is weeks at the most before he won't even be able to put so much as bread on the table,' scoffed Henry, casting his superior glance around the assembled group, but all eyes were on Margaret.

'He may not be a gentleman by birth, but he is worth a hundred of you. He has never lied to me or forced me to do as I am told. He has helped me, and been kind, and does not impose his will upon me.' Margaret looked at John who was even more captivated by her spirited display than the rest of the party. The fact that she was championing him was wondrous.

'Are your wishes the same, Mr Thornton? Do you still care for me?' she asked.

The focus of everyone's attention now moved to Mr Thornton as he stepped towards Margaret and took her hands in his.

'I have been a fool. If only I had come to see you sooner or had written to you directly. I should have known that you would have replied to my letters, if only out of politeness, even if your wishes had changed.'

'But why would you think I would change my mind?'

'I thought that once you were back in sophisticated society you would recognise the deficiencies in the man I am.'

'I know the man you are, Mr Thornton. I knew then and I know now.'

Henry tried one last time. 'You want her for the mill! It is as clear as day. Margaret is no more than an object to you, a way to enhance your social standing and increase your monetary worth.'

As John and Miss Hale were occupied examining the intricacies of each other's eyes, Hannah took her opportunity to speak.

'But my son's friendship and offer to Miss Hale were not dependent on her inheritance of Marlborough Mills. His business is not reliant on owning the land or property. I should say it was more of a hindrance to him after Mr Bell's death, knowing that he would let Miss Hale down if he were to fail. To suggest Miss Hale and my son's attachment was influenced by her inheriting the mill at some future time of Mr Bell's sad demise is preposterous.'

John and Margaret were diverted from their thoughts of each other to the knowledge that Hannah was defending them in her unique and bristly way, and it warmed their hearts. John regained his focus on the conversation at hand.

'Mother is correct. Miss Hale's inheritance of the mill is not really of consequence. It is an investor I need, not a mill. Not that I am not pleased,' he said, tightly clasping her hands that were still in his.

This brought to mind the five hundred pounds that he had been led to believe Margaret had invested in the mill. A thought struck John like a bucketful of cold water. *Lennox*. Lennox had been stringing out the demise of Marlborough Mills for months. He had supplied just enough for John to continue to provide a living for his workers, a kind of living death of his business. Now he could see why. Lennox needed the mill to continue as, while John was working day and night to keep his head above the water, Lennox had power over him. As long as John struggled on the edge of bankruptcy, he was not a potential suitor for Margaret.

'You told me that Miss Hale was the investor who loaned me five hundred pounds. Is that so? Was it her money that you used without her knowledge?' he asked.

All eyes now shifted to Henry again. 'It made economic sense to keep the mill operating. The mill and land are worth little without a business paying rent.' Henry looked at his audience. 'Very well, I will admit it. I did conceal Margaret's ownership of Marlborough Mills as I wished to win her hand, and her inheritance would make her the quarry of every unattached London beau. I wanted to secure her before she became preyed upon by fortune hunters. I was protecting her.'

'But how would that have made a difference?' asked Edith, thoroughly engrossed in the spectacle before her, which outstripped any recent theatrical performance she had seen.

John agreed with Mrs Lennox, and could not initially make the connection between Marlborough Mills and Margaret becoming the prize that Henry described.

'You felt that Miss Hale's inheritance would make her more attractive, not only to me, but to other men? London gentlemen? Owning a mill in Milton is a fine thing to be sure, but would it increase Miss Hale's charm to others? Is there more to discover about your deception? Out with it, man!' he urged.

Henry realised he had let slip more detail than was wise. He was backed into a corner from where there appeared to be no escape. He had revealed too much, and with everyone's attention directed upon him he couldn't think of a plausible excuse. His carefully constructed plan was crumbling, and there was a danger that the whole truth would be uncovered. So, with seemingly no alternative, Henry decided to appease the gathering with a little more information, and acquire some more time to think. If the entire charade was to be exposed, it would not be today; he would not suffer the ignominy of such a public humiliation.

'She didn't just inherit the mill,' he mumbled, affecting contrition to add authenticity to his words.

'Sorry?' said Margaret, gripping John's hands so tightly her knuckles blanched.

'You didn't only inherit the mill. There was a bequest of some capital as well.'

'"Capital"?' repeated the gathering in unison.

'How much "capital"?' asked Margaret shakily.

'I forget,' said Henry absently, attempting to make little of the fact.

After an initial shocked silence there was a flurry of activity as the outrageous disclosure from Henry sank in. It was quite astounding that Henry was either utterly incompetent, or underhand and lacking in honour. Mrs Shaw began to fan herself and was attended to by Edith, the Captain approached Henry with a look of absolute disgust, and John manoeuvred Margaret back to her seat beside Fanny, as he was concerned she might faint. Meanwhile, a large smile spread across Hannah Thornton's face.

It was now clear to John that Lennox had been hiding Margaret's inheritance and waiting for her to finally agree to marry him so that her estate, one that she didn't even know was hers, would belong to Lennox when they married. In that case, it must be a sizeable amount for Lennox to have gone to such lengths to keep it secret.

John knelt in front of Margaret, her hands still clasped in his, offering her some of his strength. He spoke to her softly, and although he didn't whisper, his words were for her alone. 'You don't have to have me. This information changes everything. Do you need some time to think? The last thing I want is for you to feel forced into accepting my request for a courtship when you are going through such turmoil,' he said, longing for reassurance that her mind was unchanged, but needing her to be able to decide for herself.

She fixed her unblinking gaze upon his. 'It doesn't change what is important to me. I have not changed my mind,' she said. A slow smile grew upon John's face as he comprehended that his most fervent wish had been realised, and all other concerns fell away. She cared for him.

In the distance, the front door slammed as Henry took his leave. The noise broke the spell that the whole room had been mesmerised by, and the reality of the situation seeped into John's consciousness. He reluctantly removed his hands from Miss Hale's with one last reassuring squeeze. John stood and approached her aunt.

'May I have your permission to court Miss Hale, Mrs Shaw?' he asked quietly. A horrifying thought flitted across his mind that Mrs Shaw would not agree, and he glanced back at Margaret and saw that she was looking at her aunt with expectation. In fact, all eyes in the room were now firmly settled on Mrs Shaw as they collectively held their breaths in anticipation of her decision.

'Well, I can hardly refuse now, can I?' blustered Mrs Shaw, winning a hard hug and excited squeal from Edith, and such a dazzling smile from Mr Thornton that she thought she might actually swoon herself.

Mrs Shaw agreed to a six-month courtship, the ending of which would coincide with the completion of Margaret's half-mourning period. It was quite peculiar having the terms of their courtship discussed in front of the gathering in the drawing room at Marlborough House, and yet it had been such an extraordinary few days that no one appeared to think twice about it. John and Margaret had willingly agreed, so delighted were they that Mrs Shaw had consented at all. John had marvelled at Margaret's tenacity, as she argued that it would be unreasonable to conduct a lengthy courtship when separated by almost two-hundred miles, since they had endured both the same duration and distance already. Fanny's contribution to the discussion was to offer a remedy to the dilemma that the long distance posed; she offered Margaret a home in

Milton. This solution resulted in the greatest happiness for the courting couple. As John had already broken the boundary of respectability by holding Margaret's hand, and in doing so again might lower Mrs Shaw's opinion of him, John expressed his feelings by smothering Fanny in a fierce embrace as an outlet for his thanks and affection.

Chapter 24

he was reminded that Mr Thornton, a man unknown to
him, should seek aspersions on his company's legal
activities. However, when he had gained access to the
... Mr Bell [illegible] to his bank
... when in answer's name. Mr Lennox [illegible] these
... had been ... to Mr ... several
... [illegible] sought been there who to affect

Mrs Shaw, the Captain and Mrs Lennox returned to
London the day after the meeting at Marlborough House.
Far from a tearful parting, Margaret was radiant as she
stood on the train platform to wave her relatives off, her
arm through John's and Bertie at their feet. The courting
couple walked back to Marlborough Mills, arm in arm,
attracting the attention of the townsfolk they passed who
muttered and twittered about the return of Miss Hale, and
the apparent loss of Mr Thornton to the maidens of Milton.

John had received a reply from Mr Johnson to his
hastily sent telegram, advising him that the will of Mr
Bell (deceased) had been located and was secure, and
arrangements were made for Margaret to attend the official
reading of the document. Mr Johnson had asked for a two
week delay to the meeting so that he could conduct an
internal investigation into the highly unusual management
of Mr Bell's will. And so a date was set for a fortnight
hence, and it was agreed that John would accompany
Margaret to London, with Fanny as chaperone.

Mr Johnson had been astounded to receive Mr
Thornton's telegram requesting that he identify the
whereabouts of Mr Bell's will and safeguard it. At first

he was affronted that Mr Thornton, a man unknown to him, should cast aspersions on his company's legal activities. However, when he had gained access to the will, and latterly the Mr Bell (deceased) folder, Mr Johnson spent a significant part of the evening attempting to understand what in heaven's name Mr Lennox had been doing. Josephine had been alerted to the exposure of Mr Lennox's deception, as she had been the one to accept delivery of Mr Thornton's telegram, and then later she spied Mr Johnson searching through Mr Lennox's office. It was easy for her to identify the document folder as Mr Bell's that Mr Johnson had taken back to his office to peruse.

Henry had arrived back in the capital and travelled immediately to his office, which by that time was deserted. He was horrified to find that not only was Mr Bell's folder missing, but so was the will. He had sat at his desk in a stupor. It was over. He had failed. The question now was how wide ranging his losses would be. Not only had Margaret and her money slipped from his grasp, but it was likely that his job and good name were in jeopardy too.

Margaret and John attempted to devise a routine in order to spend time together which was acceptable both personally and societally. Although it was less than two weeks since their courtship had been sanctioned, John in particular was beginning to feel the strain of perpetually being under the watchful eye of others, whether that be his mother, sister, brother-in-law, mill masters, employees, or Milton citizens in general, gawking at him and Margaret when they were in each other's company. The relative freedom that they had been allowed in the past by Mr Hale, when they had met for short periods while raising Bertie, or when she had visited him in his office, were no longer possible, and they had no opportunity to be alone together. Not that John had any designs to act improperly, he just felt that the constant scrutiny was excessive and stifling.

John had visited the Watsons' house almost every evening to see Margaret, for a little while at least, although by the time he finished work, had dinner, washed and changed and walked there, it was invariably bordering on too late to make a house call. Sometimes Margaret would set off towards the mill and meet him and Bertie halfway, so that they could walk back together and have a few moments alone. On one such occasion, Margaret had raised the subject of her inheritance with John. Although it was yet unclear how much Mr Bell had left her, like John, she too suspected that it must be a significant amount as she couldn't see Henry going to such lengths without a substantial inducement. She offered to make a financial investment in Marlborough Mills, although the amount was dependent on the size of Mr Bell's bequest. John was delighted but also uneasy. It felt wrong, and perhaps not gentlemanly, to agree to take money from Margaret, even in the form of a loan which he would repay with interest. He would not take advantage of her good will. Nevertheless, Margaret had insisted that he make plans to return the mill to its full manufacturing potential.

Margaret and John had no option but to sit with Fanny and Watson during his visits. Although the Watsons were the perfect hosts, this situation precluded any private conversations, even those not of a romantic nature, as John didn't want to discuss mill matters with Margaret in earshot of Watson who was, after all, his business rival. John wished to discuss the details of Marlborough Mills' revival with Margaret privately, so he contrived to get her to his office.

'Bertie has a new trick to show you, Margaret. Well, not really a trick I suppose, but I feel sure you will be charmed. Is it possible for you to visit us at the mill before the noon whistle one day?' he asked hopefully.

Margaret had not needed any further encouragement, and with the innocent premise of watching Bertie perform his latest manoeuvre, she had determined to visit him in the next day or two when she was not needed by Fanny.

John was engrossed in his paperwork, calculating and re-calculating how soon the mill could be running at full capacity depending on varying amounts of money that Margaret might be able to invest. A light tap on the door interrupted his train of thought.

'Come,' he said, looking up to see who might need his attention. Margaret entered the office carrying a basket, the contents of which were covered with a cloth. 'Margaret! How lovely to see you,' he said with a smile, standing immediately. He took the basket from her, and placed it on the desk.

John was still in awe of the fact that Margaret and he were courting, and he was determined to follow the rules of propriety. Margaret, on the other hand, was more inclined to bend the convention slightly, and had prepared a gift for him that was hidden in the basket.

'Will you sit with me, Margaret, so that I can show you my plans?' he said, moving the chair opposite his desk to the space next to his. Margaret willingly complied, and was quite enchanted to have to squeeze into the gap between the desk leg and John.

A copy of the presentation that John had taken to London for Henry Lennox's nefarious investors meeting was spread out on the desk, and he took the time to go through the facts and figures with Margaret. He was delighted that she concentrated and interjected with questions now and again, which confirmed that she was far superior to those fools in London.

'So you see, Margaret, with some investment, Marlborough Mills will be productive and profitable in a matter of months. It feels so presumptuous to ask when you still haven't had the full particulars of your inheritance, but once you have been informed I can put my strategy into action, depending on the sum that you are able to spare. Additional funding will mean that the mill, our livelihood when, I mean, if we marry, and that of the hands will be secure. You can see here,' he said, pointing to the interest column, 'that you'll make money on the investment in the mill. It's a higher rate than if your money remained in the bank, so it is a sound business decision. But I would urge you to seek separate financial advice so that you are happy that what I have told you is right. And I have further plans ...' John looked up for the first time to see Margaret staring at him with a perplexed expression. 'Does it trouble you, Margaret? I will not ask again if you are not happy to sponsor the project.' He felt a little sick as disappointment set in. 'I will find another way,' he said gently, and touched her hand briefly.

Margaret's chair scraped on the floor as she withdrew from behind John's desk. She moved to the centre of the room and placed her hands on her hips. She looked magnificent.

'What do you mean, "if",' she said crossly.

'Pardon?' he replied, bemused.

'You said "if" we marry.'

'Well, I don't wish to presume. A courtship is to determine whether a couple are compatible is it not?'

'I'm sorry you have not yet decided!' she spat indignantly at him and snatched up her basket, which still contained her gift of lemon biscuits. She had spent the morning making them to remind him of their kiss those many months ago and had hoped to perhaps coax another from him, but vexation led to belligerence, and she felt he no longer deserved them.

'Good day, Mr Thornton,' she said with her nose in the air, spun on her heel, and was gone from John's office before he had time to think what on earth had happened, and how he had managed to irritate Margaret so thoroughly. He gathered his wits and bounded after her, taking the steps three at a time, and caught up to her just as she was entering the yard. She had captured the attention of Bertie, who had left his sentry at the weaving shed door to greet her. While Margaret lavished her love upon Bertie, John lightly touched her elbow.

'Will you come back to the office, Margaret? Please?'

Margaret's aggravation with him was still at its height. 'I shall consider your business proposal and return when I have made a decision. Does that suit?'

John frowned. 'Very well.' And with that she left him and Bertie standing in the yard staring in her wake.

If she thought crossly all the way home and into the afternoon. Her annoyance was so complete that she hadn't been able to settle on one activity for the rest of the day. But once her ire had waned, distress had set in, and she had concealed her spontaneous bouts of weeping by remaining in her room for the majority of the afternoon, complaining of tiredness.

Despite Margaret's suggestion to the Watsons that she didn't think John would call on them that evening, their usual visitor arrived just after nine o'clock. John, wearing his sternest scowl, was shown through to the drawing room. Fanny assessed her brother, whom she noticed was not wearing his customary black work clothes, but had clearly changed into his smart blue striped waistcoat with a cravat in a similar shade. John's eyes rested immediately upon Margaret, and although that was not unusual, it was curious that she didn't return his look and kept her face averted, evidently engrossed in a book.

'My apologies for the late hour. I was unavoidably detained. May I have a private interview with Miss Hale please?' John asked formally.

Fanny first glanced at Watson and then at Margaret, who had now looked up. Fanny was no fool. Something had happened at Marlborough Mills today.

'Of course, if Miss Hale is agreeable? You may use my music room. You must leave the door open, of course,' said Fanny a little smugly, for once being able to tell her brother how to behave.

Margaret stood up abruptly and left the room, and John followed mutely behind. On entering the music room he slammed the door shut causing her to whirl around to meet his eyes. As soon as he saw her face he was contrite; he could see that she had been crying. And worse even than that – he knew he was responsible. He stepped close and grasped her hands.

'Margaret, I am sorry, but I find the word alone is not enough. I have spent months hoping that you saw me as more than a mere manufacturer, and then, as soon as you have agreed to a courtship, I prove that you were right all along, and bore you to tears with business plans and ledgers,' he said earnestly. He held her hands tightly in his, feeling as she trembled slightly under his touch.

'It's not that, John,' she replied, eyes glistening. 'It was the uncertainty you voiced about our future. I thought … I thought,' but she couldn't continue and looked away. John moved her to the piano stool to sit down and he knelt before her.

'I am certain, Margaret. Of course, I am. But if I was hesitant in voicing my wishes, it was because I wouldn't dare to presume that you feel the same, not because I am undecided. I understand my deficiencies, Margaret, and would not impose myself upon you if you found me to be lacking. But, if you wish to know what's in my heart, then I shall tell you. It's the same feeling that has been present and never diminished since I first confessed it to you. I love you like no man has ever loved a woman before. I wish for a partnership, Margaret, to share my life with you – the other half of my soul. Do you … could you … love me?' he asked.

Margaret slid her hand from his so that she could touch her palm to his cheek, and she tried to put her emotions into words. 'I believe the feeling was allowed to blossom from our friendship, although I don't know when it first came into being. But I love you, and have loved you, for what feels like an eternity,' she replied, warming his heart with her words and emboldening him to ask what he must.

'Then, will you have me, Margaret? Marry me?' he whispered. 'And hold me in your heart forever?'

'I'll never let you go. You are here, always,' she said, placing her hand upon her heart.

The stillness in the room was broken as Margaret moved suddenly, startling John, as she flung her arms about his neck and pulled him to her. She held him close with the desperation of her affection, and he reciprocated, unquestionably the luckiest and happiest man alive.

After a moment or two, John drew back a little so that he could see Margaret's beautiful face that was now an emotional rainbow of bliss and tears, and he brushed the teardrops from her cheeks with his fingertips. He glanced at her mouth, and then to her eyes searching for unspoken permission, then lowered his lips to hers. His gentle but insistent soft lips caressed hers time and again. Margaret's hands first smoothed his hair, then raked through it, sending shivers of delight down his spine, while she made the shiny spikes that she loved. His scent was of soap with a hint of his cologne that she remembered so well from his visits to Crampton. He smelled like home.

'As you hadn't kissed me for so long, I wondered if you no longer wanted to,' she said a little breathlessly. 'So I brought you some of the lemon biscuits that you liked so much before to see, perhaps, if they might have the same effect. And then it all went wrong, and I brought them back home with me again,' she said, then tried placing her lips upon his, and she found he seemed to like that even more.

'Perhaps you could try delivering them again tomorrow? I feel sure they'll do the trick,' he said, with his charming bashful smile. A knock on the door interrupted their tryst.

'Would you like some tea, John?' called Fanny, attempting to restore respectability.

'No thank you, Fanny. I will be off home now,' he said, getting to his feet and, holding hands, John and Margaret approached the door.

'Oh!' said Margaret. 'I don't think I said 'yes'! Yes, John, I will marry you,' and they sealed the bargain with another kiss.

Chapter 25

February 1856

Margaret, John and Fanny travelled to London for Margaret's appointment with Mr Johnson the attorney. It was a long journey, to travel both to and from the capital in one day, but Margaret had insisted it should be so, in order to minimise the time John would be forced to be absent from the mill. They set off on the nine-fifteen train from Milton-Northern, with all three of them feeling a nervous anticipation of what the day might hold. Following the meeting they would have tea with Mrs Shaw and Mrs Lennox before returning to Milton that evening. Although he was not permitted to sit next to Margaret on the train, the pleasing benefit of sitting opposite was that John could gaze at her without reproof as both Margaret and Fanny dozed, lulled by the rocking motion and rhythmic rattle of the train.

The doorbell jangled at Johnson, Wiley and Lennox attorneys, and Josephine smoothed her uniform skirt and apron, if not her tattered nerves. She knew who it would be as she had seen the visitor's name in the appointments ledger. She was finally going to see Miss Hale, and she felt as giddy as a goose at the prospect. Josephine opened the door promptly and smiled at the party awaiting entry. Her delight at the visitor was magnified as she comprehended that Miss Hale was accompanied by none other than Mr Thornton.

'Good afternoon, Miss Josephine. How nice it is to meet you again,' said Mr Thornton in his rich velvety voice, tipping his hat to her. 'May I introduce Miss Hale and my sister, Mrs Watson?' Margaret proffered her hand to the maid. Josephine wiped hers quickly on her apron and shook the lady's hand. She was immediately taken with Miss Hale's handsomely striking beauty and friendly disposition. Of course, she had expected no less of a woman who had captured the heart of Mr Thornton.

'Miss Josephine,' said Margaret, smiling with warmth and sincerity. 'Mr Thornton and I are truly grateful for your assistance in helping us to become reunited,' she said, and glanced up at John who smiled his agreement back to her.

'Thank you, miss,' said the maid with a small curtsy, and she led the group to Mr Johnson's room for their appointment, where Mr Bell's last will and testament would finally be revealed to his one and only heir. Henry Lennox was not in attendance, as he had been relieved of his client. Henry had temporarily removed to the coast, on the suggestion of his employer, for a period of personal reflection and to regain his vigour. Indeed, it was only because Margaret had chosen not to press charges against Henry that he didn't lose his job, nor was he investigated by the police. Whilst she was livid that Henry had manipulated her for his own gain, Margaret knew the strain that the disgrace would cause her aunt, Edith and the Captain, so she had decided to be lenient. Henry had suffered in losing his ready welcome at ninety-six Harley Street, and the respect of his family and colleagues at the law firm.

While Fanny waited in Mr Lennox's vacant office, Margaret and John listened intently as Mr Johnson revealed the contents of Mr Bell's will. Margaret reached for John's hand, and they sat in stunned silence as they were informed that Miss Hale was Mr Bell's sole beneficiary. Mr Johnson had been profuse in his apology to Margaret for the irregular management of her inheritance to date.

The legal process going forward was relatively simple as, while he had been coveting Margaret's worth, Henry had compiled a detailed list of her properties, their value, and the current rents being obtained, as well as money and investments. Margaret and John had been quite shocked at the sheer volume of Mr Bell's estate.

'Look John, the dear house on Crampton Terrace is here,' said Margaret, as she drew her finger down the list of her properties, causing an idea to materialise into John's mind that he hoped would make her happy.

Josephine entered the room shortly after carrying a tea tray requested by Mr Johnson, as he wished to pay extra attention to this client following the unseemly conduct of Mr Lennox. John excused himself for a moment as Mr Johnson directed Margaret through some legal documents which now needed her authentic signature, rather than the forged version applied by Henry. John followed Josephine into the hall. He had a question to put to her.

Margaret, John and Fanny were warmly welcomed at Harley Street for tea later that afternoon, although John was on edge as he was anxious to speak with Mrs Shaw in private. She granted him an interview, and while she could guess what he was about, she was slightly perturbed that he and Margaret were rushing things, as it was only a matter of weeks since she had agreed to their courtship. She led him to the back drawing room for privacy, and sitting on the crimson damask settee, Mrs Shaw regally invited John to speak.

'Miss Hale and I would like to make plans, Mrs Shaw, and those would be better made if we were engaged and not simply courting. I confess that Miss Hale and I would like to marry, perhaps in a few months' time if you are agreeable,' he smiled as he thought about Margaret. 'It would be advantageous to be when the weather is a little warmer, as she has the idea that she would like to walk to church for the wedding and have a simple ceremony.'

'You have asked her then?'

'I have Mrs Shaw, and she has favoured me with her acceptance. I realise that I have broached this with business at the forefront of my argument, but I must assure you that it is my love for Miss Hale and not my trade that brings me to ask for your approval, although the two things are inextricably linked as Miss Hale and I wish for a partnership in all things.'

Mrs Shaw sighed deeply, taking a moment to make her decision. 'If Margaret is in agreement, then I give you my blessing … but … no sooner than three months' time, and that is my final word on the matter.'

The party that returned to Milton on the train that evening was a somewhat tired but happy trio, and Fanny willingly surrendered her seat next to Margaret now that her brother and Miss Hale were engaged. Margaret slipped her arm through John's and leant against him as she slept on the journey back home. John realised that he had changed his mind; sitting next to Margaret was indeed preferable, especially when she was settled against him, and the faint scent of roses delighted his senses.

Margaret started to visit Marlborough Mills regularly, and whilst she couldn't guarantee to attend every day, as Fanny sometimes had plans or visitors that she was required to be present to meet, she did her best. She had agreed wholeheartedly to the sum John had requested to bring about the resurgence of Marlborough Mills. She pointed out to him that once they were married it would be his money anyway. It was a fact that troubled John, as it made him feel no better than Lennox in using Margaret's wealth for his own ends, and he was determined that her money would be a loan to be repaid back, as he had originally suggested. With the finances in place to restore the functioning of Marlborough Mills to full speed, John needed to work long hours. Margaret insisted that he need not come to see her every evening so that he could get some rest.

It was on one of her visits to the mill that Margaret finally got to see Bertie's antics which John had previously alluded to. The dog spent most of his day in the yard, as long as it was dry. For a sheepdog he was peculiarly disenchanted with the rain, and on such days he stayed with John in his office. When outside, Bertie gravitated to wherever Edwin Bailey was working, and often sat expectantly by the weaving shed door, where he was not permitted to enter, though he frequented all of the other sheds both seeking and giving affection.

John looked out of his office window and into the yard, and invited Margaret to join him. He rested his elbow on the window ledge and his chin on his hand, just as he had done many a time when daydreaming about Margaret before she was his. Well, almost his. The midday whistle had blown, and he and Margaret watched in amused delight as the natural instincts of Bertie's breed came to the fore, and he started rounding up the workers to enter the canteen. John watched Margaret's smile widen as she grasped what he was doing. Bertie began patrolling the perimeter of the yard, narrowing his circle as stragglers were unconsciously shepherded towards the queue for the canteen. His stance was hunched down, and his tongue lolled from the side of his mouth as he concentrated on his self-imposed task. Two young spinners were standing chatting, away from the amassed line for lunch, and Bertie approached them and attempted herding them into the group. The girls seemed oblivious to Bertie's actions but found themselves swept nearer the canteen, and joined their fellow workers there. Once his mission was achieved,

Bertie joined the end of the queue so that he might get his daily reward should there be any scraps of food left over.

With the mill on track to achieve its former zenith, John further explained to Margaret his innovative idea to expand the business into fabric printing. He showed her his diagram of a purpose-built printing shed, which would house several roller printing machines. He recounted to her his research on the transformation currently ongoing in the manufacturing of synthetic dyes. This diversification of the business would protect their interests, should the increasingly volatile market impinge upon their ability to keep the factory's cotton production business secure.

'I think it's a wonderful idea, John, especially if it will protect the workers' livelihoods too, and offer more jobs to those in need. But where will it go, this extra building?'

He blinked once. 'I was thinking we might build it on the site of the house.'

'The house? Marlborough House? But where will we live?' she said, in disbelief.

'May I show you my idea?' he said with a mischievous smile. 'It is not fixed, but I think you might like it.'

John, Margaret and Bertie went for a walk to the mysterious destination that John would not be drawn on. He was excited and nervous, unsure as to what Margaret's reaction would be. Margaret knew the streets of Milton well, and became more curious the nearer they came to the familiar neighbourhood of Crampton. John stopped outside Margaret's previous home.

'I wondered if you would like to live here for a time when we are married? I have very happy memories of this house, and I thought perhaps you would too,' he said.

John retrieved the front door key from his pocket, and they entered the building which smelled fusty and a little damp. It felt as cold inside the house as it did outside, and their breath formed misty clouds. The house had stood almost as a museum to the Hales since Mr Hale had died. The property had remained in limbo, unable to be sold or rented out while Henry concealed the new owner's identity, and attempted to win Margaret's hand. Margaret had been quite overcome, and at first John had not been sure if she was happy or sad. Certainly, when they walked through the house together, Margaret had been deeply moved by the nostalgia of all of the familiar and previously treasured belongings. John held her tightly and rested his cheek against her temple.

'Have I done the wrong thing, my love,' he asked gently.

'Oh no! It's the perfect thing. I couldn't have dreamt of a better way to begin married life with you than in this house where we became friends. I shan't be scared by the enormity of running a household when I have managed this house already. But will you not mind losing your grand home? What will the other mill masters think?'

He kissed her, softly. 'I care not one jot what they think. I care only about you, and selfish as it sounds, I would like to share in your happiness.'

'And then there is your mother. She didn't like this house, John. She will think it's beneath her to live here when she has previously lived in a much more splendid home.'

'I haven't discussed it with Mother yet. I wanted your approval first. But I have enquired if Fanny would welcome Mother at her house. When I was planning to close Marlborough House to economise, Fanny was happy to have her then, and she tells me that she is still of a similar mind. What do you think?' Margaret's feelings on the matter were demonstrated rather than spoken.

A further surprise for Margaret's final approval was the appointment of their new maid. John had broached the idea with Josephine at the reading of Mr Bell's will. She had travelled up to Milton on her day off one Sunday to have a tour, and Margaret had been delighted to welcome her and had shown her the town and the house at Crampton. Unbeknown to John or Margaret, as soon as the words had left Mr Thornton's lips asking if she would be interested in a position in the North, Josephine had decided that she would come and work for them. She had no recollection of being wanted before, and it was a heady experience. It would also put her in the vicinity of Mr Higgins, which brought a long dormant blush to her cheeks. Josephine confirmed her acceptance of Mr Thornton and Miss Hale's offer, and she felt quite content. She knew she would be happy in Milton.

⌒

Chapter 26

April 1856

Two months had passed since Mrs Shaw agreed to John and Margaret's marriage, and now their wedding day was only a few weeks away. The engaged couple had been so busy that there would have been no opportunity for an earlier ceremony, even if Aunt Shaw had been amenable to the idea. John had willingly left the arrangements to Fanny and Margaret, as he and his mother had other business to attend to; the day after the wedding, a demolition company was to descend upon Marlborough House and raze it to the ground. In the vacant plot a new warehouse would be built, specifically for the housing of roller printing machines capable of printing not only Marlborough Mills' own cotton, but if needs be, silk, linen and even wool. Edwin Bailey was to be the overlooker of this new aspect of the business, and the young man had nearly burst with pride at the faith that the master had placed in him.

Hannah had tried hard to change John's mind on his setting up home in the very modest house in Crampton Terrace. She didn't think it suited his position as a master and leading figure in the town, and had suggested far grander houses that he could rent or buy. However, John was unmoved by her argument. His and Margaret's decision to live at Crampton was based purely on their own happiness, and he would not change that merely for show.

John was sorry to have forced his mother from her home, but once Margaret left the Watsons' to begin her married life with him, then Fanny would welcome their mother into her household, and she was quite looking forward to being in charge. In truth, although Hannah fervently wished that her home was not to be pulled down, if it was to make way for the expansion of the factory and therefore the continued success of her son, then she would accept it. There was also the added benefit of a reasonable excuse to be away from the lovebirds once they were wed. Not being a particularly demonstrative person, Hannah wasn't sure that she had the stomach for their billing and cooing. She concluded that perhaps it was for the best that she move to Fanny's after all.

Josephine had arrived in Milton with her small trunk of possessions, and John had arranged her accommodation in a local boarding house where she would stay until a week after the wedding, so that John and Margaret could have a honeymoon of sorts alone together in their new home. With the expansion work at the mill there was no opportunity to have a holiday quite yet, but Margaret had assured John that time away was of no consequence. Josephine was to live with the new Mr and Mrs Thornton, and she looked forward to being part of a household again, along with a cook and the assistance of Mary Higgins.

Mr Thornton had described Milton to her as an industrial town that some found to be too grey and dull for their taste, but Josephine was perfectly satisfied. The smoky sky was similar to London, and as she worked all day she didn't mind that there were not as many grand houses, monuments and green spaces available. Josephine knew that she would be grateful until her dying day for the divine providence which had led her to open Mr Thornton's discarded letter. That simple discovery had helped him and Miss Hale to achieve their perfect happiness together. And now, even at her time of life, Josephine was grasping the chance to end her own loneliness forever.

In the run up to the wedding, John had attended Fanny's house to see Margaret on most evenings as excitement for the event built. Margaret had decided to make a new waistcoat for John for their special day. She wanted to surprise him with the design, and having no sense of what was fashionable and what was not, John was content to leave the choice to her. She had used one of his existing waistcoats as a template to ensure the correct fit. It had felt peculiar handling an item of his clothing, and something so personal to him. It even smelled like him, of smoky cologne.

When the wedding waistcoat was almost finished, Margaret had brought her basket of sewing paraphernalia to the music room for John to have a fitting of the new garment. She had asked him to close his eyes while she helped him to put it on, taking care where it was still pinned. He had stood still with his eyes closed and smiled as she fussed about him, occasionally feeling the light touch of her fingertips through his shirt here or there. With his eyes shut, the thrill of each brush had been magnified, and Margaret had playfully scolded him for fidgeting, though he couldn't help it as it turned out that he was quite ticklish.

Apart from the joy of spending time together, there had also been many decisions to be made, and they invariably reached agreement on a course of action together. Tonight though, John felt like the breath was being strangled from his body by the neatly tied cravat ensnaring his neck as he sat stiffly in Fanny's music room waiting for a private moment with Margaret. Fanny had allocated this room where the betrothed couple could spend a short time alone together when he visited, and John was grateful for it. But today he almost wished that his sister would be with them, so that he would be prevented from broaching the subject with Margaret that he must.

Margaret. Even to think of her by her first name was still an intoxicating experience. Soon the privilege of occasional brief interludes with Margaret would be enhanced immeasurably when she became his wife, becoming *his* Mrs Thornton. Mrs John Thornton – how incredibly magical that sounded. His mind wandered to his dear mother, the only current Mrs Thornton in his life, and the black slashes of his brows drew together causing familiar deep crevices to appear upon his forehead. It was this woman that was causing his distress. Her comments regarding his future home had caused a queasy feeling in the pit of John's stomach, ever since she had brought up the most indelicate subject last night. Hannah had no idea of the turmoil she set in motion in her son when she had voiced a question that she perceived to be perfectly decorous. She was a stickler for adhering to the most fitting behaviour, and there was no way on God's green earth that the Thorntons would be found lacking in decorum. Nevertheless, her words had caused John considerable consternation.

John swallowed uncomfortably. He now found his coat to be as equally constricting as his tie. He also felt disagreeably hot, causing a faint sheen of sweat to break out on his troubled brow. Margaret swept into the room, a glorious smile wholly for him upon her sweet mouth. Despite himself he couldn't resist, and unconsciously reflected her smile back. Margaret apologised for failing to welcome him at the door, and was chattering away when she suddenly stopped and looked at him with curiosity. She placed her delicate, cool hand upon his face and John held his breath at her touch.

'John, you don't look at all well. You are so pale and yet display signs of a fever. Do you ail? How can I make you more comfortable?' she asked, pushing him gently to sit back down onto Fanny's plush velvet settee, and plumping a cushion to wedge into his back.

'I am well. Thank you,' he replied.

Margaret looked at him sceptically. He was never a chatterbox, but his clipped response was unusual for their recent meetings, and she found the change in his demeanour to be worrying. A seed of doubt was planted in

Margaret's mind, and for a terrible moment she wondered if he was having second thoughts.

Margaret sat next to John on the settee, his stiffness contagious. John's hands gripped his thighs. Margaret reached out, gently placing her right hand over his left. He flinched. *He flinched!* Margaret snatched her hand away and looked in horror as John closed his eyes and let his head fall.

'Margaret,' he choked out, his face marred by a troubled expression. He took her now reluctant hand to hold reverently in his.

'I am well. Just … nervous. I … I wish to talk to you regarding a delicate matter. No, that is a lie. I don't wish to, but I must.' His eyes flicked between her puzzled look and back to his knees once or twice.

Margaret let out a relieved sigh. Indelicacy she could cope with, after all this was not the first time they had had to face the embarrassment of awkward issues together. She watched John struggle to swallow again, and a little giggle fluttered in her chest. How adorable this man was. Her man. She had the naughty thought to tease him for a little while but, seeing his distress, she relented.

'Well, you must out with it, John,' she said, patting his hand. He nodded almost imperceptibly, eyes closed. He struggled to know where to begin.

Margaret encouraged him. 'Just say it, dear. Surely it can't be that bad?' Margaret's mind had turned to the bedroom. He must want to talk about that. *Dear Lord.* What else could make him so shy?

Margaret had hit upon the problem at hand, but it was not the subject matter so much as Margaret's opinion that worried John. At the beginning of their friendship, it would have been the topic itself that would have had him stricken with acute embarrassment, and he realised that he had changed. Margaret had chosen him, a plain working man, above all others, and now was the first test as to whether she would regret her choice as he showed her his coarse nature. He didn't want to disappoint her, but he felt that he must be honest with her now, as he would be throughout their lives together. He was about to reveal how unworthy of Margaret he was, but he couldn't stop. He had to at least try to achieve his heart's desire.

'Try taking a breath, counting to three and begin,' she suggested.

Again, John gave a little nod. He took a breath *one, two, three* … 'My mother,' he started, staring hard at his hands, 'has been asking about the decoration and furniture for your room.'

Silence prevailed while Margaret's mind tried to determine why decorating would cause John such embarrassment.

'Oh?' she said.

'Your bedroom,' he clarified.

John had had almost twenty-four hours to contemplate the conundrum of separate bedrooms. Not only was it utterly devastating to him that he would not spend each night in Margaret's company, but he found it distasteful that he would only see her at night-time in order to satisfy his carnal needs. Indeed, he had reflected that during busy periods at the mill, when he rose early and retired late, he might go for days on end without ever seeing her.

And then, to request her company purely for the marital act? No, it just would not do. He wanted to *be* with her. He wanted to hold her innocently in his embrace, and feel her breath on his skin as he fell asleep after dusk and when he woke with the dawn.

'Margaret, you know I am a great brute. Indeed, a gentleman would not come to you with such a request, but I must,' he said, now quite impassioned. He twisted to face her. 'I would … did you … do you … umm,' he struggled to find the right words, and pushed his hand through his hair making the little tufts that Margaret had become quite accustomed to.

'That is very kind of her,' said Margaret, as it dawned on her what he was attempting to ask. She tried to put him out of his misery. 'I had not imagined having my own room, but I am aware it is the height of propriety. I suppose the house is big enough to afford the luxury. Tell me, John, what do you want to ask me?'

John blinked. 'I will confess to you, but I'm worried that you will think less of me. I don't wish to disappoint you, but I had hoped … I hoped …'

'I don't need a separate room, John.'

Relief, surprise and the need to maintain composure battled within him. 'You don't? You would be happy to share? With me?'

'Well, I wasn't planning on sharing with Josephine,' she said dryly, a teasing twinkle in her eye.

John grabbed Margaret in a crushing embrace just as Fanny's maid entered the room with the tea tray, so he retreated to his side of the settee, a self-satisfied smile tugging at his mouth. He marvelled at the power Margaret had to make everything better.

When they were alone again Margaret poured the tea, added milk and stirred as she contemplated the subject of their togetherness that John had brought to mind. They would share a house, not just a bedroom, and be able to spend time together in the evenings in their own sitting room, and not tucked away in Fanny's music room. She thought it would be lovely.

'It will be most pleasing to have our own parlour as well, and to have a little time just for ourselves, don't you think? When we are not ... sleeping?' she asked, and John graced her with a warm smile, love shining in his clear blue eyes.

'Yes, my love. It will be wonderful to have our own parlour. Tell me, what will we do in this sitting room that we would not do with Fanny and Watson?' he teased.

Margaret readily took the bait. 'Well,' she said, raising her eyebrows, 'I might like to put my arms around you, or sit with my feet curled up under me, and rest my head upon your shoulder.' She tilted her head slightly, inviting his reply.

'Show me,' he whispered, and Margaret snuggled under his outstretched arm and placed her glorious head in the hollow of his shoulder. She pulled her knees up so that they rested slightly against his thigh, and she tucked her feet underneath her, her skirt bunching up and spilling over to cover John's legs, while her rosy scent tantalised his senses.

After a minute or two in that attitude, both thinking of future evenings spent thus, Margaret giggled softly. 'And now I will scandalise you,' she announced. 'In the privacy of our own rooms I would dispense with my corset. Such contraptions are not conducive to relaxation,' she said, straightening up and assuming the necessary upright position that her constricting clothing necessitated. John's arm felt bereft in its solitude.

'Indeed, corsets will not be welcome in our room,' John said happily. 'Nor cravats,' and he ran a finger around the inside of his collar, unconsciously demonstrating the discomfort it currently caused. Margaret's eyes followed John's long, elegant finger as it swirled around his starched white collar. In her head she asked permission, but the words never reached her lips as her own finger followed the same path, squeezing between his collar, that was cinched in by the offending cravat, and his skin. The skin of his neck. It was coarse and stubbly, and her mind wandered into the uncharted territory of wondering where the prickles would end and smooth skin would begin.

John had stopped breathing, mesmerised by Margaret's touch as she tiptoed out of modesty and explored his neck. Their eyes met, stormy grey and sparkling blue.

'Yes,' she agreed, removing her errant finger from his clothing and placing it back, demurely onto her lap. 'No cravats either.'

Margaret and Josephine had worked tirelessly together at the little house in Crampton, occasionally with the added help from Mary Higgins. There had been a disagreement in the Thornton household, as mother and son had clashed over Margaret's cleaning activities. Hannah had tried to persuade John to stop Margaret from demeaning herself in carrying out a maid's duties, and even offered their own staff for Margaret's use, but John had stood firm. If Margaret wished to prepare their home herself in readiness for their married life together, then he would not stop her, and Hannah had to begrudgingly accept his decision.

Margaret and Josephine had nigh on emptied every room of the house. They had scrubbed paintwork, polished furniture, washed curtains and beaten all the rugs and carpets. John had arranged for two rooms to be freshly decorated to suit Margaret's taste, and he had been rewarded most delightfully. She had kept some furniture that had belonged to her parents, and had brought over from Marlborough House other pieces of furniture, carpets and kitchen equipment to make the house 'theirs', and a comfortable cosy place where she and John would be happy together, with Bertie of course.

John rang the doorbell, noticing how the brasses gleamed from being polished, but there was no response. He took out his key, opened the door and listened; singing coming from the kitchen made him smile. He walked softly down the hall and spied Margaret with her back to him on her hands and knees on the flagged kitchen floor. She was humming to herself as she scrubbed away, and it transported him back to that evening over a year ago when Bertie had been born.

That night, horrific in its tragedy as it was, had been the turning point in their lives, where the first building blocks of their friendship had been laid down. He coughed so that he didn't frighten her with his sudden appearance.

'John! Oh! What a mess I must look,' she said as she got to her feet, and tried all at once to neaten her hair and straighten her skirt and apron.

'You look perfect to me,' he said, with a slow contented smile as he stepped towards her, and placing his hands on her waist, he pulled her into his embrace.

'The doorbell isn't working,' she said into his neck, and she felt the rumble of his laugh.

'You know the way to my heart, Margaret. Enticing me with tales of faulty fixtures in need of attention. I daresay I can mend the doorbell,' he said, and kissed her saucily on her cherry red mouth.

'Was there a reason for your visit? Checking up on our progress? Come to crack the whip here now that your workers know that your bark is worse than your bite?' she said, with a twinkle in her eye.

'I might have simply wanted to see you,' he said, and nuzzled her neck, tickling her with his rough jaw. Footsteps approaching down the hall forced them apart just in time as Josephine entered the kitchen.

'Beg pardon, sir,' she said, punctuating her journey to the sink with a small curtsy.

'Actually, I have come for a guided tour and to admire your work. And then Fanny has insisted that I accompany you back to her house to prepare for tomorrow, and I am instructed not to take no for an answer.'

Margaret took John's hand, and the pair had a final look around the rooms that in one day's time would be their home. The house smelled of beeswax polish and lavender, and Margaret had managed to achieve the cosy homeliness that he had first admired about the Hales' house. This house was not decorated or furnished ostentatiously for show, it was warm, inviting and comfortable. It was a house to be lived in – a home to be loved in. Margaret had blushed when she showed him their bedroom, and he had held her hand tighter.

The last room that Margaret showed to John was the parlour. John sat on the familiar worn green velvet settee that had been his only stipulation for their new home. He pulled her onto his knee, and Margaret pretended to be cross with him for taking liberties.

'I can't see the harm in it. Modesty signifies that I may not have you on my knee today, but tomorrow it will be permissible whenever we choose. Isn't that an amazing thought Margaret,' he said, expressive eyebrows drawn down in contemplation. 'How many times I wished to hold you just so, on this very seat,' and he laid a light kiss on her neck. 'Everything will be all right, Margaret. We will be all right now. Now that we will have each other, always.'

'We shall be happy here, I know it.' she said, smiling happily into his eyes.

'Yes, it will do very well, for a while at least. Though I was talking to your friend Mr Beatwell regarding some new houses and his sewage infrastructure project the other day.'

Margaret rolled her eyes. 'Only you could bring up such a subject while we are engaged in a romantic tryst. And besides,' she said, wriggling as if to get off him, 'we have not moved in yet and now you are making plans already for us to leave. What happened to consulting me?' she said, now genuinely getting annoyed with him.

'Hang on,' he said, pulling her firmly back into his embrace, and looking her straight in the eye. He would not have any misunderstandings or falling out now. 'I have made no plan, and never will I without your consent, my love. I merely bumped into him in the bank, and we engaged in a conversation, and it occurred to me that we might like to invite them as our first dinner guests. He is a fascinating chap. He was telling me about some fine houses being built with their own sewer system that he is overseeing. There was no premeditation to it so don't fret. The houses have gardens, and the architecture is very modern. But do you understand the implications of the wastewater system?'

Margaret was still a little put out, but was willing to see that she had jumped to the wrong conclusion. 'Less disease?' she volunteered.

John smiled. 'Well of course, but I was thinking a little more selfishly about indoor plumbing, and the luxury of a purpose-built bathroom,' he whispered in her ear, causing a delightful warm tickling sensation.

'Oh! A bathroom?' asked Margaret, as she looped her arms back around his neck, and blessed him with one of her kisses.

'Well, if I'd known that talking about sewers and indoor conveniences would have had such an effect, I would have done it sooner.'

'Honestly John, with your history of indelicate subjects I'm surprised that you haven't,' Margaret replied and both of them laughed. 'A garden too?' she asked.

'Yes. Not very big though. But there is a space allocated nearby to be a small park. It may be that, lovely as this house is, it will get too small for us when we have a family.'

'You are planning for a family then?' she teased.

'Well, it is nature,' he reasoned.

'I think I should like you to show me the plans for these houses, John.'

'Whatever you say, my love.'

John Thornton loved Margaret Hale and, quite to his amazement, she loved him in return. He fastened the waistcoat she had made for him as a token of her love. He had been overwhelmed when she had presented him with the finished article, which was sewn so exquisitely that even his mother had been impressed by her work. Margaret had embroidered a pattern across the front of the waistcoat body and collar with a design reminiscent of the fabric that he had created for her almost a year ago. The waistcoat was made from pale gold silk with tiny green sprigs and cornflower blue flowers embroidered in diagonal rows. She had also given him a cravat and a ribbon for Bertie's collar in the same shade of blue as the flowers. Hannah had drawn the line at allowing Bertie to the wedding ceremony, and it was agreed that Edwin Bailey would mind Bertie during the service, although he might slip in at the back when no one was watching.

In half an hour John would place a ring on Margaret's finger as a symbol of his eternal love for her. In front of all their friends and family, and before God, they would pledge themselves to each other.

Hannah waited for him in the carriage that would take them to the church, giving him a few minutes' solitude to gather his thoughts. John straightened his cravat one last time. He had never considered himself to be sentimental about possessions, but he felt a momentary melancholy, and he touched the wall of the house that he would never enter again. It was the end of a chapter of his life, one of struggle and loneliness. But another was about to begin, and this time he would meet whatever life had in store for him, whether it be challenges or achievements, sorrow or joy, hand in hand with Margaret. John could hardly wait.

~~~ The End ~~~

About the author

Diana K Cooper is a nurse who has spent her career working in the North West of England. She enjoys reading, walking and writing short stories. *Second Chances* is her first novel and the realisation of her lifelong ambition - to write a book. Diana lives in Blackpool, Lancashire with her son.